If Your Colors Were Like My Dreams

Retha Knight

Burkwood Media Group is committed to publishing works of quality and integrity. In that spirit, we are proud to offer this creative fiction book to our readers; however, the story, the experiences, and the words are the author's alone.

Burkwood Media Group
P. O. Box 1772
Albemarle, NC 28001
www.burkwoodmedia.com
Printed in the United States of America

Dedication

For my partner Kisha, who said, "Write us a story, baby." And for my daughter Brianna, who shows me courage and determination everyday.

1.

Crimson

A rolling bead of sweat journeyed from the center of her brow to the tip of her nose until it broke free—the words under the puddle blurred on her phone screen. Those few words interrupted the last year of silence between them. Empress wiped the water away on her phone and wished she could do the same with the last year—wipe away all the hurt.

She was drained of excuses to avoid these family gatherings and felt a bit panicky. Her thoughts of previous gatherings enveloped her and allowed her some deep breaths between her shallow ones. The years passed in her mind like movie reels running on screens around her.

As the reels ran, her niece and nephew grew from sleeping babies on her lap to young adolescents who tried to teach the latest dances to their aging relatives. Her father's face was etched with a few more laugh lines, and flecks of gray became more prominent in his close-cut hair. She and her twin brother walked hand in hand as children and matured into well-intentioned, but neglectful, adults who were too consumed with themselves to remember the secure feeling of being inseparable.

She focused on her sibling and saw the two of them in their younger years at the lake. The high-hanging sun warmed the water, but it was still a welcomed ease from the battering Carolina heat. Her mind blew the memory of soft wind on her face when she thought of them running and leaping from the pier to experience the exhilarating feeling of a free fall before they hit the water. The lake extinguished the summer heat on their skin, and they delighted in the relief it brought. In later years, they sat on the pier on occasion and dipped only their feet into the cooling water.

As more sweat crowded her brow, Empress was forced to realize she was no longer reminiscing but procrastinating. She blotted the moisture from her face and adjusted her makeup in the rearview mirror before opening her truck door.

A car parked along the curb in front of the house and distracted her from her climbing anxiety. A statuesque man with umber-colored skin exited the car and smoothed his Golden Bulls golf shirt before walking toward the house. As if he felt her watching him, he paused his long strides and noticed her sitting in her truck in the driveway. He smiled, sent her a modest wave, and proceeded to approach the house.

Her thoughts shifted to intrigue, causing her eyebrow to shape into a question mark. While taking in everything between his black Kenneth Cole shoes and his matching pork pie hat, she appreciated the beautiful scenery, though she hadn't driven much on the other side of the highway.

She waited until the pork pie hat disappeared on the other side of the arched doorway to the house before she exited her truck.

"Aunt E," her nephew Trip shouted as if to announce her entrance into the house. He wrapped her in a tight hug and picked her up to show that he had grown stronger since she last saw him.

"Boy, put me down!" Empress yelled as she tried to mask the smile he always brought to her face.

He flexed his enlarged biceps. "Starting at tight-end this year. 'Bout to be the truth on them boys, fa sho." He gave each muscle an over-exaggerated kiss and flashed his dimples.

Empress gave in to her laughter and shook her head at his antics. "What have I told you about talking like that?"

"Sorry, Aunt E." He put his arms down at his sides and cleared his throat to impersonate what he referred to as his *inner suburbanite*. "I'm sure going to put a hurting on those young men this year, and golly, I can't wait."

"Move," she responded and gave him a playful push.

Empress took a few more steps into the house and was greeted with a hug from her niece Cammy. "Aunt E, check this out." Cammy raised the bottom of her shirt high enough for Empress to witness the sparkling butterfly in her navel. "Isn't it cute?"

"Yes, it's ... cute." A memory from months ago played in Empress's mind—her niece noticing her own navel ring, and the uproar that little piece of silver caused in her family. Cammy's fascination further contributed to her mother's frustration toward Empress. Empress still felt the sting from the day when her sister-in-law Camellia accused her of being a bad influence on Cammy. "Do your parents know about it?"

"Yep," Cammy assured her with the smile she shared with her brother.

Empress kissed Cammy's forehead and pulled her into a hug. In their embrace, she lived all the missed moments between them in these recent months. She had been keeping her distance from the honed anger of her sister-in-law.

"C'mon," Cammy insisted, leading Empress by hand into the family room where most of the others had settled.

"There she is," her father said and greeted her with his traditional kiss on her nose. "How is my baby girl?"

She assured him she was fine, but the embarrassment of being coddled in front of everyone made her run her fingers through her bushy curls as a distraction. The awkward pause that was ushered in as Pops searched her eyes to make sure nothing was hidden in her declaration deepened her discomfort. When he was satisfied, he released his glare and planted another kiss on her nose.

"Hey, baby sis," her brother, JS said, giving her a hug that lifted her off the floor like his son had done minutes earlier.

"Hey, JS," Empress replied after he released her.

The statuesque man whom Empress saw walk into the house earlier stood and extended his hand to her. "Dabney Michael."

"Empress Silver," she responded, gripping his hand.

An uncomfortable stillness filled the room as most everyone watched their interaction. From the corner of her eye, Empress saw a grin spread across her father's face, which was confirmation that he expected Dabney's interaction with her to extend well beyond this Memorial Day celebration.

The opening patio door alerted Empress to the entrance of her sister-in-law. A recognizable smell of charcoal smoke infusing with meat wafted through the kitchen as Empress peered around the corner. She gazed at Camellia's sandy-brown hair and her lean silhouette. Camellia's trademark vanilla scent overpowered the aroma of cooking food and augmented Empress's already erratic heartbeat. She felt the tingling jolt of lightning everyone was expecting to see when she was introduced to Dabney. The few words they had spoken through texts before Empress entered the house still hadn't prepared her for actually seeing Camellia. In the few moments Empress stared at her, she coveted each graze of her sandy-brown hair and caress of her lean silhouette when they were last alone a year ago. "Hello, Camellia."

"Empress," Camellia acknowledged without breaking her routine of taste-testing and seasoning dishes. Her movements were quick and curt, just as her responses were when Empress texted her to let her know she would be attending the get-together. As quickly as Camellia had entered the house, she exited back out onto the patio in the same agitated fashion.

JS marched through the patio door with fury in his footsteps. Everyone in the family room could hear their strained voices disagreeing over

Empress's presence. After agreeing to disagree by saying no more, and choosing to ignore his wife's reservations, JS hustled back through the door and commanded, "Let's eat!"

They all meandered to the patio and selected seats around the table. "Empress, why don't you sit next to Dabney," Pops insisted before she could sit between her niece and nephew.

She felt her right eyebrow turn into a question mark again, and her eyes narrowed when they locked in on her father's. She hoped her hard stare would send him a telepathic message about his meddling.

A smiling Dabney stood and pulled out the chair beside him, almost forcing Empress to accept his gracious offer.

The noises of nature surrounded them as they piled their plates with the traditional favorites of a Southern cookout. Empress listened to the lapping waves and humming boat motors on the lake behind her so she wouldn't have to focus on Camellia's spiteful glare in front of her.

"How 'bout them Carolina Panthers," Pops exclaimed to break the silence around the table.

"They are definitely heading back to the big dance again this year," Trip affirmed with a fist bump on his jersey.

"Yeah, they should do well this year since they beefed up that offensive line more," JS added.

"Are you a football fan, Dabney?" Pops asked.

"Absolutely, sir." He paused to wipe his mouth. "I'm sorry to say, though, that I'm a die-hard Cowboys fan."

"Boooooo," JS mocked.

"I know, I know," Dabney responded with a slight chuckle.

"Don't listen to him, Dabney," Pops added. "Before there was a team here, this was Cowboys country. Everyone in this house would be parked in front of the TV on Sundays wearing their Cowboys jerseys." He nodded at JS. "Don't make me break out the pictures, son."

They all contributed to the laughter between bites of food until silence settled on them again. Once more, the sounds of life outside on the lake filled the air.

"Dabney and I have been looking at locations for the next restaurant," Pops stated, breaking the silence again. "Empress, you should talk with Dabney more about this since you are managing the new location project."

"I'm going to make the assumption based on his statement that you two have been looking at locations throughout the city for the next restaurant," Empress said with obvious sarcasm to Dabney.

Dabney laughed. "Yes, that's the gist of it."

"Which company do you work for?"

"I work independently. I have a small office on the south side of town."

Cammy's interrupting phone further aroused her mother's resentment. Camellia's eyes bored into Empress, because she had gifted the phone to Cammy on her last birthday. "Wassup, girl," Cammy answered.

As Cammy stood up to take her call to a more private area, Camellia's bronze complexion flushed crimson. "Get off that phone and sit back down," Camellia snapped.

"But, Mom—"

"I said, sit down, Cammy."

"Awww, Camellia, let the girl go and talk to her friend," JS said.

The crimson deepened and added weight to Camellia's words, which sawed the air between them all. "See, JS, that's the problem. She doesn't listen to me because every time I tell her to do something, you undermine me. Soon she'll be as bad as that spoiled-ass sister of yours."

As Camellia's words smacked Empress's ears, and before she could muster a retaliation, JS took his natural position as Empress's defender. "Camellia, I told you earlier to check that attitude."

Camellia slid her chair away from the table and stood up abruptly, causing her chair to topple over. Seconds later, Empress heard keys jingling in the house, followed by a vehicle starting in the driveway.

JS shook his head and proceeded to eat his spoonful of potato salad. As he looked around the table at the stunned faces, he was met with the look of disapproval in Pops's eyes. He paused his chewing.

"Are you going to check on your wife?" Pops asked.

Empress watched the tension rise up in JS as his face tightened and his jaw clenched. He took a long look at his plate before dropping his napkin onto it. "I guess so," he answered as he stood from the table.

"Excuse me," Empress said, also throwing her napkin onto her plate and easing her chair away from the table.

With Camellia's calloused words playing ping-pong in her head, Empress walked down to the pier to put some distance between herself and her embarrassment.

The lake was tranquil, and all that surrounded it matched its tone. While the setting sun deposited shimmers of gold on the water, fireflies rose to the challenge of lighting the space in its absence. Empress removed her shoes and eased her feet into the cooling lake—the water rippled away from her like so many other things in her life.

Minutes later, she heard the acapella opening verse of her favorite song, followed by tapping hi-hats and blaring horns. Camellia's statement took a back seat to the sound of Nina Simone singing about "Feeling Good." Empress knew her father was dancing around the room, hoping she would join him soon as she always did when he played that song. It was his unspoken way of telling her to look beyond a troubling now. Through her unforgiving, awkward teen years, when she was the favorite target for her peers' taunts, "Feeling Good" became her eternal Band-Aid.

The sound of footsteps approached her on the pier and further broke her contemplation. Dabney removed his shoes and sat down beside Empress, allowing his feet to also make ripples in the water.

They sat for a few moments, taking in their surroundings and watching the water change from their presence.

Empress turned to Dabney and attempted a smile. "I thought my family was crazy," he said while shaking his head.

They shared a laugh and, swayed by their instinctive kinship, Empress rested her head on his shoulder.

2.

Amber

Empress had been home now going on two years and, though it was home, it still seemed like a foreign place to her. So much had grown in her absence: the city of Charlotte, the mindset of the people, and her as an individual. There were still remnants of the past, but newness shrouded everything and made those remains hard to find. Gentrification had completely transformed the downtown area into an upscale, urban habitat that few Charlotte natives could afford. She could only describe the feeling to herself as a muted sadness as she welcomed all that the shiny newness had brought to her hometown and simultaneously mourned all that it had taken away. As she looked out at the passersby on the bustling sidewalk to digest more of the changes, a collision between two people sparked the memory of when she first experienced unbridled love.

They met during the full bloom of her awkward period—Empress was a gawky sixteen-year-old with metal braces and thick glasses. She walked down the hallway with her textbooks tucked tightly against her like protective armor. Her sight was fixated on her steps while walking to her Linear Algebra class, so the collision startled her. Her armor of textbooks slipped from her arms, and her march was halted. As she concentrated on gathering her books back into their position of protection, a soft "I'm sorry" danced through her ears.

The hazel eyes that met Empress's were hidden behind their own set of thick glasses. She watched as the girl's skinny arms gathered her own fallen textbooks into the same protective position as Empress's. Empress outlined the soft curves of the girl's face with her eyes. The smile that had been hidden since the addition of her braces was triggered.

Camellia's returned smile was a random act of kindness Empress had never experienced in past collisions at school—the cold tingling she normally felt from anxiety warmed. They walked together at a slow pace to her Linear Algebra class and discovered mutual interests in trivial things like Scrabble and Grunge music.

Within a few weeks, Camellia was a habit to Empress like brushing her teeth in the morning. A day never ended without them laughing about something that was barely deserving of a smirk, or sharing details that required crossing one's heart and swearing on the graves of dead relatives. As they exchanged life stories during their time together, she learned that Camellia had also been the favorite target of torment from her schoolmates at her previous school. Those similar experiences drew Empress to her more.

Their seventeenth birthdays were the following summer within weeks of each other. Not much fuss came with the occasion as the two of them knew they could never conjure up enough people to attend parties in their honor. In celebration of their birthdays, and their upcoming senior year, Camellia and Empress decided to take one last day of solitude at Lake Wiley. A few weeks prior, they had found a spot that provided enough seclusion so that their reading, and mild defiance of sipping wine coolers, would not be disturbed.

When the sun began painting the sky in its setting colors, they both stopped, awed by the simplicity of its beauty. As their feet made waves for the dragonflies' amusement, Empress noticed the sleekness of Camellia's legs. Empress drank up Camellia's body with her eyes until her gaze rested on Camellia's face. Earlier that summer, they both retired their thick glasses and replaced them with contact lenses, exposing the subtle beauty that had been hidden even from its owners.

Camellia turned to face her. They watched the last of the sun's rays coat each other's eyes with gold and amber hues. Their heads tilted and their lips parted as they drew closer to one another. Camellia placed her hand on Empress's cheek as if to guide her through this foreign territory—her wealth of experience amounted to a brief encounter in the woods with a boy she met at vacation Bible school years prior.

Empress felt her appetite grow with each graze of their tongues. A heat rivaling the earlier temperatures of that summer day swept between her thighs while comfort settled quietly inside her. When their lips parted, confusion slipped between the spaces of heat and comfort. "Camellia," was all that Empress could think to say.

"Empress," Camellia responded, her eyes blinking rapidly.

The departing day gave way to the summer night, and in their silence, Empress could only think that the one thing more amazing than watching the sunset in Camellia's eyes was watching the moonlight find a home there also. A full day had passed with Camellia, and all Empress wanted was another lifetime to spend with her.

Empress's ringing phone brought her back from the summer of her first love. "Hey, Pops," she answered.

"Ready when you are."

"On my way."

Empress began the routine she had started since returning to Charlotte. Her evenings now consisted of spending a couple hours with her father. Though he was quite capable of getting home on his own, and hated her insistence at times, Empress met her father at his restaurant to ensure his safe arrival home. She knew he was only complying with her wishes for her own safety-net of sanity rather than for his protection from another ill-fated event.

She was never able to shake the guilt she felt a couple years prior for not answering the night JS called to tell her their father had suffered a heart attack while closing up the restaurant alone. On that night, Empress turned off her phone to stop his barrage of calls, because who she was doing at that time was much more important than anything JS had to tell her. It wasn't uncommon for him to flood her phone with back-to-back calls. She assumed his calls were again about how awful his life was with Camellia. She didn't need to have yet another conversation about their lack of sex, or his cheating exploits, or about how he felt like Camellia trapped him.

A few days later, at her father's side in the hospital, she prepared to relocate back to North Carolina. She had loved the life she was building to her perfection in California, where her agonizing, awkward years had been replaced by her active sex life. Her nine-hundred-square-foot apartment in San Jose, which cost more than a mini-mansion in Charlotte, coupled with a mid-level financial analyst job at Xerox, put her on the path of being a much desired power lesbian. Loneliness never plagued her long on the west coast, and that put *more* distance between her and all she left behind on the east coast.

3.

Sapphire

Her life no longer required much thought—get the kids off to school, get into the office by nine, get a workout in, get everyone fed in the evening. She knew her contributions were significant—that was proven when she had the flu and JS failed miserably at running the household—but she felt like her ritual made her more oblivious to everyone in her life, including herself. It had been about a year since anyone told Camellia she was special to them, and the hurt from losing those words compounded into anger and resentment.

Camellia sat in the parking lot of her gym and peered up into the sapphire night sky through her sunroof. The opacity of the sky calmed her and allowed her mind to drift. She realized most of her life had been an oblivious ritual.

Her father's church was the center of her life into early adulthood—Sunday morning service, Sunday evening service, Tuesday evening choir practice, Wednesday evening service, Friday evening youth service, and Saturday morning choir practice. It wasn't until she married JS, due to being pregnant with the twins, that she was granted the excuse of finishing college while raising a family for narrowing her church time down to Sunday morning service only. For her parents, that excuse painted a much better image than having a daughter who was a single baby-momma yet a faithful church attendee.

JS's entrance into her life had been unplanned and, in many ways, unwanted, but at least it came with a path to freedom. She had gone to the Silver's house that day to see if anyone had heard from Empress. It had been three months since Empress had left for Stanford University, and what started off as daily phone calls from her had dwindled to sporadic texts or emails. JS was home visiting from Chapel Hill that weekend and had answered the door. He told Camellia they, too, no longer heard from Empress daily, but she called Pops every Sunday evening. He offered to give Empress a message from Camellia when she called the following day.

Missing Empress while talking to JS showed Camellia how similar the two were. She noticed JS shared almond-shaped honey-brown eyes with his twin and how their smiles both stretched up to those captivating eyes. She reached up and touched his cheek in an attempt to feel who she was missing.

He placed his hand on hers and turned his head to kiss the palm of it. He was the male version of the girl she loved. That initial visit had reignited the embers inside Camellia that had begun to simmer for Empress.

A month later, Empress returned home during her winter break and brought with her the distance that had grown between them. Camellia still felt the anguish that had washed over her as Empress pulled her hand away when Camellia reached for it.

"Have you changed your mind about coming to California with me?" Empress had asked, resurrecting the conversation that preceded the dwindling of daily calls to sporadic communications.

"Empress, you know I can't do that. My parents won't support me if I go to school out there."

"We can figure out how to pay for it. We can get jobs and live off-campus in an apartment to save money. We can work during the day and go to school at night. We can do whatever it takes to make it work."

"Empress, I don't want to fight about this again. I just want to enjoy you while you're here since I probably won't hear from you again until the next time you come home."

"If I come home again."

"What do you mean *if*?"

"Camellia, I love it out there. I can be who I truly am there. I don't have to wait to have stolen moments in a dark coffee-house and hope no one you know sees us touching."

Camellia had leaned back in her chair and folded her arms. "So you're being who you truly are out there? How many other girls has it been, Empress?"

Empress had fidgeted with the paper cup that contained her coffee as Camellia's stare pierced her.

"You know what, Empress, go and be whoever the hell you want to be. I don't know what I'm even doing here with you. I'm not like that anyway," Camellia had spouted as she stood and began to gather her things.

"Oh, really, Camellia? Were you not like that when we were making out at the lake or during our sleepovers?"

Camellia had looked around the darkened coffee-house to ensure it was still sparsely populated with unknown customers. Through a blur of tears, she took one last look into Empress's soft brown eyes and said, "Fuck you."

The next few months resulted in secret calls to the Silver's house when JS was home to make Camellia feel she was nothing like Empress. She now realized those secret calls to mask her pain, and inflict some onto Empress, forced her to stay on her unplanned and unwanted path.

The slice of the night sky peeking through her sunroof again became her focus, and she noticed the Orion constellation in its natural position next to the Square of Pegasus. Her mind drifted to another memory of Empress.

They would stay outside for hours in the summer evenings, sometimes looking through a telescope in hopes of seeing something new and undiscovered. That was one of the many things she missed about being with Empress: taking small moments like this to appreciate the apparent beauty concealed by everyday life. For Empress, everything—no matter how minuscule—was too important not to notice: seeing the night sky lit with infinite points of light, a soft wind on their shoulders, and the beautiful things Camellia never noticed about herself. Searching for something new and undiscovered seemed metaphorical now, as she and Empress together had been something new and undiscovered to both of them.

Her life would be so different now had the new and undiscovered not frightened her so much. What path would she be on if she hadn't reached up to place her hand against JS's cheek in hopes of feeling Empress? Where would she be now if she wasn't saddled with two children and a husband who merely saw her as an obligation?

She sighed as her thoughts settled into the realization she always ran from. She was, at its simplest, a girl still in love with another girl.

Her thoughts moved to when that simplicity became her life's complication. She and Empress had rehearsed for hours so Camellia could tell her father about them both being accepted to Stanford University.

The climate in her father's study seemed colder than usual on that day. She still got goose bumps when she remembered her father's face stained with repugnance. She was stunned at how mentioning Empress dissuaded him most.

"You two are spending too much time together. It's time you grow up and realize there is more to life than that girl." He spat out the last two words as if they put an awful taste in his mouth.

"But, Papa, I got a partial scholarship, too, and that can help with the costs," Camellia responded.

Her father's eyes bored into hers, and she looked down at the ground. "The answer is no. There are plenty of good schools here for you to attend. Is that understood?"

Camellia remained silent. When her father shouted her name, she jolted and answered, "Yes, sir."

Soon after that, she retreated to her bedroom. Sitting on her bed for what seemed like an eternity, she realized she wasn't crying. Her pain pitted into a calloused wound and still lived inside her.

In the month following that frigid moment, she sat on Empress's bed for a second eternity, watching her pack for Stanford and adding layers to her internal pain.

Now, the tears she hadn't released all those years ago streamed down her face as her eyes continued to survey the night sky. So much time had passed since she made the choice not to live her own life.

In her abstract life, she would be a global journalist, traveling the world and writing about all she experienced. She would elevate everything to importance through her writing, no matter how minuscule some things seemed.

But now, as Orion and Pegasus reminded her from their native positions in the night sky, pushing aside the life she wanted had resulted in a life of minimal change. She was living the life she had been expected to live, stagnant just like those constellations.

4.

Lavender

Every woman who passed their table couldn't escape JS's scrutinizing, sexual gaze. "Check out the ass on that one," he pointed out to Empress before taking a long swallow from his bottle.

Empress held her own admiration in silence, as usual, and simply shook her head at her brother. The passing woman did have an ample ass that looked as if God picked it off a special apple tree, but she knew how demeaning it felt to be on the receiving end of stares.

"You know we share the exact same DNA, so I know your brain works just like mine. She has a nice ass, doesn't she, sis?" JS tilted his head and their trademark, devilish grin spread across his face.

Empress couldn't help but match his grin and clinked her wine glass to his beer bottle in confirmation. The two shared a chuckle and took another sly look in the woman's direction. Again, they clinked their glasses together to signify that God had done an excellent job.

These times she shared with her brother reminded her of when they were children. She remembered JS always being her loudest cheerleader, especially when she didn't know how to root for herself. Though they were twins, Empress seemed blessed with a few additional shortcomings that took a decade to overcome. At a young age, her nearsightedness forced her to wear thick glasses that magnified her eyes to twice their size and earned her the cruel nickname Eye-press in middle school. A few years later, her adorable overbite had manifested into protruding buck teeth, which required braces.

As JS lived a life of game-winning touchdowns and record-breaking track times, peppered with pretty girls all competing to be his next girlfriend, Empress sought shelter behind books in the farthest corners of secluded spaces.

Her fondest memory of JS was when one of those pretty girls was leaving their house, and she saw Empress making her way to the kitchen for a snack. "Damn," the girl said to JS with a taunting laugh, "are you sure you two are really related?"

JS looked back at his sister, who was hanging her head in humiliation. He saw the hurt push tears to her eyes. "Bye, bitch," he said to the girl before slamming the door in her face.

Empress paused her reminiscing. She looked across the table and tried to match the smile on his face as JS stole glances of the woman who had passed them earlier. Her pain threatened to show tears in her eyes, forcing her to look away from him. Though he had no idea, she knew she had hurt her hero.

Her good intentions grew into selfish ones the first night she invited Camellia to her place after she moved back to Charlotte. The tension between them had been noticed by everyone in Empress's family, though the reason was still Empress and Camellia's shared secret. After awkward silences between them at family gatherings, JS pleaded with his sister for a resolution between her and his wife.

That night invited more than just a chance at burying feelings of resentment. Empress had been greeted with the familiarity of soft vanilla as she opened her door. With a deep inhale, she was transported back to the Lake Wiley sun setting in Camellia's eyes. Camellia reached up to touch her cheek as they shared a gaze. Empress turned and kissed the palm of her hand. Her desire for Camellia ignited and fought all she knew was reasonable and right. She pulled Camellia into a kiss and back into her life.

It was when she was awakened from a satisfying slumber the next morning, by her buzzing phone, that she was reminded of the consequences of their actions. "Thank you," was followed by a heart emoji in the text from JS. Her satisfaction became panic as the weight of reality set in and forced her to realize she didn't just have the most amazing night with the love of her life, but she had also slept with her brother's wife.

The intoxicated, slurred words of JS brought her back to the present. "Time travel, sis," he declared to start his favorite drinking game with her. "The year is 1985. Madonna or Janet Jackson?"

Empress looked at her male mirror and masked the pain of her secret with a smile. "Though I have been in love with Janet Jackson since I was thirteen years old, I have to go with Madonna," she responded.

"See, I told you our brains are the same," he said and again clinked his bottle to her glass.

"Yes, bro, we are alike in so many ways," she agreed, followed by a long drink from her glass.

After they time-traveled to other years to compare the belles of before, JS began his next favorite game. He slowly perused the room as the devilish grin returned to his lips. "Her," he said with a nod in the direction of a young woman sitting alone and nursing her drink at the bar. "Get the girl. Loser picks up tonight's tab."

Empress sized up the woman for herself and unconsciously rolled her eyes. She was often picking up the tab at the end of the night as JS only chose women he knew he could easily add to his roster. "Okay, but not her." Empress scanned the other end of the bar, and when her sight caught a shimmering cheek piercing, she said, "Her." She nodded in the direction of a young woman with lavender-colored hair laughing with her friends as they watched a video on one of their phones.

"Hmmm, interesting choice, baby sis. She seems a little too dangerous for your taste."

"Watch and learn," Empress said before chugging the last of her wine and leaving their table. Her mind ran through all the opening lines she had ever used to start a conversation with a woman as her heart jogged in her chest. After years of playing this ridiculous game with JS, she had learned two things—whoever went first was often the victor, and the way to a woman's heart was almost always through her shoes.

As Empress sidled up to the bar and slid into the seat next to their selection, she took notice of the wedge, platform sneakers that looked like Chuck Taylor Converse throwbacks the woman was wearing. *First base,* she thought to herself as confirmation of her conversation starter. "A Paloma cocktail," she said to the bartender, who raised an eyebrow at her order and then nodded. She turned her head and looked back at JS, who greeted her glance with a raised bottle. When she turned back to the bar, she pretended to notice the woman's shoes for the first time. "OMG, those are so hot," she expressed to the woman and placed her hand on the woman's arm to get her attention.

"Oh … thank you," the woman responded with a smile, flashing both her cheek piercings that doubled as dimples.

"If you don't mind me asking, where did you get those? I haven't seen anything like them in the stores."

"I bought them from an online shoe store. I buy most of my shoes there because they carry unique styles."

"One Paloma cocktail," the bartender replied, interrupting their conversation.

As she thanked the bartender and paid for her drink, Empress saw the woman's head tilt in question in her peripheral vision. *Second base,* she thought to herself. Her obscure drink provided yet another conversation piece. "I'm sorry, you were saying you bought them at an online store," Empress continued, shifting her attention back to the woman.

"Yes, they make these and other crazy styles." The woman turned herself toward Empress and away from her friends. "What is that you ordered?"

"It's a Paloma cocktail. That's just a fancy way of saying tequila with grapefruit soda."

They shared a laughed, and the woman replied, "I love anything grapefruit."

Third base, Empress confirmed mentally. "You're welcome to try it if you like," she suggested.

"Really?" The woman asked and again flashed her pierced dimples.

"Absolutely."

The woman lifted the glass, extended her tongue, and slowly licked the sugary rim before taking a quick drink from the straw.

Empress's heart sped up to a marathon stride as she watched the woman run the tip of her tongue across the glass.

"That is soooo good," the woman said with exaggerated satisfaction.

"Yes, it was. ... Is. ... Yes, it is a good drink," Empress stammered.

The woman smiled. "So, what's your name, Paloma lady?"

"Empress."

"Nice."

"What's yours?"

"Tandy."

"Pretty name." Empress interrupted their banter with a sip from her drink. "It really suits you," she said to steer the conversation toward her real intention.

Tandy flashed another smile with her shimmering dimples flexing on either side. "You're a bold woman to try and pick up a random chick in a straight bar," she said before bringing Empress's drink closer to her and again licking some sugar from the rim. "I like bold women."

Losing herself again in the pleasant distraction of having her glass licked, and the many possibilities that could follow that gesture, Empress reminded herself of the few times this game went in her favor. The few others like Tandy didn't result in any long-term, meaningful commitments, which was fine, but they did result in some pure physical fun, which was even better. "Bold women are indeed a blessing," Empress responded.

"Hey, Tandy, a table just opened up for us," one of the ladies said from the far end of the bar.

Tandy nodded at the lady and then turned her attention back to Empress. "Hate to cut this short, but we're here to celebrate my friend's birthday. Why don't you put my number in your phone? Maybe we can hang out sometime, and you can show me how to make a Paloma cocktail." She took one last lick from the rim of the glass and followed it with a long drink from the straw.

Home run, Empress thought and handed over her phone.

Tandy entered her number and then walked to a table across the room with her friends. She peeked over her shoulder at Empress as she walked away and flashed her pierced dimples again with a smile.

Empress raised the Paloma cocktail to her face and licked the last bit of remaining sugar from the rim.

The pierced dimples danced as Tandy chuckled at Empress's gesture.

When Empress arrived back at the table where JS was waiting, she placed her phone onto the table in front of him to see the name *Tandy* was now one of her contacts. "Did you take notes?" she asked before taking the last gulp of her Paloma cocktail.

JS clapped his hands a few times. "Well done, baby sis. What made you choose her?"

The mischievous grin they had been sharing all night reappeared on Empress's face. "Piercings and ink means she just might like the pink."

JS clapped his hands once more and joined her in a laugh. "Well, guess I'll go back to my original plan since you got the girl." He walked over to the bar in the direction of the first woman he had selected for their game.

Empress watched as the woman was immediately melted by his hoax of modesty and attentiveness. It was a skill he seemed to master even before he learned the alphabet as a child.

A few minutes later, JS returned to their table and drank his last gulp of beer. He picked up their check. "Well, baby sis, I'm off to start the second half of my evening."

Empress shook her head at her grinning brother.

He returned to the bar to settle their bill and made plans for the rest of his evening with his new friend.

5.

Burgundy

He could not discount the beauty of the transformation, but he still struggled with digesting all the changes ushered in with it. New businesses, new housing, and new faces transformed his subdued town into an attractive, progressive city. A city that now provided empty, optimistic promises of fresh starts to the scores of people who migrated there daily.

Until the age of ten, Second Street was all that Pops thought he would ever need to know in life. Their small brick home sat in a tight row of others all displaying financial meagerness and prideful ownership. Rusting curls of wrought iron banisters lined the stairs leading up to the porches adorned with modest chair and table sets. On this one street, his family and the other Black Charlotteans of the mid-1900s maintained successful businesses, educated children, worshiped together, and shared meals in the area known as Little Brooklyn.

Pops brought the coffee mug up to his face and took a deep inhale. The early mornings of his childhood on Second Street lived in the rising bitter notes of steam filling his nose. His coffee ritual on these rare Saturday mornings, when he was able to spend time relaxing at home before going to the restaurant, were a tribute to his mother. On these mornings, he mirrored her steps of dumping two heaping scoops of coffee grounds into an uncovered pot of boiling water so that the strong smell permeated even the darkest, dank spaces in the house. It was the smell that would nudge his father to consciousness and signal him to get up and start his day. As his father wandered into the kitchen, still tucking his shirt into his pants, causing his belt buckle to rattle like a high-pitched tambourine from jostling about, Pops would watch his mother pour the coffee through a strainer into a cup half-filled with warm, sweet milk. Before taking his first sip, his father would greet his mother with a kiss on her cheek, and take his own long inhale from the cup. During their walk to open the restaurant, his father would raise his coffee cup and nod to greet the folks sweeping their porches, opening their own businesses, and passing onward to other missions as they trekked along the sidewalk.

Pops lifted his head to peer over his balcony down Second Street. He tried to merge the past of those early morning walks with his father through Little Brooklyn with the present area known as Brooklyn Village. Despite the twinge of pain he felt from remembering all that had been destroyed in this area through the classic checkmate of discriminatory gentrification, he seasoned his thoughts with thankfulness that his business was benefiting from the city's growth and that his family was profiting from his business. In his brief moment of meditation, he placed two fingers to the side of his head and then moved them to tap his heart as a tribute to his father, who had always told him to include his heart in every decision he made.

His father's heart and mind were the basis of the current success Pops Place was experiencing. When ongoing demolition surrounded them and lined Second Street, and the other crossroads of Little Brooklyn, with rubble piles that were once businesses and homes, his father had noticed some buildings remained untouched. The most obvious of those remaining was the AME Zion church, which still served as a worship place for many who were forced to move from the area as their homes became neighborhood casualties. Another obvious one was the Mecklenburg Investment Company Building that sat on the corner not far from the church, where a few struggling businesses were holding out hope of surviving the drastic changes. The not-so-obvious of those remaining was the small, insignificant building between those two historic structures. With the small offering the city gave him for their home and the Pops Place restaurant's original location, his father had made a down payment on the small, insignificant building that still served as the current location for Pops Place.

Pops took another drink from his coffee cup and thought more about his father. As most children do, he loved his parents and overlooked their many flaws. He remembered the day when he first learned that his father was merely a flawed man.

One summer on a Sunday morning, while he was sweeping in front of the restaurant, a woman he knew only as Mrs. Harris strutted up the road from the AME Zion church before service started. She was wearing a tight burgundy dress and her lips were painted the same color. "Your daddy around?" she asked twelve-year-old Pops.

"Yes, ma'am," he answered and pointed inside the restaurant.

Mrs. Harris grew a wide grin and adjusted herself in her dress before patting Pops on his head and saying, "Thank you."

After he finished sweeping the sidewalk, he walked into the restaurant and saw his father sharing the same wide smile as Mrs. Harris while they talked. When his father noticed him, he said,

"Get the tables set up for the lunch rush, son. I have to show Mrs. Harris something in the storage room."

"Yes, sir," Pops replied.

As he placed the silverware and menus on the tables, he heard the familiar sound of a high-pitched tambourine. He looked around to locate the sound's source and noticed it was coming from the storage room. As he walked closer to the storage room door, he heard the quiet whispers and panting of his father's voice mixing with the muffled moans of Mrs. Harris. That familiar, high-pitched sound was his father's jostling belt buckle.

He shook his head to free his mind of the unwanted memories of his father's many exploits at the restaurant. Again, he brought the coffee mug to his face and took a long inhale. The heat near his face reminded him of another summer day at the restaurant.

He again peered into the distance and squinted as if he could still see a faint outline of her. It was another trademark Carolina day, where the humidity intensified the heat and caused even the simplest of duties to be accompanied by waterfalls of sweat. His facile task of sweeping in front of the restaurant had him feeling as if he were going to pass out at any moment. As he stopped to wipe the free-flowing water from his face, he saw a Maya Angelou poem walking toward him.

Each step she took toward him brought a welcomed cooling throughout his body. In that initial moment, he learned she would always have the exclusive ability to give him what he needed before he even realized he wanted it. "Got something cold to drink in there?" she asked when she reached the awning at his father's restaurant.

"Yes, ma'am," he responded, holding the door open for her.

As he prepared her drink, she thumbed through a couple books he left sitting on the counter. "These yours?" she asked as he placed her drink before her.

He nodded and looked away from her—trying not to stare.

"In every human breast, God has implanted a principle, which we call love of freedom; it is impatient of oppression and pants for deliverance," she quoted.

He raised his eyes to hers and felt the welcomed cooling rise again in his body.

"Phillis Wheatley is one of my favorites," she stated through the smile he still saw every night before drifting off to sleep.

From then on, Sterlin Silver guzzled the beauty and intellect of his future wife, Hope, with more haste than he drank his Coke on that day.

Before he took his last drink from the coffee mug, he again squinted to try and see her walking toward him. When his sight conjured nothing, he closed his eyes to see her infectious smile, to hear her quote her favorite lines of poetry, to feel the weight of her beautiful mind against his chest.

6.

Teal

Empress watched as Dabney distracted almost all women by parading his swagger and style through the restaurant to where she was sitting. "I'm sorry I'm late," he said, approaching her from behind and placing a gentle hand on her back to signal his arrival.

She stood to greet him with a hug and then noticed the intrigue many women wore at the sight of Dabney. His chic look of a slim-fit teal shirt contrasting against his dark-wash jeans reminded her how she, too, had been distracted by him. Empress blurted out her first thought after her intake of him. "Why are you single?"

Dabney raised his eyebrows, causing his eyes to widen. "Excuse me?"

"I'm sorry. I didn't mean to sound so blunt, but meeting a successful, handsome, single man in this city is almost like spotting Big Foot walking through Midtown in a dress." At least that's what she heard from the few single straight women she had spoken to in passing.

He placed the back of his hand over his mouth to hold in the water he had just drank. "Well, Ms. Empress, I could propose the same question to you."

Empress smiled and waved her hand as if to dismiss his compliment while looking away with embarrassment. Though she had long outgrown the unforgiving awkwardness of her teenage years, she still sometimes struggled with flattery. "Are you going to tell me, or do I have to guess?"

"I'm curious to hear your guesses."

"Well, you're obviously not gay, because I'm sure you wouldn't be single for long on that team either."

Dabney laughed. "No, I'm not gay."

"You have a criminal record. A long one filled with all kinds of crazy shit."

Again he laughed. "Nope, never been in trouble with the law."

"You're into kinkier stuff than that dude was in the *Fifty Shades* books."

Dabney smiled and shook his head. "Nope."

"Well I'm out of guesses," Empress said and leaned back in her chair while taking a sip from her water glass.

"I just haven't found the right person," he responded.

Empress made the sound of a tire deflating. “Considering every woman in here is ready to slit my throat to sit at this table with you, I’m sure there have been plenty of people to choose from.”

“Quantity doesn’t always equate to quality.” He paused to take a sip from his glass before continuing. “So now that you have berated me with your insane guesses, allow me to put the ball back in your court. Why are you still single?”

She looked beyond him and felt her fingers tighten on the water glass as that question always made her cringe. “I guess I just haven’t found the right person either,” she answered simply.

“Well, Ms. Empress, maybe our luck is changing,” he replied, lifting his glass to her.

She raised an eyebrow, but clinked her glass to his out of politeness.

As they looked over the menu, Dabney asked, “So how do you like being back in Charlotte? Your father told me you lived in California for some years after college.”

“It’s cool, quite different than when I left here. I like how it has grown and gotten more progressive, but I hate that so much is gone now that I grew up with.”

“Yes, Charlotte is looking like a shiny new penny now. When I came here from Atlanta with my family as a kid, I hated it. It was so slow and quiet compared to ATL. Now folks are flocking to here from there."

"Nothing compares to Cali, though," Empress responded. "The first time I saw the mountains growing out of the ocean, and the houses in the hills, I was in love. "

"If you liked that, then you would fall in love with Manarola, Italy also."

"Wow, you've been to Italy?"

"Yes, I had a girlfriend during my last couple years of undergrad that was from there, and we went once." Dabney said, his last few words quiet.

"Did she move back there after college?" Empress asked, assuming that was the cause of his pain.

"I think she may have. We stopped dating not long after that trip."

"Damn, was her family worse than mine?" Empress said from behind a smile.

Dabney again placed his hand over his mouth to hold in the latest sip of his drink as he laughed. "Yes, you could say that," he said after swallowing. "Apparently, she neglected to tell them I was Black, so we had a rather awkward *Guess Who's Coming to Dinner* moment." He paused as it was obvious the memory still caused him discomfort.

"I'm sorry to hear that. It's awful that something as insignificant as race can still place significant barriers in our lives."

"Absolutely. I can't blame her, though. She was forced to choose between her family she has known and loved her whole life and a guy she had only known for a couple of years. To add the complications of race is a hard choice for anyone to make."

"I guess it can be," Empress replied and shook her head a bit.

Dabney narrowed his eyes at her curiously. "Did something similar happen to you?"

"No, not at all. I was just remembering a story my aunt told me about my grandparents that was sort of similar."

Dabney's brow wrinkled. "Your grandparents chose each other over their families?"

"Sort of.... For a little while, at least."

The lines on his forehead deepened as his eyebrows rose.

"My mother's parents met in Cuba when my grandfather was a Marine stationed there. He saw my grandmother singing in a bar and fell in love with her. A few months later, they married, and she left her family in Cuba to come here to North Carolina with him after he got out of the military. I guess he thought it wouldn't be an issue since interracial marriage was finally legal here then."

Dabney blinked a few times.

"He was White, and most of his family was very Confederate Southern White. Apparently, he also neglected to tell his family that his new wife wasn't just Cuban, but that she was Afro-Cuban."

"Oh ... wow," he replied, replacing his wrinkled brow with wide eyes.

"Yep, so all of the plans he had to build them a house on his family's land and raise their own family there vanished. His family told him to choose, and he chose her and his children."

"That was admirable of him."

"I guess it was until he regretted his choice. My aunt told me he started drinking a lot and became abusive, so my grandmother finally left and moved to California to raise her and my mother."

"I'm sorry to hear that. Have you ever met him or anyone from his family?"

Empress shook her head. "He died before we were born." She took a sip from her wine and then continued. "My mother purposefully chose to attend JCSU here in Charlotte to reconnect with him, and that's when she learned he had died. She reached out to his few family members that still lived in the area, and, when they realized who she was, they refused to acknowledge her as being his daughter and cut contact with her."

"Well, it's awesome that your grandmother is such a strong lady."

"Yeah, she was, to my understanding. She also died just before we were born, but my aunt tells me she was an amazing lady. She actually rekindled her singing career for a few years after she moved to California, and she sang backup on a couple of Celia Cruz's albums."

"That is amazing. Sounds like you come from some good stock, Ms. Empress," Dabney added with a smile before taking the last sip from his glass.

Empress shrugged and half smiled back at him.

"So about the next restaurant," Dabney said, shifting to their next subject. "I think it might be good for you to talk to my friend Nya. She's a small business expert, and she gives seminars to business owners once a month at the convention center."

That sounds boring as hell, Empress thought to herself. "Oh, that sounds interesting," she said to Dabney.

"Are you available next Saturday to attend her monthly seminar?"

Empress racked her brain for excuses to avoid spending a Saturday listening to torturous lectures about how to run a business. When no sufficient excuses bubbled to the surface, she reluctantly replied, "Sure."

"I know it doesn't sound like the best way to spend a Saturday," he said. "But trust me, Nya does a great job of keeping everyone entertained while simultaneously informing them. She uses a lot of advanced digital media in her presentations, so it's not just her on stage lecturing."

"Mm-hmm," Empress replied to show she wasn't convinced.

"Seriously, you will really enjoy it. And afterward, we can all have lunch so you two can talk more. She has a lot of good insight and experience."

Empress unconsciously squinted one of her eyes at the thought of having lunch also. It was bad enough to give up her Saturday morning, but to prolong the pain into the early afternoon was asking a lot.

"Trust me," Dabney declared with a smile.

"Okay. One condition."

"Name it."

Empress leaned across the table and focused on his eyes. "You buy me a PopWich bar from the truck across the street at the park," she said and broke her serious expression with a smile.

"Ummm ... sure," Dabney replied with a slight laugh. "Can you please tell me what the hell a PopWich bar is, though?"

Empress let out a sarcastic gasp and placed the back of her hand on her forehead as if she were warding off a fainting spell. “Lord, he doesn’t know what a PopWich bar is.”

Dabney laughed and shook his head at her.

“A PopWich bar is one of the greatest inventions of our modern lives. It’s a hybrid of gelato, an ice cream sandwich, and a dipped cone.” Empress paused and nodded at him.

Dabney shook his head again. “Why are you nodding at me?”

“I just realized why you are still single. The minute you tell a woman you don’t know what a PopWich bar is, she runs away screaming.”

Dabney let out a clamor of laughter.

“Do you at least wait until after you sleep with them to tell them you don’t know what a PopWich bar is?” Empress continued.

“Okay, Ms. Empress, this damn PopWich bar better be all that you are hyping it up to be.”

“Oh, it is. If I’m spending half of a Saturday listening to some boring business lectures and also agreeing to have lunch with—no offense to your friend—the person that gave those boring lectures, then hell yes, it’s worth it. Trust me.” She said the last sentence in a mock of his baritone voice.

“Really, now you’re going to mock me after insulting my PopWich bar knowledge.”

They continued to trade their Charlotte living and overall life experiences through the end of their meal. After they settled the bill, Empress continually tapped her fingertips together. "PopWich bar," she said before scooting her chair from the table.

Dabney laughed and grabbed her hand to lead her out the door.

As they approached the PopBar truck parked with the other food trucks outlining Romare Bearden Park, Empress pointed to one of the pictures on the truck and turned to face Dabney. "PopWich bar. Learn it. Love it."

He laughed again and held up two fingers to the lady in the truck.

They walked through the park in silence, enjoying their PopWich bars and occasionally stopping to read about the life of Romare Bearden and his artwork inspirations.

"So what did you think?" Empress asked as Dabney licked the stick of his PopWich bar.

"Not bad," he said in between chewing the few remaining nuts.

Empress widened her eyes. "Not bad? That's what you say the first time you see the Mona Lisa in person and realize how small it is. Your first PopWich bar should be like when you see a sunset on the ocean. Mind-blowing."

"I think you experience things on a different level than most people do," he replied with a smile.

"Life is too short not to find the beauty and wonderment in most things. We're all so distracted these days with our devices, social media, and reality TV that we have forgotten the feeling of amazement. I try to find that feeling by giving importance to simple things."

"That's deep," he said and fixated his eyes on hers. "It's refreshing to talk to someone on this level. Most of the women I go on dates with only want to talk about those distracting things you mentioned, or they treat the date like a job interview where they want to know your career aspirations and five-year life plan."

This is a date? Empress thought to herself with alarm. "Yeah, it's cool to just hang out and talk to someone without classifying it as a date. It takes away all that weirdness and pressure," she said, trying to shift their togetherness to something else.

As they rounded a corner of the park, they saw children playing in a fountain with their parents looking on and taking pictures. The back wall of the fountain was lit up in the transitioning colors of a rainbow, which made Empress smile. Even if the lighting didn't have the same significance as it possibly would in California, she still saw it as welcoming progress for this city.

Dabney misread the smile on her face. "Do you want to have kids someday?"

"Huh? Oh ... I guess ... someday." She paused as a glimpse of Camellia's face flashed before her. Thoughts of commitment and a life raising children were only built with her in Empress's early adulthood years.

"I think having a family would be really cool."

Empress turned to Dabney and raised her eyebrows. "Now that's deep."

"Why is that deep?"

"That's not something you hear men say, really."

"Yeah, I know," he agreed and looked slightly embarrassed. "I just dig what my parents have. They have been married for over thirty years, and they raised three children. They really hold each other down."

"That is cool," Empress reassured him to lessen his embarrassment.

He focused on her eyes as if he were reading an unspoken message. As he leaned in and tilted his head to kiss her, a buzzing interrupted his mission.

Empress leaned away from him to get to her buzzing phone. "I'm sorry. This might be Pops letting me know he's closing up for the night." The name on the text read Tandy. Empress jogged her memory back to the night when she and JS hung out.

"Paloma cocktails tonight," Tandy's message read.

Empress replied back with a grinning emoji and her address. She tried to contain her budding smile as she looked back up at Dabney. "I'm sorry, but I have to go."

"Is everything okay?"

"Yes, I just have to make sure Pops makes it home safely."

"I can come with you."

"No," Empress said with more alarm than necessary. "I mean, we usually spend this time alone together talking through some father-daughter stuff."

"Oh, I understand." Dabney dropped his shoulders a bit.

Empress walked closer to him and landed the kiss he attempted earlier. It was more customary than sensual. "Thank you for a fun evening."

"Thank you," he said with a widening smile.

As she walked the few blocks to her place, she sent Pops a text. "Heading home now. Are you still at the restaurant?"

"No, your brother brought me home," Pops replied. "Did you have fun tonight with Dabney?" he continued and added a smiley face.

“It was cool. Love you. Good night.”

Pops replied with a heart-eyed, kissing smiley face.

7.

Onyx

"Though many in our society may be unraveling this country's moral fibers with the passage of liberal laws where men can marry other men, and smoking marijuana is now an acceptable pastime, we don't have to stand by and allow them to destroy all that is good and decent. Our responsibility is to be the voice of sanity and reason to those who choose to stray from all God wants us to be. Just because we have the unpopular opinion that same-sex relationships are indeed the abomination God deemed them to be, and just because we want to abide by the laws of God and not the misguided ones of man, we still have the right to let our voices and to let God's voice be heard. My brothers and sisters, it is our obligation to God to show our opposition to the passing of such travesties that are corrupting our children and humankind as a whole."

The tension was crammed between them all, making their car ride from church more uncomfortable. From behind her, Camellia heard her daughter's voice pierce the awkward silence. "That's not right."

"What did you say, baby girl?" JS asked her.

"I said that's not right, Daddy." She paused as if to arm herself with confidence before making her next statement. "And, honestly, I don't want to go back to Abuelo's church anymore."

"Cammy, don't give your opinion on things you don't understand," Camellia snapped.

"I understand a hate speech when I hear one," Cammy snapped back.

"A hate speech?" Camellia questioned.

"I'm done, too," Trip added. "That was way over the line."

"I think the kids are old enough to make their own decisions about their faith. If they no longer want to go to your father's church, then we shouldn't force them."

"Wow, big surprise, JS. Again, I'm made to look like the bad one while you side with the kids."

"Camellia, this has nothing to do with making you look like the bad one. It's just about doing what's right."

"And since when did you become the revival of Harvey Milk, JS? Since when did you decide to march with the gays?" Camellia turned her face toward the window to allow the passing cars to distract her. "Since when do you care about anyone other than your damn self," she whispered to herself.

"I just don't think it's right that gay people should be treated any different than the rest of us. They are just asking to be considered equal, like all minorities do," JS answered.

"There is no difference," Cammy added. "My friends that are gay are just that; they are my friends who also happen to be gay."

"Yeah, there's a gay dude on the football team with us," Trip added. "And that dude is the truth. He hit this guy so hard in a game last year that called him a fag—that dude probably still doesn't even remember his own name. As long as the gay dude doesn't push up on me, I'm cool with him."

"We should be proud of the fact that we've raised such open-minded children who are willing to stand up for what's right. We shouldn't have to worry about what the congregation will think of us," JS said.

Camellia looked at JS from the corners of her eyes and then cut them back to the distractions outside the window. She saw his reflection in the glass and noticed the dimple he shared with his sister. A smile tried to break through her hardened expression at her brief thought of Empress.

"I don't think I should go back to your father's church either," JS continued. "I know some gay people, and I think it's hypocritical of me to support some place that preaches about oppressing their rights."

Again Camellia's eyes rolled over to him. She wondered how much discussion he had with his sister about her gayness. She shook her head to try and remove the thoughts of Empress's exploits and exhaled loudly through her nose.

As he turned the car into the driveway of Camellia's parents' house, JS announced, "Best behavior, everyone. We don't need to discuss our objections to your grandfather's sermon. We are just here to have a nice quiet dinner, and then we can go home." After he shut the car off, he turned to the back seat and raised his eyebrows at his daughter.

Cammy folded her arms and exhaled loudly through her nose as her mother had done.

Trip laughed.

"Shut up, Trip," she yelled with her frown deepening.

"Don't get mad at me because Dad called you out."

"He wasn't just talking to me. He was talking to all of us."

"Yeah, but he made it a point to look at you and your big mouth."

Cammy swatted her brother on his bicep, which caused him to laugh more.

"Best behavior, dammit, everyone," JS tried to say sternly through his budding smile from his son's comment.

Camellia got out of the car and closed the door with more force than was necessary. She walked reluctantly to the house and shook her head at the charade of this family dinner thing.

****

The sound of silverware hitting plates was the only indication the family was having dinner together. "We have been missing you all at church lately," Camellia's father, Emmanuel, finally stated to break the piercing silence.

"Yes, Papa, we've had some other commitments to attend to with the kids' senior year in high school coming up."

"I can't think of any commitment that is greater than God," Emmanuel snapped.

Camellia dropped her head and concentrated on the food on her plate.

"Sir, with all due respect, Camellia has been working really hard to get the children prepared for their most challenging year of school. She's trying to ensure they have as many opportunities available to them as possible, and that requires a lot of their time," JS replied.

Camellia raised her head to look at JS and saw the sternness etched into his face. He hadn't defended her since they were first married. She felt her expression soften.

The loud clink of Emmanuel's silverware dropping onto his plate startled everyone at the table. He narrowed his onyx-colored eyes and met the challenge in JS's stern expression. "Faith in God provides opportunities. Your children would know that if you tried to raise them the right way."

"Would anyone like some more chicken?" Camellia's mother, Isabelle, asked awkwardly.

"Our children are beautiful and brilliant," JS responded to Emmanuel, disregarding Isabelle's offering. "And you would know that if you took any kind of interest in their lives, or even in the life of your daughter."

Emmanuel accented each of his words with a pound of his index finger on the table, causing the dishes and glasses to clink in angry harmony. "I will not be talked to in that manner by anyone in my own home. Especially by you."

Camellia gripped JS's forearm. He turned to face her and was met with a distant memory of kinship in her eyes. She gave him a slight nod to signal their solidarity in leaving. "Kids, let's go," he ordered, turning back to Emmanuel.

Isabelle stood up to walk with them to the door as Emmanuel stood and walked in the opposite direction into another room.

"Thank you for coming," she said to them before giving each a hug as they walked out the door. When Camellia was the last to reach her in the procession of goodbyes, she placed her hands on either side of Camellia's face, tears welling in her eyes. "Te quiero, mija."

"Te quiero, Mami," Camellia replied through her own tears.

They rode with silence sitting between them in the car as they each gave in to their distractions of things outside, texts, or games on their phones. As JS turned into their subdivision, Cammy again was the first to break the silence. "That was some really good behavior, Daddy."

Camellia looked over at JS and smiled.

JS returned her smile and followed it with all-out laughter. "You got jokes," he replied, looking back at Cammy.

"Dad, you know it was killing her not to talk while we were there," Trip added.

Laughter collided in the space between them as JS pulled the car into their garage.

8.

Fuchsia

The residue of the recent storm clung to the sticky evening air. In the two-block walk to the restaurant, Empress felt sweat forming on her brow and lip. A scorching Carolina summer day cooled by rain could make an inconvenient mess out of one's hair, but there was no replacement for the tranquility it brought to the city. As she passed the window of a dimly lit gallery, she looked over to view her reflection to ensure the Carolina humidity was not making her appear like she was auditioning for the role of the Joker.

She noticed her expanding curls and the glisten growing on her brow in her passing reflection, but she didn't notice the approaching woman consumed with her phone until it was too late. The collision between the two women sent Empress to the pavement. The boost in confidence she received from the gallery window also collapsed.

"I'm so sorry. I was texting ... and ... I'm so sorry," the woman stammered as she helped Empress pick up her items.

"It's fine," Empress responded, her head weighed down from embarrassment. While gathering her things, she noticed the woman was wearing fuchsia stiletto heels—much too daring for Empress to attempt, but she had an appetite for women who did. Her gaze slowly traveled up to the woman's face. Firm calves hinted there was a set of matching thighs under her skirt, holding up an apple ass, curving into a slender waist, rounding out to perfectly protruding breasts, and topping it all with a God-weeping smile. She accepted the woman's extended hand and tried to contain her budding smile. "Nice shoes," was all she could think to say next.

"Thanks. It's kind of my addiction. I alternate between my addictions of good food and fierce shoes." Her laugh seemed laced with nervousness. "Again, I'm so sorry for bumping into you. Are you okay?"

Empress's awe led her into a short, seductive daydream that included the woman and those stilettos. The smile she was trying to contain spread across her face as the vision became more lucid.

"Are you okay?" the woman repeated.

"Yes," Empress replied more to her sinister thoughts than to the woman's question.

"I'm late for meeting some friends for dinner, but I feel awful about knocking you down." The woman bit the corner of her bottom lip and tilted her head. "Perhaps I can make it up to you another time. Maybe I can buy you a drink or dinner sometime?"

Dinner? ... The restaurant! The mention of food jolted Empress's thoughts back to the present and reminded her of her original mission of meeting Pops to walk him home. "I'm sorry; I have to go," she said, breaking into a light jog to Pops Place.

Pops was locking the restaurant's front door when Empress snuck up behind him with her gun-shaped fingers pointed in the small of his back. "Give me your money, old man," she ordered in her poor attempt of a deep voice.

"You're late," Pops replied, continuing to secure the restaurant. "And who are you calling old," he added. He bent down to kiss the tip of her nose.

They walked in silence. Empress was preoccupied during their five-block walk to his building. Her sly smile returned as her mind conjured every curve from the woman's shoes to her illuminating smile. She loved the way adoration made her feel, even in instances like this one where there was no possible follow-up. Since she moved back, her dating life had resembled a white crayon drawing on white paper—nothingness. So these real moments of adoration had been few.

"A quarter for your thoughts," Pops offered. He chuckled to himself. "I still remember the look on your little four-year-old face after I offered you a mere penny for your thoughts."

"I need to see the money first," Empress responded with her palm out.

"Always the money maker," he said with a prideful smile. "So what has your mind so occupied that it has managed to keep you quiet? Usually, by now, you would have filled me in on everything that happened to you today from being cut off in traffic to the way the produce looked at the farmers market."

"Just thinking about some what-ifs."

"What-ifs?"

"Yeah, you know, like what if you did this instead of that, or what if you went this way instead of that way, and what could have possibly been different."

"Hmmmm, such heavy thoughts might be worth more than a quarter."

Empress opened her palm again and smiled at her father.

"I'll write you a check," he said before placing his arm around her shoulders. "So where is all this what-if thinking coming from? Are you having some regrets?"

She tilted her head and ran her fingers through her hair. “No, it’s not regrets so much as it is just wondering what the other outcome could have been. Don’t you ever think about what your life would be like now if you had made different decisions?”

“Let me think.” Pops tilted his head to mock his daughter. “What would my life be like if I hadn’t married the most beautiful woman in the world, who gave me the most beautiful daughter in the world? Well, I can think of one good thing that would have come out of doing that differently.” He paused and read Empress’s face. “My damn feet wouldn’t hurt every night, because I would drive home instead of walking there.”

She gave him a playful push. “We’re walking because I promised your doctor I would make sure you got more exercise.”

Pops waved his hand in dismissal. “I have a gym membership for that.”

“Yes, but you actually have to go to the gym to get some exercise.”

“That’s some BS. Just having the intention of exercising should automatically make you healthier.”

They both laughed.

"Seriously though ..." Empress continued, "don't you ever think about the possible occurrences if you had done some things differently?"

"Sure. I think everyone does to some point, but it's important to not dwell on the what-ifs, because that can take away from living in the present."

"But don't you think we have to ask these questions every once in a while to make our present better?"

Pops pulled her closer to him by her shoulders and kissed her forehead. "I always knew my baby was a genius. You're always thinking. You get that from your mother. She was always pondering life, and our existence in comparison to the universe, and the meaning of everything." He looked into the darkness ahead of them.

Empress saw her father squint as he looked into the darkness. She wondered if he, too, was conjuring her mother's image with his memories. "She's one of my what-ifs," she confessed. "Like what if she were still here, and how things would be different."

Her father looked down at her and again placed a lingering kiss on her forehead. "She's my everyday what-if, too, baby girl."

"That reminds me, I talked to Aunt Faith the other day."

"Oh yeah," he answered. "How's she doing?"

"She's good. She will be here next week. She wants to know if the lake house is available, or if she should get a hotel room here in the city."

"The lake house? Why does Faith want to stay way out there?"

"I don't know. I offered her to stay at my place, and I would sleep on the couch, but she didn't want to be a bother to anyone."

Pops rubbed the back of his neck. "She can stay out there if she wants, but I don't see how that makes much sense. I'll talk to her about it."

Empress's buzzing phone interrupted them. She read the text message from Tandy, "Paloma cocktail?" Tandy fell far from the category of infatuation. Adoration wasn't even a remote feeling with her, even when they had sex, but Tandy was a satisfying distraction from the what-ifs. Empress replied with a thumbs-up emoji and a half smile on her face.

Pops shoved both hands into his pockets. He lowered his head and raised an eyebrow. "That smile on your face must mean you have plans later."

Empress dropped the smile from her face. "Perhaps."

"Good. You should be enjoying your life more and not questioning it so much. Plus, Dabney seems to be a good guy."

Empress felt both her eyebrows rise as her eyes darted around in search of her next response. “Yeah, he is, I guess.”

They approached the front of Pops’s building, and Empress was grateful for the distraction. Pops pulled his daughter into a tight hug and gave her a final kiss on her forehead. “Enjoy yourself, baby girl. Worry about the what-ifs when you’re old and looking back on a well-lived life. The what-ifs won’t matter so much then.”

She watched him walk into the building and waved as he disappeared behind the elevator doors. The half smile again curled up one side of her face as she thought about the distraction that would soon be at her place.

9.

Purple

"Please, Camellia? I need you to do this for me."

"JS, I need to get to the gym to meet with my trainer."

"Please, Camellia? I wouldn't ask if I absolutely didn't need you to do this. I meant to grab the paperwork on my way out this morning, but I forgot. I'm dealing with too much here at the restaurant to come back home and then take the paperwork to Empress. She has a meeting at the bank in a few hours, and she needs those papers."

Camellia let out an exasperated sigh.

"Please, Camellia?" he asked again, desperation in his voice.

His question reminded her of the moment he came to her rescue at her parents' dinner table a week ago. She felt indebted to return the favor of him being there for her. "Sure, JS," she answered, reluctance hanging on her words.

"Thanks. You can just leave them outside of her door. The key card to get into her building is on my desk."

****

She hadn't seen Empress since the Memorial Day fiasco. Her heartbeat thumped in her ears on the elevator ride. A chance encounter with Empress was unlikely, but of course, it was a possibility. Tension raced through her body, and she realized its intensity when she heard the papers crinkling in her clenching hand.

As the elevator doors opened, she peeked her head out to peer in both directions of the hallway to check for an Empress sighting. When she saw she was alone, she took soft footsteps down the hallway toward Empress's door. As she bent down to place the rolled-up paperwork gently against the door, the door swung open.

"Camellia," Empress said, surprised.

"Hello, Empress," Camellia responded as she slowly stood up straight.

"What are you doing here?"

"JS forgot to grab the papers before he left the house this morning, so he asked me to drop them off to you."

"Oh … thank you," Empress stammered.

They stood through an awkward pause, both not knowing what to say next.

Before Camellia could move into her excuse of needing to leave, she heard the familiar chorus of a song flowing from behind Empress. "Still a Janet Jackson fan, huh?" she asked with a smile.

"Always," Empress responded, returning the smile.

Another pause settled between them, but this time they each seemed to allow the music to transport them back to shared memories.

"Empress, I'm sorry about what happened at the cookout."

Empress shook her head. "It's okay."

Their eyes connected. "How have you been doing?" Camellia asked.

"Pretty good. This next-restaurant-location stuff is a little stressful at times, but it's cool. I'm finally putting my project management skills to work."

"I thought you were focusing on the financing."

"I'm juggling both things right now. The way the city is growing, I'm thinking about opening up my own construction management firm. So this is giving me some great experience."

"Wow, that's amazing. You always have been so ambitious."

"I guess. I just have a lot of spare time lately, so I'm trying to find productive ways to fill it."

Empress's eyes darted around as if she was searching for something. "How have you been, and how are the kids?"

Camellia recognized Empress's grasping to stay in the place of familiarity and warmth with her last question. "I've been okay, and those children are driving me crazy. It was so much easier when they truly were kids. I don't know if I'm equipped to deal with mini-adults that are just as stubborn as I am."

They shared a laugh before they heard another voice intrude into their conversation. A malevolent reminder that the last year they spent apart allowed for more than just distance between them.

Empress looked away from Camellia. She ran a hand through her bushy curls before she peered over her shoulder in the direction of the soft voice that called her name. "I'll be there in a minute, Tandy," she called back to the voice.

Camellia felt her shoulders drop, and her expression hardened. "Guess you have found some other things to consume your time as well," she replied before walking back to the elevator. As she waited for the elevator doors to open and rescue her, she unconsciously looked back at Empress.

Empress stood in her doorway with her arms folded across her chest as if she was guarding her heart against more inevitable ache.

Camellia heard the ding to signal the approaching elevator and waited an eon for the doors to part. As the doors closed behind her, she felt her hardened face crumble.

****

The sky was a thin purple veil slowly draping over the city by the time Camellia returned home. She walked through the kitchen as she entered the house and noticed the dirty dishes in the sink. Anger etched onto her face. She stomped over to the stairs and yelled up them, "Cammy, get down here and load the dishwasher."

A mini mirror of Camellia looked down from the top of the stairs, wearing the same anger, her arms folded in defiance. "None of those dishes are mine. I haven't eaten here at all today," Cammy replied with annoyance lacing her words.

Camellia was taken aback at the blatant display of defiance. She folded her arms also. "This is your week to keep the kitchen clean, so it doesn't matter who dirtied the dishes."

Cammy pursed her lips and expelled a hard breath through her nose. "This is some bullshit," she said, turning her head away from her mother.

"What the hell did you say?" Camellia asked with the same strength in her words as when she initially yelled up the stairs.

"I said this is some bullshit," Cammy repeated, rivaling her mother's tone.

Before Camellia could charge up the stairs toward her daughter, JS intervened and rushed between them. "What's going on?" he asked as his head bounced back and forth between the fuming women.

"Your daughter just cussed at me," Camellia said, glaring at the top of the stairs.

His head jerked back and his eyes darted back and forth. "Maybe you heard her wrong. What did she say?"

Camellia rolled her eyes over to JS and her head slowly followed. "She said this is some bullshit."

His eyes expanded and shifted toward his daughter. "What? What's bullshit?"

"Daddy, it's not fair that I have to do the dishes when I haven't even been in the kitchen today," Cammy responded with her eyelids batting and her bottom lip slightly puckered.

JS looked back at Camellia and then looked away abruptly. "Cammy, don't ever disrespect your mother like that," he ordered with a sternness he rarely used toward his daughter.

"But, Daddy—"

JS held up his hand. "Go do what your mother told you."

Cammy redeposited the anger on her face.

JS raised his eyebrows and silently pleaded with her.

As Cammy did a reluctant walk down the stairs, Camellia did a hastened one into their bedroom.

Camellia flung the shower door open with such force that it almost shattered. She took off her clothes and threw them toward her hamper with just as much force. The water's scalding heat in the shower didn't rival the lava that was coursing through her. She put her head under the hot water and felt a river of fire rushing down her back. She wanted to feel anything worse than what she was feeling inside her.

JS was sitting on the bed when Camellia exited the bathroom. He seemed shocked by her nakedness. He fixated on the water droplets falling from her breast and then moved his gaze to his lap.

Camellia turned to face him while wrapping a towel around her body. "JS, I told you that spoiled-ass sister of yours was a bad influence on Cammy. She has never talked to me like that."

JS just nodded in agreement.

"And the next time you need someone to do something for you in regard to her, don't even think about asking me. I don't want anything more to do with your inconsiderate-ass sister. *Puta culo lesbiana perra*!"

He again nodded, still wearing the same glazed look of someone not listening. When she turned her back to him and focused her attention on finding something in one of her drawers, he walked behind her. He kissed one of her exposed shoulders and traveled his lips across her back to kiss the other one.

She was reluctantly receptive to his affection because she wanted to exist in any different space than where she was mentally, so she didn't move away. "What are you doing?" she asked in a hushed voice.

"Trying to make you feel as good as you look," he responded and pulled her by her waist to feel his erection.

She reached up to open her towel and allowed it to drop to the floor.

JS dropped to his knees and burrowed his face between her thighs until his tongue reached its target.

Camellia's body stiffened at the immediate feeling of pleasure. She closed her eyes, and flashes of light gave way to colors that flooded her memories. She felt Empress's hands pulling her body so that more of her face was immersed in Camellia. Her thighs quivered as the memories gave way to sound. She heard Empress's satisfied humming. Her body exploded as the sound gave way to taste. Empress's warm mouth covered hers with her sweetness as the explosion quaked into euphoria.

JS kissed away the droplets of water from Camellia's back and again pulled her close to him.

Camellia reached between her legs and rubbed his hardness before guiding him inside her. Any further escape was welcomed.

His first stroke heightened her remaining tingles and beckoned a moan from him. The rare times they had sex were often unplanned and unbridled. These rare occasions, where they both were gifted a path to escape paved by whatever the other was running from, were the only times she felt any connection to him.

She felt the buildup of compounding pleasure in each deepening stroke as he cupped her breasts and rolled her nipples between his fingers. He softly bit down on her exposed shoulder that initiated their connected encounter and a deeper moan escaped him.

They were motionless, each descending from their heights of physical gratification and retreating into their disconnected realities.

He slid out of her, placed his forehead against the back of her neck, and softly kissed her shoulder blades.

Camellia threw her head back and rested it atop his. She was conscious and clear in her present existence. An existence where she fucked her husband while thinking about Empress making love to someone else.

JS walked into the bathroom to wipe himself off, and in the process said, "I'm going to talk to Cammy and make her apologize."

Camellia looked over at him through her dismayed thoughts and saw only the similarities he shared with Empress. She nodded and pretended to go back to the task of looking for something in her drawer.

10.

Chocolate

He never took the time to understand why it was the silence that always jarred him awake. On these rare mornings, when silence placed a hand on his shoulder and nudged him, his mind would race with excitement. The sweet sound of silence equated to his home being vacant. He was often awakened by either Camellia's rants, the bickering between his daughter and wife, or the loud jeers and cheers from his son as he watched any sports competition.

JS bolted up from the bed, wearing only his pajama bottoms, and rushed into his Saturday morning routine from childhood. He grabbed the milk and a large bowl from the kitchen and danced his way to the basement. After moving Christmas lights and Halloween headstones around in a box, he found his stash. His smile expanded to his eyes as he pulled out the brown box of Count Chocula. With one hand, he turned the television to the old-school cartoon channel, and with the other, he filled the bowl with his favorite cereal.

Halfway through his first bowl of cereal and a cartoon he remembered with fondness from childhood involving a baby goat that was literally eating its owner out of house and home, he heard the garage door open and close. The bickering he was accustomed to between his wife and daughter was muffled, but still prevalent. *The truce has ended,* he thought, rolling his eyes.

JS sat his half-eaten bowl on the table beside the open Count Chocula box and stared at it as he awaited the arrival of his feuding wife and daughter. As their voices drew closer at the top of the stairs, he watched the milk turn more chocolatey in the bowl. He sighed. His favorite part of drinking the remaining chocolate milk after eating the cereal was now not going to happen.

As Camellia and Cammy made their way downstairs, JS picked up on pieces of this morning's feud. It was something about a dress as best he could make out. He ran his hands across his face to break his gaze from the transforming milk and tried to focus on his daughter's complaints about her mother being unfair.

"Daddy, all I want is a nice dress for the Senior Kick-Off formal. I make straight A's and don't get into any trouble. I think I at least deserve to be rewarded by picking out my own dress."

"Tell your dad how much the dress was that you feel you deserve for doing the things you're supposed to do anyway."

JS shifted his attention back to his daughter after his wife's interruption and tried not to linger on the bowl of transforming chocolate milk.

"It was seven hundred and ninety-five dollars, JS," Camellia explained before Cammy could answer.

JS felt his eyes widen at the dollar amount and was now distracted from his bowl of chocolate cereal milk.

"I have two hundred dollars saved and will use that to help pay for it," Cammy answered in her defense.

"That's good, but you're only another five hundred and ninety-five dollars short," Camellia replied. "I told you we could find a nice dress for about three hundred dollars, and that's more than reasonable, considering you won't wear this dress past the one night."

Left without other reasoning to throw back at her mother, Cammy resorted to her fall back declaration. "Daddy," she whined.

Again, JS rubbed his hands over his face. He dropped his head and allowed his hands to travel to his now-aching neck. As he raised his head to address the fuming women before him, his son signaled his arrival with rapid footsteps coming down the stairs.

"What up, fam," Trip said before dropping on the couch beside JS. Noticing the box on the table, he said, "Oh hecks yeah, Count Chocula," before grabbing it and the milk and heading back upstairs to the kitchen.

JS watched the stairs until the brown-haired, grinning vampire on the box was no longer in his sight. His eyes dropped to his bowl of mushy cereal surrounded by the chocolate milk that hadn't yet been absorbed.

Camellia and Cammy looked at the stairs and then back at JS, who had irritation carved on his face. When he stood up from the couch, they both took a step back.

JS stomped up the stairs to the kitchen. His son greeted him with a nod and a smiling mouthful of Count Chocula. As he walked toward the garage, JS snatched the half-empty box of cereal from the counter. He grabbed his car keys and left the house.

****

The unexpected sound of keys jingling against her door startled her from the couch. After she checked the peephole, she stepped aside while her frowning brother stomped by her and headed to the kitchen. Empress shook her head after closing the door and settled back into her Saturday morning ritual.

JS sat beside her on the couch, shook the remaining cereal into the bowl, and placed the empty Count Chocula box next to her Franken Berry box. They both focused their attention on Bugs Bunny taking his turn at getting the best of Wile E. Coyote.

Two cartoons later, JS ate his last spoonful of cereal, and his wide smile returned as he lifted the bowl to drink the remaining chocolate milk. "Ahhhh," he mouthed and followed it up with a small burp.

Empress looked over at her buzzing phone to read the text she had just received. "Cammy wants to know if you're over here."

JS took in a deep breath and expelled it hard through his nose as he rubbed his eyes.

"And the next time you storm out of the house wearing only pajama bottoms, make sure you're also wearing underwear," she added and placed a pillow over the front opening of his bottoms.

"Remember those Saturday mornings when Mom would cook banana pancakes and bacon for breakfast?" JS asked, still rubbing his eyes.

Empress felt joy and pain collide in her chest and form a tight ball in her throat at the mention of their mother. "She loved these old cartoons." Her words were quiet.

"Yeah, she did," JS responded with the same look of wounded nostalgia on his face. He wiped his eyes one last time and then asked, "Do you think things would be different if she were still here?"

"Oh yeah," Empress replied with a nod. "Aunt Faith is a great close second, but there was no one like Mommy."

JS laughed a little. "She would cook just enough pancakes for herself and act like she was upset when we didn't want any and asked for the cereal instead."

Empress joined his laugh. "Yeah, she knew there was nothing that was going to replace Count Chocula and Franken Berry on Saturday mornings for us, and she wanted the pancakes for herself anyway."

"Remember that morning she made us watch all of those *Fat Albert* reruns? Damn, that was torture."

"You got so mad because every episode ended with a lesson and a song about the lesson," Empress said as her laugh got the best of her.

JS joined her laughter until the recollection of loss seemed to settle in him again. He trailed into silence and rubbed his eyes. "I would watch a million episodes of that corny-ass show just to have one more Saturday morning with her."

"Yep," Empress replied, settling into her own recollection.

"I don't know how much longer I can do this," he admitted aloud.

Empress looked over at him and watched the weight of his statement push his shoulders down.

"All I've been trying to do is give my kids what Pops and Mom gave us. I mean, not just giving them nice things, but giving them memories like Count Chocula and cartoons." He paused. "I miss that smell of banana pancakes filling the house. I knew everything was good when the house smelled like that."

Empress nodded to the smell of comfort and safety. The sweet, savory memories of banana pancakes were interrupted as her phone buzzed again to signal Cammy's unanswered text.

"Tell her I'm here," JS surrendered. "I'm sure she just wants to know where I stand on this whole dress nonsense," he added before picking up their bowls and taking them to the kitchen.

"Dare I ask?" Empress inquired while she responded to Cammy.

"Cammy and Camellia are now at each other's throats over some ridiculously expensive dress that Cammy wants."

"How much is the dress?"

"It's like eight hundred, and no, Auntie Empress, you will not be buying it for her either."

"Eight hundred U.S. American dollars?" Empress asked with shock.

"Yes," JS answered between laughs.

"Oh, hell no, you don't have to worry about me buying that."

"It seems like all they do is fight. Hell, all Camellia does is fight with everyone these days. I don't blame you for keeping your distance from her." He paused. "By the way, what happened when she came over yesterday? I still don't know much Spanish, but I understand cussing when I hear it in any language."

"Nothing much," Empress answered, pretending to be interested in the latest cartoon by laughing and pointing. "She just continued her rant from the Memorial Day cookout." She laughed again to further distract him. "Remember this one?" she asked.

JS shifted his attention and joined her laughter. "Yeah, the house of tomorrow with the crazy inventions that we are supposed to have by now."

They watched a couple more cartoons in silence—each more distracted by their thoughts than what was on the screen in front of them.

"Well, I guess I'll head back into battle now to settle this latest dispute. This is one of the rare times Camellia and I are actually going to agree on something," he said as he walked to the door.

"Wait!" Empress ran to her bedroom. "Put these on under your pajama bottoms," she said, holding up a pair of gym shorts as she walked back into the room.

"There's no way I'm going to fit into these," JS responded, holding up the shorts. "Big J won't be able to breathe in these too-tiny shorts. And hot pink ... really?"

"Ummmm, yuck, for referring to your penis as *Big J*. And think of all of the attention Big J is going to get in jail if you're picked up for indecent exposure for having him out and flapping about as you walk to your car."

JS snatched the shorts from Empress. "Jealous," he said as he walked by her and headed for the bathroom.

"Not at all. I keep my Big J in my top drawer."

11.

Mahogany

Empress spotted Dabney excusing his way through the crowd when she arrived at the convention center. He was doing his usual of capturing the attention of every woman around him as Empress walked over. Their customary hug as a greeting again had all the women sizing her up in measurement of themselves.

As they walked into the auditorium, Dabney guided her with his hand resting on her lower back. He acknowledged acquaintances along their way to two empty chairs in the front of the room. After they sat, Empress said, "Please don't feel like you have to babysit me. Go and talk to your friends if you want."

"I'm good," Dabney responded with a smile.

Empress smiled back at him, though she still felt an underlying annoyance about giving up half of her Saturday.

"Good morning, everyone," came through the speakers as a woman walked to the front of the room.

Her navy skirt had been replaced by a pair of taupe slacks that hugged her hips and then flared beyond them. Her suede stiletto heels were now mahogany instead of fuchsia. Remnants of the seductive daydream Empress had about the woman after their collision on the street expanded her smile.

After a refreshing hour of lecturing on small business innovation in an ever-changing technological economy, the woman thanked everyone for listening. Empress felt her heart rate gradually increase to the point where she could hear it beating between her ears as the woman gravitated closer to them. As the last few attendees filed out of the room, she walked over to them.

She and Dabney greeted each other with a hug. "Empress, this is my friend Nya Morrison."

"I guess we can't cheat fate twice," Nya stated, extending her hand to Empress.

"You two know each other?" Dabney asked.

"Not exactly," Nya and Empress responded almost in unison.

"It's very nice to meet you again, especially under better circumstances," Nya said while shaking Empress's hand. She then answered the puzzlement on Dabney's face. "We literally bumped into each other on the street about a week ago, but we didn't get to make a proper introduction because Empress ran away from me."

"I'm sorry, I was late for meeting my father," Empress answered.

"Empress's family owns the Pops Place restaurant on Fifth Street, and they're looking to expand. I figured it would be worthwhile for her to come and learn from the entrepreneurial expert."

"Your family owns Pops Place?" Nya asked, her eyes widening and a hand rubbing her stomach. "I wake up sweating after dreaming about that crab macaroni and cheese. Can you cook like that?"

Empress laughed and shook her head. "My father has tried to teach me the tricks of the trade, but I have ten thumbs in the kitchen. For some reason, only the men in my family inherit the cooking gene," she said, reflecting on how naturally the skill came to her brother under her father's tutelage.

"Well, I'm happy with just having an inside hookup to that crab mac," Nya said.

"Speaking of food, how about lunch, ladies?" Dabney asked.

"Sounds good to me," Nya replied.

Empress watched Nya walk away to gather her things. She loved the way the flared legs of Nya's pants swung back and forth with her swaying hips like a bell keeping time in a melody. As she watched, she heard Dabney explaining how long they had known each other and how they grew into being friends after a few awkward dates. The last statement pulled Empress back into the moment. "You two dated?" she asked Dabney.

"Sort of. I was interested, but she wasn't. She said the last thing she needed was a boyfriend after just breaking up with her girlfriend, so we agreed to be friends."

Girlfriend, Empress thought, her heartbeat elevating.

At a nearby pizza place, Empress ordered a gluten-free veggie-lovers pizza with vegan cheese. When the server turned his attention to Nya to take her order, she replied, "Bring me an actual pizza full of gluten, cheese, and as much meat as it can hold." After the server left their table, Nya turned her attention to Empress. "I commend you on being so health-conscious, but I can't do it all the time. I love, love, love food, and the less healthy it is, the better."

"I'm not overly health-conscious either. I can't be with a restaurant like Pops Place in the family. This is the only place I've found that can make a vegan pizza that reminds me of when I lived in California, so I order it more so for nostalgia than healthiness."

"Cool, how long did you live there?"

"Just over ten years. I went to college out there and then stayed after graduation."

"Empress didn't just go to some college out there," Dabney interjected. "She graduated from Stanford with a dual-degree in Finance and Applied Mathematics," he added, crowning his last statement with a nod.

"Very impressive, Ms. Empress," Nya responded, matching Dabney's smile.

Empress felt her skin flushing from Nya's props. As a distraction for herself, she tried to change the subject to something more neutral. "For someone that loves food, you certainly don't look as if you do." She pondered her words after she spoke them and quickly realized the subject of Nya's well-toned body was definitely not on the list of neutral distractions.

"Aw, thank you. You know that saying about how you can't out-exercise a bad diet? Well, I'm doing my damndest to try and outrun one."

Empress chuckled and asked, "How so?"

"I run about five miles most mornings, and if I know my eating was totally out of control during the day, I run again in the evenings. I have a couple of fifteen-mile days every few weeks due to my love of food."

"Nya is being modest," Dabney again interjected. "She has run the New York, Boston, and London marathons."

"Holy shit!" Empress exclaimed with wide eyes.

Nya laughed while shaking her head. "It's not that big of a deal. I'm not one of those elite runners with sponsors and such. I just have always loved running, and I love to travel. So, I figured why not kill some birds with a few stones. Do you run, Empress?"

As their server returned and filled the table with their orders, Empress thought back to the days following her hospital stay at the age of seven. Early one morning after, her aunt walked into her room with a new pair of blue-and-pink running shoes and said, "Let's trade some pain."

At the end of their first half-mile—with her heart pounding in her ears, her breath lost between her lungs and mouth, and her legs aching—she stopped and said, "I can't."

Her aunt walked to her with tears rimming her eyes. "Empress, often our emotional pain far outweighs our physical pain. When that happens, we need to trade the emotional for the physical, because the physical goes away sooner." She extended her hand to Empress, and from there, they ran the next two miles hand in hand, each wiping away a blend of tears and sweat that showed the emotional and physical pain they were trading. It was then Empress learned the tool that would aid her in dealing with the loss of her mother, ridiculing classmates, and Camellia's exits from her life.

"So, Empress, do you run?" Nya again asked after their server left.

"Only for therapy," Empress replied.

"I know what you mean. A good run can make you find the best in the worst day."

"You should run with us sometime, Empress," Dabney suggested, again inserting himself into their conversation.

"Sure, maybe, but I'm nowhere close to being a marathoner. I usually just stick to my goal of three miles in under thirty minutes."

"I will stay right beside you the whole time, and we can do what you want to do," Dabney responded.

"I will stay beside you, too," Nya added.

Again feeling herself flush, Empress tried to change to another neutral subject. "So, how does one become an entrepreneurial expert?" she asked Nya.

Nya laughed a bit as she chewed her mouthful of extra cheese meatzza-pizza. "*Expert* is quite an overstatement," she replied after swallowing.

"Again, Nya is being modest," Dabney inserted. "I don't think it's a coincidence that over the years of Nya giving her seminars and providing her services and insight to the city manager's office that there has been about a twenty percent increase in sustained small businesses across this area."

"Now that's impressive. How did you get started doing this?" Empress asked.

"Well, unfortunately, to become an *expert* at something"—Nya responded, adding quotation marks with her fingers—"you usually have to fail miserably at it a few times." She paused to take a drink. "After college, I took my Management Information Systems degree into Corporate America in hopes of electrifying the world with my big ideas. Instead, I got a very rude awakening. Most corporations don't want big ideas. They want you to do the one thing they hired you to do, and they want you to do it over and over again. After switching companies about every six months for almost three years to find that right one, I figured out the issue wasn't the companies. It was me." Nya interrupted her story with a bite of her pizza. "So I started my first business, which was sort of like an art distribution company, where I would meet up with local artists who wanted to get their work out there. I put shows or festival booths together for them to display their work to potential buyers and took a commission when the work sold."

"That sounds cool," Empress commented.

"It was, because I love art. I even tried my hand at producing a few pieces to sell. The problem was there wasn't enough business, so I had to do a lot of part-time gigs just to support the business and to make ends meet."

"What was the next business?"

"Website design. After I stopped doing the art thing and shut down my website, I found most artists still needed websites to display their work. So I did that for a little while, but again, I found myself working part-time jobs to make ends meet because artists don't have a lot of money when they are first starting."

"Wow, so what did you do after that?"

"Then I started doing some bookkeeping for those same artists and a few other small businesses. That one seemed to be the most lucrative, because a lot of small business owners don't like the accounting details that come with having a business." Nya paused again to eat a mouthful of meatza-pizza. She swayed a bit and closed her eyes while chewing to exaggerate her enjoyment of her unhealthy choice.

Empress and Dabney laughed as they watched Nya sway to music only she could hear.

"So how did bookkeeping lead to seminars?" Empress asked as Nya settled back into seriousness.

"Well, when I was maintaining some of the individual websites and using accounting software to do the bookkeeping, I realized many small business owners were dedicating their time to running and growing their businesses. Your family maintaining your existing business while expanding to a new location is an example. What you all do best is make kick-ass crab mac and cheese, and other great dishes. What you have to do to have a successful business and keep folks coming back for that crab mac is marketing, payroll, accounting, technical support, and a host of other things that can get in the way of doing what you all do best. When you take all those things into account, maintaining and growing a small business is very costly and time-consuming."

Empress nodded.

"So, when I looked at owning a business from that perspective, it occurred to me that my successful business could be making other small businesses succeed."

"That's an insightful perspective," Empress responded.

"Thank you," Nya said, her eyes lingering on Empress's.

"Nya built and maintains a platform that includes bookkeeping, marketing, point-of-sale, mobile applications, and a host of other integrations that help small business owners remain competitive as the technology and trends change that aid and grow their businesses. She put together an incredible business model that not only supports growing businesses but also helps new grads get some real-world experience in new technologies," Dabney added to his previous accolades for Nya.

Nya smiled a bit with her eyes still fixed on Empress's. "I couldn't afford to pay anyone much, so I went to the local universities and found college students who would trade a bit of their time and new learnings for real-world experience. And, abracadabra, an internship program was born."

"You are truly incredible," Empress added, settling into Nya's intent gaze.

"Yes, she is," Dabney replied.

Empress's eyes broke from Nya's as Dabney's intrusion reminded her he was still with them. "So how long have you two been friends?" she asked Dabney to include him into their conversation.

"I guess it's been close to six years now. We met when Nya was recruiting on UNCC's campus for her internship program while I was in grad school." He looked over at Nya, widened his smile, and shook his head as if he wasn't sure he should continue his story.

Nya shook her head in return and added a smile of her own. "He tried to convince me that he wasn't hitting on me and was genuinely interested in being considered for the internship, though he couldn't answer any of the basic software design questions I asked him. I honestly don't even think he knew how to turn on a computer at all."

They both laughed, and Empress joined them in a hesitant chuckle as she tried to gauge if more had happened between them.

"Hey, when you're fishing, sometimes you have to try all of your bait to get a bite," Dabney commented between laughs.

Nya gave him a playful push. "I should have gone with my first instinct because you were the worst free labor ever."

"So when did you two date?" Empress asked with an abruptness that surprised them.

"Date? Who said we dated?" Nya asked. She looked over at Dabney and saw a guilty grin spreading across his face. "You call late-night binge drinking after work *dating*? No wonder your ass is still single."

Dabney pursed his lips and narrowed his eyes. "Come on now."

"Come on now, what," Nya replied.

"You know we had a couple special moments during those nights out."

"Boy, please. A couple drunken kisses in the back of an Uber sure as hell isn't dating."

Again, Dabney pursed his lips. "Empress, don't believe that. She was all over me in the back of those Ubers."

"Is that right?" Empress asked through a tiny, forced smile, trying to hide her building agitation toward Dabney.

"No, Empress, don't believe that bullshit. Dabney knows damn well he is not my type and those *special moments* were nothing more than drunken antics."

"Let's agree to disagree." Dabney smiled and held his hand out to Nya.

"Let's agree you're full of shit," Nya replied and shook his hand.

Empress laughed. "So we now have two reasons as to why Dabney is still single."

"Now, Empress, don't you start, too," Dabney said, still laughing.

"No, Empress, please continue," Nya insisted.

"Dabney didn't know what a PopWich bar was until a couple weeks ago."

Nya fell back into the booth and looked upward. "What in the hell is wrong with you." She turned and faced Dabney. "How had you never had a PopWich bar?"

"Here we go again." Dabney shook his head.

"It is the perfect combination of everything that makes ice cream great," Nya continued.

"I know, right?" Empress added. "Especially when it's half dipped in dark chocolate and rolled in pistachios."

“Hmmm, I’ve never tried it with pistachios. My usual is a full milk chocolate dip rolled in caramel popcorn pieces.”

“Well, ladies, I hate to end this wonderful time with you on the infinity of PopWich bar combinations, but, Empress, we have to get across town to meet up with your father.” Dabney leaned over and kissed Nya on the cheek. “Truce.”

“Truce,” Nya said and laid her head on his shoulder.

As they all gave departing hugs on the sidewalk in front of the restaurant, Nya stated, “Empress, we should exchange numbers so you can send me any questions you have. Plus, I still owe you for knocking you down.”

“Sure,” Empress replied, containing her urge to attempt a backflip for the first time ever.

“We’re parked over this way,” Dabney commented after their number exchange. He placed his hand on the small of Empress’s back as he had done at the lecture.

“Okay, I’m back over this way,” Nya said as she began to walk in the opposite direction.

Empress peeked over her shoulder to look back at Nya. The melodic tempo of the bell played in her head as she watched Nya’s swaying hips.

12.

Red

Her drive to the airport was accompanied by unseasonable overcast skies and persistent, brisk winds that seemed to push her car between the lanes of the highway. It reminded Empress of the June Gloom weather in California during the late spring and early summer months. Whoever said *it never rains in Southern California* had never visited there during the June Gloom, when a constant drizzle fell in the mornings until the early afternoon. She read in an article when she lived there that the June Gloom months triggered the highest amount of suicides during the year. It frightened her to think maybe that was the real catalyst of these annual visits her aunt made to celebrate her birthday.

Her thoughts moved to many years ago when she first lost her mother. Empress felt remnants of the overwhelming weight of numbness that flooded her body when her mind migrated through those unsettling memories. It was such an unfair and powerful feeling for a child of seven to endure. She remembered her body being limp as the simplest movements seem to take more energy than she could muster. The days passed while she stayed in her bed with her body coiled into the tight ball it formed after her father told her, from behind his tears, that God needed her mother in heaven. It was after those days of not eating, moving, or talking, and her father bathing her after uncontrolled bodily functions, that he walked into the nearest emergency room shrouded in helplessness with Empress draped across his arms and shouted, "My baby needs help!"

The next day, her Aunt Faith had arrived at the hospital. A physically worn and depleted Pops welcomed her with a sobbing hug that showed she was a much-needed lifeline for both him and his daughter. After Faith wiped his slowing tears away, she crawled into bed beside Empress and held her until she again showed signs of life.

When Empresss was able to move again, she reached up to touch the side of her sleeping aunt's face, as she often did when her mother lay beside her in bed to help her fall asleep. To both her aunt and her departed mother, she said, "I love you."

As Empress walked into the airport's baggage claim area, she spotted a slender woman towering over people. Her wedged sandals added a few inches to her close to six-foot stature. Her floppy red sun hat bounced as her head darted in every direction in search of her bags on the carousel. Her white flowing sundress adorned with tiny red flowers stopped just short of her large calves, which were a signature of the miles she still managed to get in weekly. Empress snuck up behind the woman and tapped her on the shoulder. "Excuse me, ma'am, may I have your autograph?"

"I'm sorry, but I don't give out autographs," her Aunt Faith replied as she turned around with a smile. Faith placed her hands on the sides of Empress's face and stared into her eyes after they broke from their hug. "How are you?" she asked with the concern and sincerity she always showed for Empress.

Empress placed her hands on her aunt's. "I'm doing well."

Her aunt searched Empress's eyes for signs that showed anything different from her words. "Good," she said when she was satisfied with her inspection.

"What's up with this weather?" Faith asked as they walked outside. "I come here to escape the June Gloom for a while."

"Well, it looks like you brought it with you this time. It should clear up soon, though. The weather in North Carolina is almost as erratic as a Kardashian marriage."

Brisk winds continued to force trees into awkward yoga poses and swirl fallen flower petals into circle dances as they left the airport. "It's still beautiful here, despite the overcast skies," Faith noted as spatters of rain flattened on the windshield. "I love how healthy it looks here with green covering everything."

Empress looked over at her aunt and smiled.

"What?" Faith asked.

"Someone recently told me I experience things on a different level than most. I see where I get that from now."

Faith reached over and placed her hand on top of Empress's. She squeezed Empress's hand. "You are everything your mother hoped for."

Empress felt her heart thump in her chest. The melodic sound of her mother humming Celia Cruz's "Te Busco" in her ear to lull her to sleep filled her head. Unconsciously, she hummed along with her internal melody.

Faith dropped her head a bit and closed her eyes. The song seemed to move her into memories that lived on her like slowly mending wounds. "That was your grandmother's favorite song."

Empress tried to bring Faith back from her visit with pain. "Have you ever thought about going to visit Cuba to find remaining family members?"

"Sometimes I do, but most of the time, I think why bother."

"What do you mean, why bother?"

"When your grandmother told her father she was pregnant with us, and marrying a white American, he told her to leave and never come back. And of course, she never could due to that and other things happening there."

"That's awful," Empress said, shaking her head.

"It was. And I know there were times when she deeply missed her family back in Cuba, because she would tell us stories and show us the few pictures she still had. But she never dwelled in that sadness for long. She loved her life here, although it was hard at times."

Sensing her nostalgia giving way to sadness again, Empress changed the subject. "I talked to Pops about you staying at the lake house, and he's fine with it."

"Great," Faith responded and half smiled back at Empress.

"He wants to talk to you more about it, though, because it's so far out. I think he likes it when you're here. He seems so much happier."

Faith bounced her crossed leg, and her dangling foot shook side to side. "It stopped raining already," she said, looking out the window.

Empress looked out the window as well. “Yeah, I told you the weather here is bizarre. The sun will be out shortly, and the only reminder of the rain will be the overwhelming humidity.” She thought about the change in her aunt’s mood when she heard the “Te Busco” melody. In that mix of conflicting emotions, Empress sensed her aunt’s reach into sentimentalism and how that briefly overshadowed her pain. She changed to the Rumbon radio station and allowed more salsa music contributors like Hector Lavoe and Papo Lucca to give her aunt a blithesome jaunt through her memories and missed moments with her Cuban ancestry.

As they rode the rest of the way, Empress occasionally saw her Aunt Faith bounce her head and sway her shoulders in rhythm to a stirring song.

****

“Your view of the city is gorgeous,” Empress heard Faith yell from the balcony.

“Thank you. I don’t spend as much time as I should just enjoying it,” she replied.

“You really should. If I lived here, I would stay on this balcony,” Faith continued. “This city is so calm and clean.”

Empress heard her buzzing phone vibrating against her living room table. One buzz after another indicated she had received multiple text messages.

"Your phone is going off," Faith told her.

"Yep, I hear it. Can you bring it to me, please?"

"Sure." As Faith walked in the bedroom with the phone it buzzed an additional time, which prompted her to glance at the screen. Her eyebrows raised and she bit her bottom lip. "Wow, it looks like someone is trying to get your attention," she commented, handing the phone to Empress.

Empress felt her face flush when she saw the picture on her phone. Tandy's vagina was on full display. She scrolled through the succession of additional body-part pictures and read the texts that followed. "Hope to see you tonight for some Paloma cocktail time. She misses you." Empress looked back up at Faith and then quickly looked away.

Faith shook her head and waved her hand. "No judgment here."

Empress looked back down at her phone and ran her fingers through her hair. She was not only embarrassed but irritated. "Nope," she responded to Tandy. "Plans with my fam tonight."

Tandy replied with a sad face emoji. "Maybe tomorrow night?"

Empress sent back the short response of, "Maybe," and threw her phone on her bed. She tried to erase her irritation with a smile when she looked up at Faith. "Are you ready to go? Pops should be closing up the restaurant soon."

"Ready when you are," Faith responded. "You okay?" she asked.

"Yeah," Empress answered, turning back to get a shirt from her closet.

****

He was securing the building when he heard the approaching vehicle pull up to the curb.

"Get in, old man," Empress ordered after she rolled down the window.

A smile sprouted before he could control it. "You have one more time to call me old man, little girl," Pops said when he slid into the front seat. He leaned over to kiss the tip of her nose and was slightly startled by the person in the backseat. "Hey, Faith," he said, trying to maintain his composure.

"Hey, Sterlin," Faith replied.

"How about dinner at one of our old favorites to inaugurate Aunt Faith's visit?" Empress asked them.

"Which one?" Pops asked.

"Casa Antigua," Empress suggested.

"Sounds good. I haven't seen Ernesto since we were there a few years ago. It would be good to chat with him," Pops responded.

"Sounds good to me, too," Faith added.

"Cool. Casa Antigua it is," Empress answered.

They rode a few minutes in silence before Pops noticed the music playing on the radio. He raised an eyebrow at Empress.

When she noticed him looking at her, she asked, "What's wrong, old man?"

"I think you hit the wrong button on your radio, because I know you are not seriously listening to the Fania All-Stars."

"The Fanta who?" Empress sarcastically asked.

Pops and Faith laughed.

"Your mother tried and tried to get you interested in Latin music, and you resisted her every time. She finally gave up when you got your first Discman, and you constantly had those earphones on. I bet she is loving seeing this." Pops stayed with the memory of watching his wife move between the furniture in their living room as she danced to the songs on her favorite *Latin-Soul-Rock* album. In his memory, she tried to lead their bashful daughter into following her steps. He looked over at Empress and saw remnants of the little girl drawn into shyness from her awkwardness.

"I think I'm to blame for the Fania All-Stars," Faith said from the backseat. "My niece was just trying to reintroduce me to our Cuban heritage."

"Is that right?" Pops responded, still looking at Empress.

"Yes, and the fact that I'm more cultured than y'all assume. I listened to more than Prince and Michael Jackson on that Discman," Empress responded.

"Oh yeah, that's right," Pops added, snapping his fingers. "You used to listen to George Michael a lot too." Amused by his statement, he doubled over in laughter. "My mistake. I forgot how cultured you were."

Faith contributed to his laughter.

"You know," Empress said, talking over them, "it would be a shame if you two comedians had to walk the rest of the way to Casa Antigua."

As they pulled into the restaurant parking lot, Faith asked, "Will JS and his family be joining us?"

"Dang, I forgot to tell him we were coming here," Empress answered. "Let me call him, and I'll join you inside shortly."

Pops opened the truck door for Faith and extended his hand to her. His budding smile matched hers as their eyes met.

"JS, we're at Casa Antigua," they heard Empress say into her phone. They looked away from each other.

As they walked through the restaurant's door, they heard a loud, "Aaayeee," from across the room.

"My friends," a man yelled in a thick Cuban accent. A large man with a bushy mustache and a trailing ponytail greeted both Pops and Faith with tight hugs.

"Good to see you, Ernesto," Pops said after their hug.

"It's great to see you also, my friend. You're looking good, man." He turned his attention to Faith. "But, my friend, you do not compare to this vision beside you." He lifted her hand to kiss it. "*Como has sido, hermosa?*"

Faith's cheeks blushed a bit as he kissed her hand. "*He estado bien,*" she replied. "*Como has estado*, Ernesto?"

"*Estoy mucho mejor ahora,*" Ernesto replied through his toothy smile.

"Okay, Latin lover, can we please have a table," Pops interrupted.

"Ha," Ernesto replied and put his arm around Pops's shoulders. "Of course, my friend. Right this way," he said, escorting them to a large round table. He pointed at the man behind the bar along their walk and said, "Bodega Pago Asterisco 2014."

The man nodded and searched for the bottle of wine.

"My friends, you are going to love that wine. It's awfully close to Cuban." He stopped a young lady passing by with a tray of half-empty plates and glasses. "*Pan caliente y agua,*" he said to her.

Empress approached the table and greeted Ernesto. "Hi, Mr. Dominguez."

Ernesto wrapped Empress in a suffocating hug. "You have got to be kidding me. Look at little Empress. You are so beautiful. EJ is not going to believe this." He turned and waved someone over from across the room.

An imposing young woman with thick hair, long eyelashes, and modestly painted high cheek bones approached their table.

Ernesto greeted the young woman with a kiss on her cheek and an arm around her shoulders. "EJ, you remember the Silver family, don't you?"

"Yes, hello, everyone," EJ replied. "It's good to see you all again."

The Silver family sat stunned in silence for a few seconds until Empress ushered away their awkwardness. "EJ, you look amazing," she commented, pulling her into a hug.

EJ kissed her on the cheek. "Thank you, momma. You're looking really good yourself." Reading the bafflement on the others' faces, she continued. "It's been about a year since I transitioned."

"Oh," Pops remarked and smiled to try and mask his discomfort. "Congratulations," he said, not knowing how else to reply.

Faith and Empress both looked at him with raised eyebrows due to his klutzy statement.

Pops looked down at his menu with embarrassment.

"Yes, it's been quite a journey," Ernesto added and again kissed EJ on the cheek.

"Hey, family," JS said, approaching the table. He hugged Faith around her neck before planting a lingering kiss on her cheek. Then he walked over to Ernesto with an extended hand. "What's up, Mr. Dominguez?"

"Look at this handsome grown man," Ernesto exclaimed, greeting him with his customary big hug.

Over Ernesto's shoulder, JS noticed the intriguing woman beside him. "Hello," he replied and extended his hand to her.

"JS, you remember EJ, don't you?" Ernesto asked.

"Sure, where is he?" JS replied, still grasping the woman's hand.

Empress put her hand over her eyes and shook her head again.

"Hi, JS," EJ replied.

JS's eyes widened. "EJ?"

"Yep, it's me," EJ responded from behind a seemingly nervous grin.

"Holy shit," JS replied. "You look incredible."

"Thank you," EJ answered with a sense of relief.

"How?" JS asked. "I mean, what ...?" he said before catching himself again. "When?" he finally landed on.

EJ laughed at his stammering. "It's been about a year now."

"Wow," was all JS could say before taking his seat.

A server interrupted them with full wine glasses and a basket of warm bread.

"Looks like you updated the menu, Ernesto," Pops said, changing the subject.

"Yes, that's all EJ. She runs the daily operations now at all three locations. Business has been great since she took over."

"We added some fusion dishes to diversify the patronage. Like the pollo masala mojo is a blend of traditional Cuban and Indian dishes."

"That's so cool. I want to order that," JS declared. "I would love to do something like that at our next location. Like blending soul food with Spanish food."

"Now, son, we talked about this. We need to stick with what keeps the people coming in before we can think about changing things," Pops replied.

JS pursed his lips.

"Instead of ordering, do you all mind if I bring you an assortment of dishes for you to try? I'll throw in some traditional ones also," EJ asked.

"That sounds wonderful," Empress answered.

"Enjoy, my friends," Ernesto said as he and EJ walked away.

Faith grabbed JS by the hand. "How are you?" she asked.

"I'm good, Aunt Faith," he answered.

"How is your family?" she continued.

"Everyone is good. The kids are almost done with school. Trip is trying to get a football scholarship to any college, and Cammy is just itching to leave Charlotte."

"That's good," she replied.

"Soooo, a lot has changed here," Empress added.

"Honey, yes," Faith replied. "But you can feel the happiness and positivity in the air here."

"Yeah, I dig the vibe in here," JS added, looking at EJ interact with patrons across the room.

"Excuse me, everyone," Pops said before leaving the table. The decorative and structural changes of the restaurant disoriented him during his search for the bathroom.

"Everything okay, my friend?" Ernesto asked as he walked over to Pops.

"I thought the bathrooms were over here."

Ernesto guided him with an arm around his shoulders. "We moved them over here."

"Thanks." Pops was again disoriented when he walked into the bathroom. He was expecting to see the row of stalls and urinals he remembered.

Ernesto was standing at the end of the hallway when Pops exited the bathroom. "Are you sure you're okay, friend? You look like something is bothering you."

Pops attempted a smile. "Lots of changes around here." He turned and pointed in the direction he came. "Four individual bathrooms now. That had to cost a pretty penny."

"It did, but we want everyone that comes here to feel comfortable and just enjoy themselves while they're here. It was another one of EJ's ideas, and it seems to be working."

Pops nodded. "Speaking of changes ... EJ ... wow," he said with the same baffled look he had at the table.

Ernesto laughed. "Yes, lots of newness here, my friend."

"How did you handle it when he told you?"

"When she first told me she was transitioning, it was a lot to take in," Ernesto admitted. "But we had already been through so much a few years back, so I understood."

"What do you mean?"

"EJ was at Pulse nightclub in Orlando that night when all those people were killed." He paused as if to steady himself through the trauma of that horrific night. "She was texting me and hiding in a storage closet until her phone cut off. For the next eight hours, I didn't know if my child was dead or alive." He shook his head and cleared his throat. "I don't wish that feeling on any parent." He pressed his fingers into his eyes to wipe them. "When she finally was able to call and let me know she was okay, that's when she told me she felt more like herself as a woman. I told her I loved her and was just happy she was alive."

"Wow, Ernesto, I'm so sorry to hear that," Pops responded.

"Thank you, but I still feel blessed after going through all that. A lot of parents didn't get the good news I got about their child still being alive." He wiped his eyes again to clear the welling tears. "Don't get me wrong, I had a lot to adjust to and it wasn't easy. I was so worried about what people would think about me as a father supporting his child with transitioning." He landed a heavy hand on Pops's shoulder and laughed a little. "You know that doesn't go over well in our cultures, my friend." He cleared his throat again. "But then I had to think about how scared EJ must have been this whole time, and how much she was about to endure just to be comfortable with herself. What kind of father would I be if I didn't support her through that?"

Pops looked away from the realness of the moment.

"My friend, if we don't change, then the world will leave us where we are stuck," Ernesto stated and patted Pops's shoulder.

Pops nodded, smiled, and walked back to the table. He saw EJ explaining what each dish was to his family as they were placed on the table. Again, he shook his head and tried to rid himself of the realness of the moment.

"You okay?" Empress asked as Pops sat back down at the table.

He nodded at her. "Just catching up with Ernesto."

"Oh my goodness, you all have to try this pollo masala mojo," Faith said, interrupting them. She swayed her shoulders and danced a little.

The rest of the family laughed at her antics.

"And this wine is insanely good," Empress added.

They exchanged compliments and suggestions on which food to try next as they ate. When each one encountered a dish they liked, they mimicked Faith's dance for everyone's amusement.

"How is everything?" EJ asked, coming back to check on them.

They nodded or raised their glasses, all their mouths full.

EJ laughed. "Glad you are enjoying everything. Please let me know if you need anything else."

Moments later, after most everything had been devoured on the table and they were all too full to swallow another bite, Pops asked a passing staff member for their check.

Ernesto and EJ appeared at the table a few minutes later. "How was everything, my friends?" Ernesto asked.

"So good. Awesome. Delicious," they said, talking over one another.

"Glad you enjoyed everything," EJ replied.

"Ernesto, I asked a young lady to bring our check so you all can finish cleaning and close up. I know how it is when you have those lingering customers that don't want to leave."

"Nonsense, you stay as long as you like, and your meal is on us. We enjoyed seeing all of you this evening."

“That’s so nice. Thank you so much,” they responded, again talking over each other.

“Thank you for coming in this evening,” EJ expressed.

“Don’t let so much time pass before we see you again, my friends,” Ernesto said before walking away with his arm again wrapped around EJ.

They sat around the table, looking at one another before concluding it was time to leave.

“Y’all go ahead,” JS said as they all stood. “I’m going to talk with EJ about some of their changes.”

Empress raised her eyebrow at JS, and Pops shook his head.

“I’ll catch up with you tomorrow, Auntie,” JS said and planted another kiss on Faith’s cheek.

After they climbed into Empress’s truck, Faith declared, “That was so much fun.”

“It sure was. It’s amazing how well they are doing after all those changes,” Empress added.

“Yes, it is,” Faith agreed.

“All the changes aren’t good. Ernesto told me the new bathrooms set them back, and I noticed not many of their usual customers were there tonight,” Pops interjected.

“Aunt Faith, do you still want to go to the lake house tonight?” Empress asked, changing the subject.

"I guess it's too late now to drive way up there," she responded.

"You can stay at my place tonight, and I can take you in the morning," Pops offered.

"Thank you, Sterlin. That will be fine."

Empress shrugged. "Okay, enjoy your stay at the Old Man Motel."

Faith broke into a laugh that rivaled the one they had on the way to the restaurant.

"Watch it, little girl," Pops said, joining the laughter.

13.

Magenta

It was hard to look at her sometimes, because she and her sister, Hope, shared so much. Pops picked up a couple of pomegranate seeds and put them in his mouth. His teeth slowly punctured the seeds' skin, releasing the juice.

His mind rambled back to the first time he ate a pomegranate and the apprehension he had when he first saw the peculiar-looking fruit. Hope slit its skin into fourths and then held it under water as she broke it apart. She pulled some little jewel-looking beads from the inside and scooped them into a bowl. He remembered thinking how he wasn't sure what pieces they were supposed to eat, but that he would mask his confusion for as long as possible to appear as modern as she was. She picked a few seeds from the bowl and told him to close his eyes and open his mouth. It was then his ritual of unconscionably obeying her began. He felt her slender fingers slide the seeds into his mouth. "Slowly bite them," she whispered into his ear. As he bit the first one, the unexpected, tangy juice flowed and dribbled a little down his lips. Still, with his eyes closed, he felt her tongue run across his lips, and then the softness of her lips pressed against his. It wasn't his first kiss with anyone, but it was his first kiss with the right one.

"Where did you go, Sterlin?" Faith asked, forcing him back to the present.

"Just got lost in my head for a bit," he responded.

They had been spared many of the plagues of aging like excessive weight gain and an abundance of gray hair. It was as if God had been purposeful in limiting the hardships that can come with aging in replacement for their common loss of Hope they both endured years ago and would be saddled with for the rest of their lives.

"So, birthday girl, what would you like to do for your upcoming day?" Pops asked to shift himself outside of his mind.

Faith fidgeted with her magenta-painted fingernails a bit before answering. She shrugged. "I don't know," she answered.

Pops smiled at another passing memory. "Remember that time when we all drove to the beach with about twenty dollars between us."

She joined him in the smile and nodded. "You got that cheap little tent for us all to sleep in on the beach because we couldn't afford a hotel room. And we had a wonderful dinner of those hot dogs that had probably been in that store since Jesus was a baby."

"Yep, and I ended up sleeping in the car because the tent was too small for even the two of you."

They both laughed and Faith nodded again. "That's what I want to do."

Pops tilted his head and raised an eyebrow.

"I want to experience something I've never done, just as we did then," she said to clarify. "But I want to eat food that was made in this century."

He nodded and placed more pomegranate seeds in his mouth. Again, he bit each one with slow intention.

"You still love those things just like Hope did," Faith commented.

He nodded and smiled, reliving highlights of his memory that reminded him why he loved them.

She shook her head. "I find them so annoying. All the preparation you have to go through just to eat them doesn't fit the modest satisfaction of actually eating them."

He thought of how different Hope and Faith were internally, though externally, they were identical. Hope was like the simmering embers of a slow-burning fire. Faith was constant combustion, igniting all in her path with her explosive personality.

Faith rubbed her right eye with her index finger as she yawned, the same way her sister did when she was too tired to even hold her head up.

"I better let you get some sleep," Pops said as he began to stand.

She placed her hand on his and gave it a gentle squeeze. "Please sit with me a little longer."

He sat back down and looked at her hand on his. Seeing her slender fingers wrapped around his made him feel secure and sparked affinity, which scared him. Another memory slid from the hidden crevices of his mind—the first time a year ago when the feeling of her slender fingers against his face brought the unthinkable to thought and prompted their first kiss. His feelings of security and affinity were immediately replaced with the heat of embarrassment. He pulled his hand away from hers and picked up more pomegranate seeds.

"Empress seems well," she remarked, sensing his discomfort.

"Yes, she does. I think it might have something to do with a new guy I introduced her to."

Faith's eyebrows raised. "A new guy?" she asked in clarification.

"Yes, I've been working with a really smart and nice young man named Dabney on plans for the new restaurant. I think he and Empress hit it off at the Memorial Day cookout."

Faith looked away from him.

"What?" Pops asked.

"Her happiness has never been tied to a guy before."

"Yes, I know, but there's a first time for everything, I guess," Pops said with a slight smile.

"Yeah, I guess." She paused. "JS seems well also."

Pops rolled his eyes, closed them, and shook his head. "JS is still the same as he always has been."

Faith laughed a little. "I remember when Hope called me after their first day of school. She said JS had to sit in the corner the whole afternoon because he was trying to kiss girls on the playground during recess."

Pops rolled his eyes and shook his head. "I wish he would just get it together and realize his potential. It's almost like he needs a sense of chaos to even function."

"I'm sure he will. Some of us have to learn things the hard way." Faith again rubbed her right eye with her index finger as she yawned.

"You better get some rest," Pops suggested and again stood to leave the room.

"How long are we going to do this, Sterlin?"

"Do what?"

"Pretend."

"Pretend what?"

"Pretend like there isn't something between us."

Pops sat back down. He rested his elbows on the table and steadied his head in his hands. He couldn't escape the realness of this moment.

"I'm not saying we need to act on any impulses again, but we should at least be able to talk about this." Faith tapped her index finger on the table. "Why else did you want me here?"

"I don't know," he admitted. "I wanted to see you alone, but I know that's wrong."

"Is it, though?"

He dropped his hands from his head and looked at Faith. "Give me a little more time. Let's just celebrate your birthday, and maybe we will talk about it after that."

Faith tightened her lips and shook her head. "Don't worry about taking me to the lake house in the morning. I'll find my own way." She stood up and walked across the room to turn off the floor lamp. "Good night, Sterlin."

"Faith."

"Good night," she replied again while pulling back the bedding.

Pops stood to leave but hesitated on taking a step toward the door as a last check on how serious she was about him leaving the room.

When she walked over to the door and waited with her hand on the knob to close it behind him, he realized her seriousness.

"Good night, Faith," he said before she closed the door in his face.

14.

Gold

The clothes strewn about her bed and floor indicated her current mental state. There had only been a few texts between them, mostly business questions, since they had met. But the many moments Empress spent scrolling through her social media accounts made her feel like she knew more about Nya. Many pictures with lots of people at lots of events gave Empress lots more intrigue.

Once her reeling mind felt a mild level of satisfaction with her attire of cropped black jeans, a white silk shirt, and peep-toe ankle boots, she left for the restaurant.

During her drive, she remembered her evening routine of walking home with Pops and how she hadn't informed him of the change in plans.

Pops answered her call on the first ring. "Hello, baby girl."

"Hey, Pops, I'm not going to be able to walk home with you this evening. Is there someone there that can make sure you get home okay?"

"Yes, there is someone here that can make sure I get home okay, and his name is me. I'm a grown man, little girl," he replied.

"Okay, grown man, can you please let me know when you have made it home safely?"

"Not a problem, I'll call you when I get in."

"Actually, could you please just text me?"

"Hmm, my daughter doesn't want to talk to her father as she does almost every evening? Does she, by chance, have another date?" Pops asked with a hint of excitement.

"Please text me when you get home, Pops."

"I will, and tell Dabney I said hello."

"Yeah, sure," Empress responded with nonchalance.

She arrived at the restaurant as their phone call ended, and, in her vanity mirror, did a once over to ensure her hair and makeup were still intact.

As she walked to the restaurant, she also remembered Faith being in town. "Hey, Aunt Faith," she texted. "Forgot, I have plans tonight. Are you good?"

Faith replied with a thumbs-up emoji, followed by, "Come up to the lake house tomorrow morning so we can have breakfast together."

"Will do."

As the hostess escorted Empress to the table where Nya awaited, she realized her fine casual dining interpretation was incorrect, as described on the restaurant's website.

Nya sat at the table wearing a black strapless dress with a lace overlay accented with rose gold earrings and the fuchsia stiletto heels from their first encounter.

"I'm sorry," Empress apologized as she approached the table. "I think I'm too casual for fine casual dining."

Nya's eyes scanned up to Empress's face. "You look perfectly fine to me," she said with a smile.

As Empress took her seat, she again looked around the room to confirm she was indeed underdressed. She appreciated Nya's attempt to put her at ease but still felt embarrassment enveloping her. Her thoughts were interrupted when she heard Nya say, "Red or white?" She looked at Nya, confused.

"Are you a red or white wine drinker, or would you like something else?"

"Oh. I prefer red."

"Can you please bring her a glass of the 2010 Blackbird Arise Red Blend?" Nya asked the server. "Trust me," she added, shifting her attention back to Empress and winking.

The ambiguity of their meet-up left Empress at a loss for words. Small talk had never been natural for her, and not understanding the context of this situation didn't help matters.

"So, Empress—interesting name, by the way—what do you do when you're not bumping into people on sidewalks? You learned so much about me the other day, but I didn't get to learn a lot about you."

"That was my father's doing," Empress replied with a slight eye roll.

"Your father makes you run into people on sidewalks?" Nya asked.

"No," Empress replied, laughing. "I meant he's the one who named me."

"He gave you a lot live up to."

"Yes, he did. Whenever I ask him about it, he says it was his way of setting me up for greatness."

"Well, from just looking at you, I think you achieved what he set you up for."

Empress hesitated. "Thank you." She didn't know how to take Nya's compliment.

The server returned to take their orders, and, as Empress scoured the menu, Nya informed her of her favorite dishes. "Do you mind if I order for us," Nya asked.

Empress shook her head and then felt a half-smile stretching on her face.

As the server left to fulfill their orders, Nya again asked, "So what do you do when you're not bumping into people?"

"I'm currently working with my family on opening the next restaurant location, but usually, I do contract work as a financial and investment advisor."

"Cool, and what do you do for fun?"

Fun? The word echoed in Empress's head as she tried to link its meaning to a recent activity in her life. She rolled her eyes upward as she usually did when conducting a mental search for something.

After some seconds of silence, Nya said, "I've never seen anyone be stumped by the word *fun*."

"I'm sorry, it's just been so long since I've done anything that would be considered fun."

"Well, what do you like to do?"

"I like going to see movies. I think there's still something special about watching them on the big screen with a bucket of popcorn."

"Cool, I like going to movies as well. What was the last good one you saw?"

Again Empress looked upward. She thought about the last movie she saw that left an impression on her. Camellia's laugh crept between her thoughts, and, before she could analyze its intrusion, she remembered seeing that laugh as Camellia gave into the amusement on the screen before them. Empress ran her hand over her hair. "I honestly can't remember the name of the movie, or much of what it was about, but I remember it being very good for some reason."

"Wow, your majesty, you are truly an interesting enigma," Nya replied before taking a drink from her glass. "Luckily, I like puzzles," she added.

As Empress pondered Nya's statement, the server returned with their orders. "So what do you do for fun?" Empress asked after the server walked away.

"I love to settle into a good book. Movies are great, but there's nothing like living a story through your own mind."

"Yeah, there's nothing like a good book."

"Yes. It's almost as good as having dinner with a beautiful woman," Nya responded.

Empress bit her bottom lip and felt her brow wrinkling. "I may be misreading you, but I'm getting the impression you're hitting on me."

A sly, seductive smile Empress recognized well from wearing it herself on many occasions now showed on Nya's face. "I was wondering how many more hints I was going to have to drop."

Empress emptied her wine glass in one large gulp just as their server approached the table to check on them. "May I get you another glass?" she asked as Empress placed the glass back on the table.

"You can bring the whole damn bottle," Empress replied in all seriousness, extracting a laugh from both Nya and the server.

Empress was at a loss for words again, and once more, Nya broke the thick silence between them. "Did I misread you?" she asked.

"No, I'm just a little shocked is all."

"Why are you shocked? The day we ran into each other, I noticed you checking me out. And I saw the way you looked at me when you and Dabney came to my lecture. Apparently, you didn't notice me doing the same."

"I guess I'm just not used to someone being so open about their sexuality in this area. When I lived in California, the rainbow flag was flown on more buildings than the state flag was, so the atmosphere there was different compared to here."

"Yes, the atmosphere here is more sexually repressed than I'm accustomed to also, but the only way it will become liberated is for more of us to show we're not ashamed of who we are and we are nothing to fear."

Empress looked beyond Nya and into her own thoughts. She was by no means ashamed of who she was but was afraid of seeing the disheartened look in her father's eyes that was sure to show if she came out to him.

"You're not out, are you?" Nya asked, sensing Empress's retreat into her thoughts.

"I am ... to a few," Empress answered. "My brother knows, and my aunt knows."

"So, your brother and aunt are the only people in your family that know?"

Again, Empress regressed into her thoughts. "Yes," she responded, not wanting to divulge how her brother's wife also knew.

"Interesting." Nya shrugged. "Well, we all have to walk our own paths in life." She took a sip from her glass before continuing. "Closet living has never been the life for me. I kicked the door off of my closet at fifteen when my mother walked in on me and a friend doing 'homework,'" she said, adding quotation marks with her fingers.

Empress's eyes enlarged into perfect circles, remembering her nearly caught moments with Camellia during their sleepovers in high school. "What did she do when she caught you?"

"She was nice enough to close the door quickly. After we scrambled around to get dressed, my friend ran out the front door right past my mother, who was sitting in the living room in shock. I went into the living room too, and all my mother could say was, 'You said you two were studying.' So,

I replied with, 'We were studying anatomy.' For some reason, she didn't find that amusing."

An overwhelming laugh erupted from Empress, and as she tried to gain control of it, a baffling snort escaped her. She covered her mouth in embarrassment.

"Coming out to my mother was very easy after that," Nya continued. "And once I came out to her, I didn't give a damn who else knew."

"So, do you identify as a lesbian?"

"Yes." Nya tilted her head. "How do you identify?"

Empress paused. She never gave much thought to her sexual identity since she focused so much on concealing her attraction to women. She thought back to a Human Sexuality class she took in college and tried to remember her self-assigned rating on the Kinsey scale. "I guess I identify as a lesbian also." She took a drink from her glass and tilted her head as Nya had done. "What about those special moments you and Dabney had when you first met?" Empress asked.

Nya waved her hand. "Like I said, those were just drunken antics. I had just moved to Charlotte about a year before that, and the girl I moved here with wanted to spread her wings in this new city and suddenly didn't want to be in a relationship anymore. So, I was heartbroken and finding all kinds of ways to distract myself from the pain then. Those couple of nights with Dabney were just a couple of very many distractions."

"So is your ex still here spreading her wings?"

"Yep, she is still here spreading her legs to all of Charlotte. We used to run into each other at a couple of the gay spots here, but it just became too much drama with her, so I stopped going to them."

The server returned to their table to clear their plates and ask about their dessert interests. "I wouldn't mind something sweet," Empress remarked, looking at Nya and trying her own hand at flirty banter.

"I would like to taste something sweet also," Nya said, returning her sly, seductive smile.

The server looked back and forth between the two of them like she was watching a ping-pong match. "I'll bring you a dessert menu," she stated, unable to mask her discomfort.

"It's still early. Would you like to do something after dessert?" Nya asked.

"Sure, what do you have in mind?"

"I don't live far from here, so maybe we can go to my place and continue exchanging awkward stories."

"I'm game, but I'm sure I don't have anything to tell that's as entertaining as your coming out story."

****

Black-and-white photos of authors hung around Nya's living room, and books lined an entire wall many people would have considered prime real estate for a mounted television. "Make yourself at home," Nya said to Empress as she moved into the kitchen.

Empress walked over to the books to read some of the titles. Nya's collection showed her eclectic flair as the included works varied between styles and genres. Eric Jerome Dickey's *Between Lovers* sat next to Charles Dickens's *Great Expectations*, and to the right of that was *Black Boy* by Richard Wright. As Nya handed Empress a glass of wine, Empress said, "You know they have e-books now."

Nya shook her head. "Not the same," she replied as she made her way to the couch. She pushed a button on her phone and the rich voice of Nina Simone filled the room with lyrics about "Feeling Good."

Empress chuckled to herself and sat on the other end of the couch.

"What's so funny?" Nya asked.

"This is one of my favorite songs, thanks to my father."

"Wow! She's beautiful, has good taste in music, and she seems to come from a good family."

Nya raised her glass in a gesture of approval before taking a drink. "Why is this one of your favorites, thanks to your father?"

"He always plays this when I'm feeling down about something, and he dances around like a buffoon until it makes me smile."

"Sounds like a great guy."

"He is," Empress replied.

They sat in silence, listening to the music transition to the next artist. "Lingerie" by Lizzo filled the air.

"So," Empress said, "you read actual books, listen to music by strong women, and almost gave your mother a heart attack at fifteen. Anything else I should know about you?"

"What else would you like to know about me?" Nya asked.

Empress searched her mind for another subject while she took a sip from her glass. She felt Nya's gaze on her skin but continued to look straight ahead at the dam of books holding all that was modern at bay. "This is really good wine," she noted as a distraction.

"Yep," Nya replied as she moved closer to Empress's end of the couch. She lifted a fallen lock of curls from Empress's face and brushed her fingers through her thick hair. "You seem nervous," she whispered in Empress's ear.

"No, not at all," Empress lied. She closed her eyes as Nya's fingers traced the contours of her face and guided their lips together. Empress tasted the sweetened warmth of Nya's mouth as their tongues touched and then felt a cool rush of liquid wash down her chest. "Shit!" Empress yelled, springing to her feet. The red wine on her white silk shirt resembled a bleeding angel wing.

"Nope, you're not nervous at all," Nya said, making her way to the kitchen. She returned with a damp cloth and a box of baking soda.

"I'm sorry," Empress apologized, diverting her eyes away from Nya's in embarrassment.

"No, I'm sorry. Apparently, I'm making you extremely uncomfortable this evening."

Empress continued to pat, scrub, and blot the stain on her shirt. As Nya's words registered with her, she realized the unintended message her awkward behavior was sending. Without moving to her next thought, and then on to the inevitable what-ifs that would follow, she began to unbutton her shirt.

"The bathroom is over there if you want to rinse your shirt," Nya said, pointing to the opposite side of the room.

Empress's shirt fell to the floor as she walked over to Nya. She placed her hands on Nya's waist and pulled her closer. Again she was greeted with the sweet, balmy warmth of Nya's mouth. With each kiss, almost forgotten areas inside her were ignited. Her skin tingled in anticipation of Nya's traveling hands. Her body felt oxygenated from Nya's kisses.

Nya led her by hand into the bedroom, turning off lights along the way so that the only illumination came from the busy city. She unzipped her dress and pulled it down her body to slowly reveal the black lace underwear beneath. She grabbed the waistband of Empress's jeans and pulled her on top of her as she slid back onto the bed.

They explored each other throughout the night, causing an oblivious reckoning with time. When the morning sunlight broke between the surrounding buildings, it painted gold slivers throughout the room. The gold slivers reached Empress's body just as she quivered from the onset of another orgasm. In the calm that followed, she realized this was the first time in a long while when Camellia's face was not her last thought before falling asleep.

15.

Blue

"Why do you keep staring at me?" Empress asked from behind a coy smile.

"I think I know why you keep smiling. I'm just trying to figure out who is making you smile," Faith replied.

Empress waved her hand to dismiss Faith's insinuation. "I'm just in a good mood."

"Girl, please. I'm not too old to remember a satisfying sex smile."

"Aunt Faith!"

"Am I right?"

"Yes, but do you have to be so loud about it," Empress whispered.

Faith waved her hand. "If more people walked around with smiles like yours, and stopped being so uptight about something that makes us all feel good, this world would be a much better place."

Empress smiled wider and shook her head at the blunt honesty of her aunt's wisdom.

"So was it your friend that sent you all of those pics of her lady parts?"

"No, it was someone else I met recently." Empress trailed off, looking around the diner they had just walked into. The windows were dingy with dead flies collected along the sills. It looked like the same dirty water had been used to clean the counter and floor. The customers scattered throughout the restaurant sized them up—the two fancy colored ladies obviously weren't from the area.

"Good. Leave that pussy-pics chick alone. She seems too messy," Faith continued while they waited to be seated.

Empress's mouth dropped open and her eyes darted to Faith, breaking her surveillance of their surroundings. "Never in my life did I ever think I would hear you use the P-word. And can you please never use it again?"

"What's wrong with me saying pussy? We both have a pussy, and that girl who sent the pics obviously has a pussy."

Empress placed her hand on her face and shook her head while laughing.

"Pussy," Faith whispered through her teeth as a server approached to seat them.

"How many?" the server asked from behind tired eyes and a seemingly withered will to care.

"Two, please," Faith replied.

"Follow me," the server said.

The noticing eyes of the other customers followed them through the restaurant and stifled Empress's amusement. "Aunt Faith, why are we here?"

As the server placed their menus on a table in the center of the room, Faith asked, "Can we please sit at a booth in the back?" Empress noticed a younger woman waiting on customers farther into the restaurant.

The server rolled her eyes before walking toward the booths in the back. She motioned toward an open booth as a signal for Faith's approval.

"Thank you," Faith replied. "This is fine."

The server slapped the plastic menus on the booth table before walking away.

"Aunt Faith, I really didn't plan on dying today," Empress whispered from across the booth.

Faith smiled and put her hand on Empress's fidgeting fingers.

"I'll be with you ladies in a minute," the younger woman said as she cleared a nearby booth of empty plates and plastic cups.

Faith turned her head and widened her smile at the waitress.

Empress looked over at the woman and then back at Faith. Her eyes shifted back and forth several times in search of some reason for them being there.

"What can I get you ladies to drink?" the younger woman asked after she came to their table.

"Just two cups of coffee will be fine," Faith answered.

"Would you like cream and sugar?"

"Sure," Faith replied.

Empress felt her eyes continuing to ricochet between them. At first glance, there were no similarities between the two. The pale, blotchy skin of the younger woman was no comparison to Faith's smooth, tawny-colored skin. Faith's thick black hair cascaded to her shoulders while the young woman's brown hair sat stringy and lifeless against her face. The younger woman had wide, sad blue eyes while Faith's were the shape of almonds and near in color. Yet, with the younger woman closer to them now, Empress noticed the faint familiarity in their thin noses and strong jawlines that jutted out into pointed chins. She read the younger woman's name tag—Karina.

Faith turned her smile back to Empress.

When the woman walked away, Empress asked, "I'm almost afraid to know this, but who is Karina?"

Faith patted Empress's hand again and her smile grew wider.

Karina returned with two cups of coffee and a chilled decanter of creamer. “Are you ladies ready to order?” she asked while placing the items on the table.

“I think we will just stick with the coffee for now,” Faith answered.

“Okay,” Karina responded. “I’ll be back to check on you.” She looked back over her shoulder as she walked away as if she, too, had noticed something.

“Who is she, Aunt Faith?”

Faith gently squeezed Empress’s hand. “That is your aunt. She is my father’s youngest child.”

Empress looked over at Karina, who was busy waiting on another table. Though she saw their few similarities minutes prior, she still couldn’t believe it. “Are you sure?”

Faith nodded. “Her name is Karina Deale. Her father was also my father, David Deale. He was married to my mother seventeen years before Karina was born.”

Empress’s mouth dropped open as her eyes again shifted over to Karina.

“Isn’t Ancestory.com something,” Faith said and then laughed.

“Holy shit,” was all Empress could say. She saw Karina making her way back over to their table and tried to compose herself.

"You ladies doing okay?" Karina asked.

"Yes, thank you," Faith answered. "There is one thing, though."

Empress felt her eyes grow to the size of silver dollars as she anticipated Faith's next statement.

"My name is Faith Deale, and this is my niece, Empress. David Deale was my father, also."

The stun landed on Karina's face as it had on Empress's. She looked at Empress, and then again at Faith, and then again at Empress. "I don't understand," she replied.

"Your father, David Deale, was married to my mother many years before you were born."

Karina looked at both women and then looked around the room as if to see if anyone had overheard their conversation. "I still don't understand what you want from me."

"Nothing, dear," Faith said. "We want nothing at all. I just wanted you and my niece to have this information."

Empress extended her hand. "It's nice to meet you, Karina," she said with sincerity.

"Nice to meet you also," Karina replied, shaking Empress's hand while wearing the same look of befuddlement.

Faith slid a piece of paper across the table to Karina. "This is my cell number. I'll be staying about ten miles away from here in the Lake Norman area for the next few days if you'd like to talk more."

Karina picked up the paper and nodded at Faith.

"This should cover the coffee," Faith continued and handed Karina a twenty-dollar bill. "Ready, Empress?" she asked, scooting out of the booth.

Empress nodded and began to scoot also.

The other customers watched them as they walked through the restaurant again, and some looked back at Karina as if they were trying to decode the look of confusion on her face.

As they exited the restaurant, Faith said, "Now we can go and get some breakfast for real this time."

Empress looked over at her aunt and then back at the restaurant. She saw Karina through one of the dingy windows watching the two women who had just jarred her small world. The wide blue eyes she wore looked even sadder.

****

The lake waves lapped against the restaurant's pier, causing occasional water splashes to leap in the air and sparkle in the sunlight. Empress pondered the times she and JS jumped from the pier behind their lake house as children. She thought about how crazy it seemed now learning some of her lost relatives were only a few miles down the road.

"Oh my goodness." Faith broke into her happy dance as she chewed. "This seafood omelet is the best I have ever had."

Empress watched as her aunt enjoyed herself.

"How is your food?" Faith asked. "You haven't eaten much."

"It's fine," Empress replied. "I'm still digesting everything that happened earlier." Empress paused to take a drink of her coffee. "Do you think she will call you?"

Faith shrugged. "Who knows? That wasn't the point to all this."

"What was the point?" Empress asked.

"Like I said, it was to give both of you the information." She took another bite of her omelet and followed it up with a drink of her Bloody Mary. "Plus," she continued, "tomorrow, I will be fifty-nine years old, and that's something I never thought I would live to see."

Empress crinkled her brow.

"I'm sure you have heard some stories about my younger years."

Empress shook her head. "No, not really."

"Well, let's just say that I was hell on wheels with a rocket strapped to my ass."

Empress shook her head and laughed.

Faith squinted as if she were focusing on something in the distance. "Hope was supposed to be here turning fifty-nine tomorrow also."

Empress watched as Faith steadied herself with another drink from her Bloody Mary. She felt the same tight ball in her chest that was there when she and JS talked about the banana pancake mornings with their mother.

"This meant a lot to Hope. She originally came back to Charlotte to try and find our Deale relatives." Again, she took a sip of her drink. "To me, David Deale was a mean, worthless piece of shit who didn't deserve to live after the way he treated our mother. But Hope was the compassionate one. She figured he acted that way for some bigger reasons. And it was important to her to know him and understand where she came from."

The tight ball in Empress's chest had grown and pushed all her emotions to the surface. Empress felt tears welling in her eyes.

Faith wrapped her fingers around Empress's hand. She lifted her glass with her free hand and nodded at Empress to do the same. "Happy birthday, Hope," she said around her own tears. "We love you and miss you dearly," she concluded before clinking her glass to Empress's.

Empress blotted her breaking tears after their toast to her mother. She sniffed back her remaining emotions and watched as Faith did the same.

"So," Faith said while fanning her face, "tell me about this new person who had you grinning like Bill Cosby with a pocketful of Quaaludes at The Playboy Mansion."

An unexpected laugh escaped Empress. The sudden clash of humor and sadness in her made it hard to control herself.

Faith joined in her laughter. "Come on, now."

Empress tried to contain her laughter, but still had the occasional tremor each time she started to speak. "Okay, for real now," she said, trying to get it together. "I officially met her about a week ago after one of her seminars."

"What do you mean, you *officially* met her?"

"It's crazy, but we literally ran into each other one night on the street about a week before that. We didn't formally meet then, though, because I had to rush off to meet Pops at the restaurant."

"Wow," Faith said, leaning back in her chair as if the news had blown her back. "So, your lives randomly intersected twice?"

Empress blinked a few times. "Yes, I guess so."

"That's huge."

"Why do you say that?"

"Because there are no coincidences, honey. Everything happens for a reason. It was destiny for you two to meet."

Empress pondered the thought. "Well, damn," she said at the realization her aunt could be right.

"So you met her after one of her seminars? What does she lecture?"

"Sustaining and growing small businesses. A guy helping us with the next restaurant named Dabney introduced us after the seminar."

"Ah, the infamous Dabney," Faith responded.

"What do you mean?"

"Your father told me about Dabney the other night. He thinks you two are dating."

Empress exhaled hard through her nose. "I know he does."

"Oh well." Faith slurped up the last of her Bloody Mary. "Tell me more about her."

"Her name is Nya. She's brilliant. She really loves learning, and she reads actual books. And she's very funny; she had me laughing most of the night. And OMG, she is ..." Empress paused and shook her head before finishing her sentence, "She is so damn pretty."

Faith again wrapped her hand around Empress's. "I have never ever seen you light up like that before. This lady might be the one."

Empress smiled and shook her head. "It's way too early to say all that."

"Honey, it's never too early to think about your happiness. Especially when you find someone to contribute to your happiness."

Their conversation was interrupted by Empress's buzzing phone. After she read her text message, her brow furrowed, and she let out a questioning, "Hmmm."

"What's wrong?" Faith asked.

"Nothing really. Pops just texted me that he had to go down to Charleston and that he'll be there all weekend. He said something about having to pick up some equipment from a restaurant depot down there."

Faith leaned back in her seat. She rolled her eyes and tightened her lips as if she was trying to swallow her rising words.

"I'm sorry, Aunt Faith, but I made plans with Nya tomorrow night, because I know you and Pops usually spend your birthday visiting Mommy's gravesite and reliving memories about her. I can cancel with Nya so we can do something together."

"No, you will not cancel your plans with your future wife," Faith responded and raised one side of her mouth to a half smile. "I'll be fine. I honestly wanted to spend most of my time at the lake house, because there is still so much of Hope there."

Empress placed her other hand on top of Faith's. "I love you," she said to both her aunt and her departed mother.

The lapping waves and splashing water droplets continued to provide a quiet symphony as they finished their breakfast.

On their ride back to the lake house, Faith's phone vibrated. Her lips slowly curled into a smile as she read the text.

"Was that her?" Empress asked.

"Huh?" Faith answered.

"Was that Karina?"

"Oh ... no," Faith stammered. "That was an old friend of mine wishing me an early happy birthday."

"Oh." Empress sensed something more. "Was that an old boyfriend?" she asked, smiling also.

Faith's smile grew wider. "Unfortunately, no. He's just always been a friend."

16.

Silver

His six-foot-five frame felt as if it were shrinking down to the size of a frail child as he walked through the door. The smell of a recent mountain rain hung in the logs that made up the cabin and intertwined with the forest fragrances of wet pine and wildflowers.

Pops looked down at the spot beneath his feet and shrunk further into frailty. He still saw the specks of blood mixed with his tears as he had punched the floor until his knuckles swelled and were covered with broken skin all those years ago. The site of that memorial of pain traveled to his gut and made him feel slightly nauseous. He felt soft tremors rise up his spine, which caused his hand to tremble as it had done on that day after being pummeled into the unflinching wood floor.

His wife of nine years had just died, and she had almost taken their daughter with her. The pain of those broken, bleeding knuckles was the first sign he was still alive, and it was the first time the pain of loss was finally outweighed by some other feeling. The robust wailing he allowed himself in that time of agony pierced his ears as it echoed off the walls and called back to him. As his tears splattered and parted the small puddles of blood beneath him, he welcomed them. He could feel again; he could hear again; he could heal now.

On that day, the cabin became his place of refuge when life cruelly reminded him that he was a single father who knew little about raising children and that he was a man cut in half after the abrupt loss of his wife. It was here he learned to exist and to cope. The only distractions he allowed himself in this place of solace included the colorful stories of Thomas Wolfe's life in this town of Asheville, the lyrical poetry of Langston Hughes, and the grounding lessons of the Bible. Here, he could always reset and remember what it now meant to be Sterlin Silver—a widower always fumbling through parenthood, who had an affection for well-written words and an indebtedness to quiet.

He looked around the cabin and saw his books strewn about the floor, his plaid blanket gathered in a corner on the couch, and his coffee cup still sitting on the table. Here, time was still, and that's what he loved most. Here, he didn't have to think of life's immediate ails like when JS almost didn't graduate from high school because his grades were lower than the letter Z. When Empress was the constant target of ridicule in her teen years. When he had to close the restaurant briefly due to the economic recession. When he realized he would never again feel the depth of love he had for his wife. Here, he controlled sound, and light, and existence.

Over the many years, the cabin existed as an extension of his life when he required solitude. He would mask his escapes to this place with excuses, to his children and others, of restaurant-related excursions and conventions. He required this place to get quiet and understand how Sterlin Silver fit into the world overall.

He soon realized the frailty he felt standing in his sanctuary doorway predicted his upcoming vulnerability. For the first time, this extension of himself was going to be introduced to someone else. He agonized through the decision of inviting Faith to come here. The gravity of sharing his intimacy with someone else was massive enough, but who he was sharing it with carried a weight greater than anything he could imagine.

There had been women through the years, many of whom were wrapped in the aspiration of becoming the next Mrs. Sterlin Silver, but none of them knew him like Faith. She was the only woman who understood all he had lost in Hope, because she, too, had experienced that loss. Faith allowed him the patience and time he needed to reach adequacy before pondering the next level. He initially loved her as his sister-in-law, but, after they both lost Hope, he grew to love her as an individual woman and not the combined duo of them.

He wanted to give Faith something no one else ever had from him, including, and especially, his late wife. He wanted to give her a piece of him where he had cried, laughed, and healed. He wanted to give her this mended version of Sterlin Silver.

He trembled as he thought about the potential circumstances this could bring to him and, especially, his family. Would he and Faith become the new, altered version of him and Hope? Would his children understand that she was not a replacement of their mother? Would everyone accept the two of them together?

A tear ran down his cheek as the weight he was bearing pushed his six-foot five-inch frame farther down to where he almost looked a foot shorter. He didn't want to hurt anyone with his selfishness, if it was indeed selfishness. He just wanted to feel love again, to keep healing, to ascend to that next level. And Faith felt like that healing next level to him. Yes, there was no denying the identical appearance she shared with her sister, and there was no denying others would base their togetherness just on those external similarities, but

Faith was different. Faith was fire and combustion. His next level would be the composition of a harmony combining his jazz and her rock 'n' roll.

His tears fell to the same place on the wood floor as they had done all those years ago. He looked down at his hands, but this time didn't see the bleeding knuckles. He saw Faith's fingers wrapped around them, giving an extra squeeze as a small transference of comfort to him. Through his tears, he saw Faith and Hope's combined smiles and then only saw Faith's smile.

He picked up the books strewn about the floor and walked them over to the bookshelf across the room. He folded up the blanket on the couch and put it in the hallway closet. He moved his coffee cup to the kitchen and washed it along with the other few dishes he had used prior.

After his minor chores, he gave one last lingering survey of his coveted, quiet place. When he rested with contentment in his decision to share his refuge, he added an offering for Faith by placing a silver vase of wildflowers and a strawberry cream cake on the living room table. In her favorite color of red, the words, "Happy Birthday, Faith," were written on the cake.

He picked up his phone and took a long, steadying breath. "I'm in Asheville," he typed to Faith. "I want you here with me. I bought you a ticket for the 4:30 flight from Charlotte to here. Please come."

17.

White

"This is it," Empress said, walking through the space. "There's no way Pops won't love this, and JS is going to shit himself when he sees it."

Dabney laughed. "I figured you all would like this for the next location. There's already a full kitchen layout in the back, an upstairs you can use as a more intimate bar for private events, and this ample area down here can be configured in any number of ways."

"Can we make the offer today and expedite the closing if they accept?" Empress asked.

"I don't see why not. We just need to work out the details so that I can have everything in place when I contact the seller," Dabney replied.

"Cool. If you have time now, we can go to the coffee shop next door and talk through the details."

"Sounds like a plan," Dabney replied. "I'll join you over there after I reset the alarm and lock up."

While Empress waited on Dabney to join her, she sent a text to Faith with a happy birthday caption and a video of Magic Mike doing a seductive dance.

Faith replied back with a kissing, eye-popping emoji. "Thank you, my beautiful niece."

As Empress took a sip from her mocha, she saw the flashing dots indicating that Faith was sending her another text. A black-and-white photograph of newlyweds popped up on her screen. She saw the thin nose and pronounced, pointed chin David Deale had passed onto his daughters with closer inspection. The woman beside him wore the same thick, curly hair and almond eyes that were signature traits of all in her bloodline. The young couple displayed innocence and naïveté in their smiles as they hadn't yet encountered the cruelty that would transition them into bitter strangers. Empress smiled at all they were.

Subsequent texts came from Faith as Empress studied the picture. "Karina sent this to me. She found it in some of her father's old things. Didn't realize it was him until meeting us yesterday. Crazy."

"Very crazy. Good birthday so far?" Again, flashing dots displayed before a thumbs-up popped up in reply from Faith.

"Cool," Empress sent back.

As she went back to studying her young grandparents, Dabney approached the table with his latte. He read the intrigue on Empress's face. "Are you okay?" he asked as he sat down.

Empress held her phone up for him to see the picture also.

He raised an eyebrow. "Your grandparents?"

Empress nodded with a slight smile.

"Wow," he said, bringing the phone closer to his face. After studying the picture for a few seconds, he said, "Your grandmother was beautiful." He paused to take a drink of his latte. "You look a lot like her," he added.

"Thank you."

"Where did you find the pic?"

"That's sort of a long story I'll have to tell you about another time. In short, it came from my aunt who I met for the first time yesterday."

Dabney raised both eyebrows and blinked a couple times. "I look forward to hearing that full story."

Empress checked the time as he handed her back her phone. It was still early in the day, but she wanted to ensure she allotted enough time to get ready for her evening with Nya. "So what do we need to go over," she asked, rushing onto their reason for meeting.

"Well, I just need to confirm if you want to offer the asking price and note any additional information you want to include in the letter of intent. So far, the letter is pretty standard since there will be no additional asset transfers outside of what is already in the space. Here is what I have so far." As he handed his tablet over to Empress, he gazed at her and half smiled.

"What are you smiling about?" she asked.

"It's cool learning personal things about you," he said and widened his smile.

Empress half smiled at him and proceeded reading the letter of intent. She didn't want to completely douse his hopes, because she didn't feel like explaining herself to him, and inevitably to Pops. So, she chose to do what she did best: evade. "The letter looks good, and the asking price is in our range. Are you ready for me to sign it?"

"Yep, you can sign in the box at the bottom."

Empress scribbled her finger across the tablet and handed it back to him. "So, I guess now we play the waiting game."

Dabney placed his hand on top of hers. "We can have an early celebration while we wait, because I'm sure the offer will be accepted."

Empress looked down at his hand on top of hers and tried to maintain her half smile.

"The Jazz Room is doing a tribute to Latin music tonight. We can check that out and then have dinner afterward. Plus, I have to hear this story about you meeting your aunt for the first time."

Remembering her need for her Dabney dating façade, she replied, "That sounds good." She paused as she plotted how to also see Nya. "Can we just do the concert though? I have an early day tomorrow."

Dabney's lips pressed together. "Sure," he replied with a hint of disappointment. "I'll pick you up around seven."

****

Empress picked up her handbag, assessed the quickest exit from their row, and scooted to the edge of her seat as the horn section in the jazz band blared the emphatic final notes of the concert. She had been constantly checking her phone and contributing mostly short answers to her conversation with Dabney. When the audience stood and applauded fervently after the concert, Empress excused her way down their row and headed toward the door.

Dabney followed slowly behind her. "You okay?" he asked when they met outside on the sidewalk.

Empress was again checking the time on her phone. "I'm sorry, what did you say?" she asked.

"I asked if you were okay," Dabney answered, his words clipped.

Empress felt the seconds of each minute slipping closer to 9:30 but resisted the urge to recheck her phone. "I'm sorry," she said again. "I just have something I need to take care of at home."

Dabney nodded and began walking toward the parking deck.

They walked to the car in silence and rode to Empress's building with only soft music filling the space between them.

"Good night, Empress," Dabney said, his tone annoyed, as he stopped in front of her building.

Again remembering her need for him and trying to disregard the digital reminder of 9:25 displaying on the console, Empress leaned over and pulled Dabney's face closer to hers. She kissed him intensely. "I'm sorry," she said before exiting the car.

She hurried over to the front desk of her building to pick up the food she ordered as the concert ended. In the elevator ride up to her place, her phone buzzed. "Just parked in the deck," Nya's text read.

During her rush of plating the food, lighting candles, and continually straightening things that were already in their rightful place, she heard Nya's knock at the door.

"Wow," breathed Empress when she saw Nya dressed in an off-the-shoulder top, skinny bell-bottom jeans, and white stilettos.

Nya smiled as she reached to embrace Empress.

As they parted, Empress saw a look of puzzlement grow on Nya's face. She leaned closer to

Empress and sniffed the side of Empress's neck. Her eyebrows raised, and a question appeared in her narrowing eyes. "What's wrong?" Empress asked.

Nya shook her head a bit. "You smell like Dabney," she noted when she walked in. "He's been wearing that Versace cologne for as long as I can remember."

Empress sniffed her shirt also to smell the remnants of the cologne she hadn't noticed before.

"I guess I should have asked this before assuming, but are you two dating?" Nya asked with a slight waver in her voice.

"No," Empress responded immediately. She paused and thought about how to proceed with her answer. "Well, not for-real dating."

Nya's eyes narrowed again.

"He wants us to be dating, but I'm not interested in him, as you know."

"So why not just tell him you're not interested?"

Empress released a long breath. "It's complicated."

Nya shook her head again and exhaled hard through her nose. "Look, Empress, I really like you a lot, but I don't do messiness and drama."

Empress paused to think about her next response. "My father thinks Dabney and I are dating."

Nya nodded. "And you're not out to him."

Empress ran a hand through her hair. "I can't come out to him right now."

Nya nodded again. "Have you slept with Dabney?"

"Hell no," Empress replied immediately. "I've only kissed him a couple times."

"Well, there's something else we have in common," Nya uttered with a slight laugh. She shook her head as if she were contemplating a contradiction. "I know we all have to walk our own paths in life, but remember, I told you that closet living has never been for me. So, please understand I'm not going into the closet for anyone. If I ever meet your father, or anyone else in your family, I will be who I am. It's up to you to tell them who I am to you. And Dabney already knows who I am, so it's up to you to tell him about us."

Empress nodded.

Nya leaned over to kiss Empress. After they parted, she asked, "Can you please take off that damn shirt? That Versace cologne is getting on my nerves."

As Empress made her way to the bedroom, Nya grabbed her hand. "Where are you going?" she asked.

A look of confusion landed on Empress's face. "To change shirts."

Nya's sinister smile curled up on her lips. "I didn't ask you to change. I asked you to take it off."

Empress unbuttoned her shirt and allowed it to fall to the floor. "Déjà vu," she affirmed.

Nya's smile dwindled and her gaze became more intense. "Keep going."

Under a thin veil of discomfort, Empress unfastened the clasp of her bra and dropped it to the floor also.

Nya licked her lips as she took in Empress's naked breasts. "Keep going," she said again.

Her heartbeat echoed in her ears as she inched her pants down her hips and onto the floor with her other clothes.

"Keep going," Nya whispered.

Empress's heartbeat was now a drumroll tapping between her ears. Her panties tumbled on top of her pile of abandoned safety.

Nya walked over to Empress. She interlaced a hand with Empress's curls and pulled her closer. She backed Empress to the door and scouted the curves of her naked body with her free hand.

The door's cold wood against her back contended with the heat of Nya's surveying fingers. She felt herself weaken from the internal collision of exhilaration and humility. As Nya's mouth met hers, the probing fingers searched inside her. Exhilaration overtook humility.

Sucks and kisses traced the path of her fingers down Empress's body. Nya's undulating tongue replaced her probing fingers.

Intoxication gagged Empress, causing only a stifled moan to ooze from her mouth. Her heartbeat tapped on every nerve, making her body concede to rapture.

"You are so beautiful." Nya ran her hands over the curves of Empress's trembling body.

When sight and sound became coherent, and realness allowed humility to surpass exhilaration, Empress wrapped her arms around her breasts.

"Why are you covering up," Nya asked.

Empress shrugged. "Embarrassment."

"Why are you embarrassed?"

"I've never felt this exposed before. It's scary, almost."

"What makes it scary?"

Empress considered the word to describe what scared her most. She looked into Nya's eyes and replied, "Trust."

Nya nodded. She removed her clothing in the same slow order Empress had. She unwrapped Empress's protective arms and connected them around her nakedness.

Empress received her vulnerability with a kiss that traveled from Nya's neck to her shoulders.

18.

Copper

It was quiet. This space was often a comfort to him, and now it disturbed him. Faith had disturbed the calm he was used to, and he was unsure if he ever wanted to hear it again.

He looked around the room as he tried to settle into this new reality where quiet was a distraction. He now saw Faith in everything. He pulled the blanket up to his face to smell her. The scent of lavender filled him and ignited his memories from the evening before.

She had replied to his text with a smiley face and confirmation of her taking the flight to Asheville. As he waited at the airport for her arrival, he placed his trembling hand in his pocket to hide his nervousness. When he saw the red flopping sun hat migrating through the crowd, his keys jingled like a timekeeping tambourine as his fingers tapped against them.

“Hey, Sterlin,” Faith said.

He pulled her into an embrace as instinct overtook thought. He kissed her as insatiableness overtook restraint. "Hi," he replied after they parted.

"I guess you have changed your mind from the other night."

He grabbed her hand, interlaced his fingers with hers, and nodded.

The rolling points of the Blue Ridge Mountains passed in the distance as they rode in silence from the airport. The additional time he asked for and his noncommittal word of *maybe* were culminating to this moment. He noticed Faith's crossed leg bounce as her dangling foot shook side to side, and he wondered if she, too, was trying to displace her doubts in the distraction of the mountains.

The road they turned onto was hidden between towering pine trees providing a protective canopy of camouflage for the unknown that lay beneath them. Faith grabbed anything within her grasp as the tires slipped and regained traction repeatedly against the gravel up the steep winding road. At the end of the road, the trees gave way to the cabin sitting watch over one of the places where the earth punctured the sky.

"Wow, Sterlin," Faith gasped as the rolling points of the mountains seemed more tangible.

He smiled at her and was met with only her smile. He was relieved to no longer see the combined duo of Faith and Hope.

The mixture of wet pine and wildflowers permeated the air as they entered the cabin. Faith inhaled deeply before exploring the few rooms. Her heels tapping against the floorboards as she walked through the space matched the quick cadence of his erratic heartbeat. When Faith saw the strawberry cream cake next to the silver vase of wildflowers on the living room table, she placed a hand on her mouth. "You remembered?"

"Of course, I remembered your birthday. I know it's tomorrow, but I figured we could start celebrating now."

Faith shook her head. "You remembered that I love strawberries."

Pops nodded. "Years ago, you told me the story about how you couldn't really eat them when you were a child because Hope was allergic. So, on the first night in your own place, you ate strawberries for dinner."

Faith walked over to him. She placed a palm on his cheek and a gentle kiss on his lips. The unflinching wood beneath his feet, where his blood and tears once puddled, now held a new memory. "Thank you," Faith said.

"You are very welcome. This is also my way of saying thank you for being so patient with me." He put his hands in his pockets again and looked down at the spot beneath his feet. "I can't promise you that I'll go fast, but I can promise that I want to go forward with you."

"I'm just happy we're going in the same direction now," Faith replied.

He pulled her closer to him. "Well, birthday girl, what would you like to do?"

She wrapped her arms around his neck and widened her smile. "I want to eat strawberry cake for dinner."

Pops laughed and nodded at her request. "Your conventional is to be as unconventional as possible."

"I wouldn't be me otherwise."

"And I wouldn't want you to be any other way." Her identifying mixture of lavender and patchouli permeated his nose and caused him to hold her tighter.

The mountain tops were painted purple as the setting sun sank behind them and set the sky aflame in copper. "God is amazing," Faith remarked as she placed her plate of half-eaten cake on the small table between them. She closed her eyes and began to rock in her chair.

“I’ve never heard you mention God before,” Pops said before taking another bite of cake.

“Well,” Faith responded with her eyes still closed, “we’re on better terms now.” She rocked a little more before continuing. “For so many years, I couldn’t believe in God, because I felt like so much had been taken from me. We lost our mother, and then I lost Hope. It was hard to believe God would allow anyone to endure that much pain.”

“So what changed?” Pops asked, placing his plate beside hers to join in the soothing, rocking motion in his chair.

Faith opened her eyes just enough to see Pops through thin slits. “No judgments?” she asked.

Pops turned his head to her and nodded. “No judgments.”

“It was a drug called ayahuasca.”

Pops raised his head a little more to show his looming question.

“I went on this spirit healing retreat with some friends years back, and while you’re there, you have two ayahuasca ceremonies. The ceremonies help you deepen your connection to the earth and universe and purge impurities from your body. Plus, you can get astronomically high.” A slight laugh escaped her.

Pops laughed with her. “So, you got really high, and now you believe in God?”

Faith shook her head. "I wish it were that simple." She paused and continued rocking. "My first ayahuasca ceremony was serene. Very dark and relaxing, no crazy hallucinations or anything like that." Her eyes opened again to thin slits, and she stared into the hastening darkness. "I was actually rather disappointed with the first ceremony. I told the medicine woman who instructed us that I could have gotten that effect with some good weed."

Pops chuckled, also watching the approaching veil of the night sky. "How did she reply?"

"She told me the first ceremony was preparatory to allow the mind and soul to connect." Faith slowed the motion of her chair with an outstretch of her long legs. "She was right, because that second ceremony was truly a trip." She shook her head a bit like the memory seemed almost too much to relive. "In the second ceremony, my mind found the buried torments in my soul and elevated them to the surface. It was crazy to feel fear, hyper-mania, anxiety, depression, animosity, and violence all at once. My body couldn't take it, so I started convulsing and vomiting. During the commotion, the instructors rolled me onto my stomach so I wouldn't choke. And when I finally had nothing left in me, I apparently tried to stand up but only made it to my knees. Then the only part I vividly remember from that whole experience showed. I saw my mother and

Hope sitting on either side of me. It's like they were waiting to help me stand up."

"Did they?"

Faith nodded. "I believe they did. I stood up with no help from anyone in the room and didn't waver at all." She allowed the chair to resume its natural rocking cadence. "Since then, I feel more connected and grounded, and not like the fragmented, flighty mess I was before. So, yes, I do believe there is a God. I still don't believe in religion, though. Too many rules and oppressions for me." Her head rolled toward Pops. "What about you, Sterlin?"

"You know I'm a good old Southern boy." Pops chuckled some. "When I wasn't helping my father in the restaurant on Sunday mornings, I was on the front pew with my mother." He paused and shook his head a bit. "My father needed to be on that front pew too."

Faith's eyes widened. "I've never heard you mention your parents before."

Pops shrugged. "There isn't much to tell. They lived in Charlotte most of their lives and didn't go to many other places. They didn't like it when I married Hope, because they thought she was too fast. And they really didn't like the fact that she was mixed with white and Cuban. Afro-Cuban to them still meant not Black."

"If they thought Hope was too fast, then they would have thought I was Satan in drag."

They both laughed.

"I loved them," Pops continued and shrugged again. "But you know I was absolutely in love with Hope and nothing was going to change that. So, I continued to work in the restaurant with my father after Hope and I got married, because I knew they needed me to, especially when he got sick. I gradually took over everything and took care of them also until they passed."

The weighted memories pulled Pops into a place of darkened silence. Faith's rocking chair let out a sputtering creak as she stood, and her bare feet pattered through the quiet. She straddled his lap, causing his rocking chair to also pierce the quiet with adjusting screeches.

They united in affection through kisses and escalated to fervor. He stood with Faith connected to him as an essential ornament and walked them both into the bedroom.

And now, during this irrefutable morning after, it was quiet. And as the rising sun peeked over the mountain tops, he sat in the disturbing quiet, smelling her scent, looking around his sanctuary for her.

Soon after, the door opened and closed. Faith bounded into the room dressed in running shoes, leggings, and a tank top. "Those hills are killer, but it is so beautiful out there, Sterlin. I only ran a few miles, and I saw so many animals and wildflowers. And the trees are absolutely gorgeous. Did you know there is a river just over one of the hills? It might take a little time to hike down to it, but we should go fishing or something. I haven't been fishing in a really long time, so I hope you know how."

Pops stretched out across the bed to lay on his side and propped his head up with his hand as Faith's words rushed like the river she was describing. A laugh escaped him and swam through her rushing words.

"What's so funny?"

"You."

"Why am I funny?"

"Woman, you are a whirlwind of energy. You remind me of Empress when she was little." He laughed to himself. "When I would ask her what she learned at school, her eyes would light up, and she would say 'We learned this and did that, and then Mrs. Such-and-So said this, and I didn't think that was right, so I did some research to check.'" He paused again to laugh. "That one question would turn into an hour-long conversation of her just talking." His eyes shifted away from Faith and into his own thoughts. "She still does that sometimes on our walks home from the restaurant, but not as much."

Faith smiled. "Hope always said Empress was a mini-me."

"Yeah, she did say that. I never noticed it until now."

Faith bent down to kiss him. "We seem to be having a lot of firsts in this time together. Like I've never seen you this relaxed before."

Pops lifted his head and his smile expanded. "Well, woman, you really helped with relaxing me, and this is where I come to rest and recalibrate."

Faith kissed him again. "How about I take a shower, and we can relax some more this morning?"

"Sounds good to me," Pops said through his wide smile. "But don't relax me too much, woman. I still want to show you Asheville before we head back to Charlotte."

As Faith prepared to shower, her phone vibrated. "I found this in his things after he died, but didn't realize it was him until now," Karina's text read. A black-and-white picture of her young parents followed the text. Faith raised her hand to cover her quivering lips.

Pops sat upright with alarm. "What's wrong?"

Faith handed her phone to him.

His eyes shifted between the picture and Faith's tear-streaked face. He pulled her onto the bed with him and allowed her tears to coat his chest. "Are these tears of sadness or happiness?" he asked.

"Both."

"Well, for the happy tears, happy birthday."

19.

Orange

It had almost been a year to the day since she had broken her own heart. She remembered the orange sun streaming onto her face between the parted drapes, just as it had illuminated the lake the day they fell in love. She felt Camellia's warm breath on her shoulder and heard a soft moan of recollected satisfaction flow past her ears. Empress knew God had created this last moment of perfection for her to keep always. "I love you more today than I did yesterday," she had admitted aloud to herself.

Camellia had circled her arms around Empress's waist and drew her closer. "I love you, too."

"I love you more today than I did yesterday, so I can't do this tomorrow."

Camellia released a small chuckle. "Well, luckily, we don't have anything planned for tomorrow."

"Camellia, I can't ... anymore." Her tears hit the pillow below her heavy head. "When I see you and my brother's children, all I see is everything I wanted for us. You are currently living the life I used to dream we would have together, but you're living it with him."

God's perfection had been broken. Camellia sprang upright. "Empress, you left me! Within a couple months, I dropped off of your list of priorities. You stopped all communication with me. JS was there when you weren't."

"Camellia, I left to go to school. Remember, that's what we both wanted. We both applied, we both were accepted, but only one of us followed through on the plan to go." Empress wiped her own tears away and reached up to wipe away the one running down Camellia's face.

Camellia moved away and began to look around the room for her clothes. "Our plan was to be together, Empress. There were schools here we could have gone to together."

"Camellia, how were we ever going to be together when you are too afraid to even live your own life?"

"We're together now!"

"No, we're not. We spend a few hours a week together when you can find the time and an unsuspecting lie to tell your family. Outside of those hours, you go home to them. I'm in a relationship with you, and you have several more important relationships to deal with."

Camellia snatched up her few remaining pieces of clothing. "Well, now you see how the shit feels." Half-dressed and seemingly broken, she stormed out of the superficial life they had built a few hours at a time together.

Empress opened her palm to hold the morning sunlight spilling over her bedroom as she did on that day a year ago. She didn't understand why the memory of her last moment with Camellia kept replaying in her mind. It was like a clamoring gong blaring the emotion of guilt over the melody of glee that played whenever she thought about Nya. When she looked at the beautiful mold of Nya's dark-brown body sleeping beside her, the gong clamored.

She bent down to kiss Nya's exposed torso and traced her kisses down to her thighs. Nya's sweet, sapid essence intoxicated Empress.

Nya responded with oscillating hips. She guided Empress's hands up to her breasts and added a resonating, "Mmmmmm," to Empress's melody of glee.

The familiar essence of Nya pushed Camellia further from Empress and quieted the gong. She felt this moment of perfection being etched in her mind.

Nya added lyrics of praise to the melody upon reaching her pinnacle. When she relaxed on the other side of heightened pleasure, she traced the contours of Empress's face with her index finger. "Good morning to you, too."

Empress pulled the comforter up to cover their naked bodies. As Nya nestled into the crevice of her arm, Empress matter-of-factly said, "You know we forgot to eat dinner last night."

Nya laughed. "I feel like what we did was much more sustainable than food."

"I definitely agree with that." She wrapped her arms around Nya. "But how about some breakfast? I can order something from the diner across the street. They have these creamy grits that taste like the best of everything, and these loaded hash browns covered in cheese, bacon, and anything else you want. And their banana pancakes taste just like my mother's."

Nya lifted her head and looked at Empress.

"What's wrong?" Empress asked.

"Nothing. It's just that you don't really talk about your mother. That's the first thing you have said about her other than she passed away."

Empress diverted her eyes away from Nya's. Her vulnerability from realizing she hadn't noticed the mentioning of her mother was too much to see. "Her birthday was yesterday," Empress uttered, feeling the full weight of the moment.

Nya nestled again into the crevice of Empress's arm and splayed her limbs across her. "So, she liked banana pancakes?"

Empress rubbed Nya's back. "Yep, she did. JS and I were just talking about how she tried to get us to love them, too, but we always opted for cereal instead." She paused and again ran her hands over Nya's back. "When I first moved back to Charlotte, I went over to that diner across the street one morning, and that's when I first tried their banana pancakes. Those damn pancakes made me think about all of these childhood memories, and, before I knew it, I was crying like a baby in there." She paused to clear the impending lump from her throat. "The owner of that place is a woman who knows my father, so when she saw me crying, she sat down with me to see what was wrong. When I told her about the pancakes reminding me of my mother, she said, 'Tell me something good about your momma.' I told her about watching cartoons on Saturday mornings with my mother when she would eat banana pancakes. So now, about once a month, I eat banana pancakes there. When the lady sees me, she says, 'Tell me something good,' and I share some other random, happy memory about my mother." She again cleared her throat. "I guess that serves as my warped version of therapy."

Nya pressed her fingertips into Empress's skin gently. "What was your favorite cereal?"

Empress laughed at the odd question. "It was, and still is, Franken Berry."

"What was your favorite cartoon?"

"*The Power Puff Girls.* Buttercup was my favorite."

"Do you have any Franken Berry cereal?"

"Yep, there should be at least half of a box left in the kitchen."

Nya lifted her head to meet Empress's eyes. She kissed her forehead and each of her eyelids before landing on her lips. The bed shuddered as she bounced out of it with the comforter wrapped around her.

As Nya walked out of the room, Empress asked, "Where are you going?"

Nya turned her head and looked back at Empress over her shoulder. "To eat some Franken Berry and watch *The Power Puff Girls.*"

God allowed her another moment of perfection. Empress wrapped a sheet around her body and followed Nya out the bedroom.

As they sat on either end of the couch, each bundled in their made-up togas with bowls of Franken Berry lifted to their faces, Nya glanced at her phone. "Shit," she said with sudden alarm. "I didn't realize it was that late."

"What's wrong?" Empress asked around a mouthful of cereal.

"I have to do a lecture in an hour." She unwrapped the comforter from around her before dashing into the kitchen with her bowl.

Empress strolled behind her as she tried to keep her sheet intact and finish the last spoonful of cereal.

As Nya dressed in the clothing she had left piled on the floor in front of the door, she asked, "Would you like to come with me to my lecture? Today's topic is Techniques for Improving Customer Engagement to Expand Your Social Footprint."

Empress thought about all the nice ways she could say no.

"I'm just kidding," Nya replied. "I know you didn't even want to come to my other lecture. Dabney told me."

Empress smiled. "It's not that I didn't want to come. Lectures have always been a struggle for me. Yours was the first one where I stayed awake."

"That's because you were too busy mentally undressing me," Nya added as she walked over to Empress. She trailed kisses over Empress's exposed shoulder before landing on her lips.

"The real thing is way better than my mental picture was," Empress responded. She circled her arms around Nya's waist. "Do you have any plans later?"

"Unfortunately, I do. There's a reception I have to attend tonight with some colleagues for the Charlotte Regional Business Alliance." Nya's eyes rolled up. "In a couple days, though, some of my friends are having their annual Flirty Fourth party. I know we haven't known each other that long, but I'd really like for you to meet them, and the party is a lot of fun."

"Flirty Fourth?"

"Yeah, it's just what they call their *Fourth of July* cookout." Nya kissed Empress's neck and whispered, "Please," into her ear.

Empress nodded slowly.

"I promise you will enjoy it." Nya pulled Empress to the door by her hand. "Thank you for a wonderful dinner-less evening," she said before giving Empress one last kiss and walking out the door.

****

Something bothered her, but she was unable to locate its source. It shrouded her, made her impervious to fatigue and pain.

"Dang, Camellia, you are bringing it today," her trainer Lea noticed.

She pushed the up arrow to increase her speed on the treadmill. Seven point five displayed on the console, her best pace ever.

"Damn, girl," Lea said.

She felt numb as the seconds counted down the last minute of her time. Her mind leaped around to the possible reasons for her mental disconnect. JS and her were on limited speaking terms, but that was a regular cycle between them. She and her daughter were still clashing, but that, too, was nothing out of the ordinary. She hadn't spoken to her parents since that awkward family dinner a few weeks ago; again, nothing out of the norm there. As the treadmill slowed to a crawl, her mind continued its search for the source.

"How are you feeling?" Camellia heard Lea say, but was too distracted to comprehend.

"I'm sorry, what?"

"I asked, how are you feeling? That was some serious work you just put in, girl. Do you have enough left in you to keep going with the workout?"

Comprehending now, but still very disconnected, Camellia nodded.

As they stacked weights on either side of the bar at a nearby bench press, Camellia noticed Lea had found her own distraction. She turned to look in the direction of Lea's gaze. A woman with a towel draped around her neck, occasionally blotting the dripping sweat from her face, stared back at Lea from behind a half smile. Camellia watched as Lea's natural expression of happiness disintegrated when she saw the woman across the room.

"Let's get to it, lady," Lea said, pulling her attention back to the task of securing the weights on the bar.

The weighted bar posed little challenge to Camellia, just as the treadmill had done. Her preoccupied mind was the only part of her engaged in a workout. As she pushed the weight away from her chest one last time to complete her set, she heard an unfamiliar voice say, "Hey, Lea."

A visibly frustrated version of Lea struggled to replace the bar in its cradle after Camellia's set. "Are you okay?" Camellia asked, sitting up on the bench.

"Yes," Lea responded with a depthless smirk. "That was my ex ... sort of," Lea blurted. "I mean, she's definitely my ex-wife, but we sort of got back together, but now we're not really together."

Camellia eyes widened. She had never seen Lea's regal confidence stifled and wasn't expecting that response at all. "I thought you were with Richard," Camellia asked.

"I am." Lea paused. Her eyes rolled up. "Or I was."

Camellia sat motionless, waiting for the rest of the explanation. Though she knew her probing was chipping away at Lea's confidence, she still felt some need to understand Lea and her ex-wife's relationship.

"Richard and I were good until a few weeks ago when my ex-wife came by the house to get some things she left after we separated. We started talking, and that led to reminiscing, which led to other things, which led to me telling Richard we need to take a pause."

"Does Richard know that you have"—Camellia's tone dropped to a whisper and her eyes darted around to see if anyone else was listening—"an ex-wife?"

Lea's eyes tightened as her brow furrowed. Her head jutted forward as if she didn't understand Camellia. "Yes, Richard knows I have an ex-wife."

Again in her whispered tone, Camellia asked, "So, you're bisexual?"

Lea raised an eyebrow. "I actually identify as pansexual."

Camellia again looked around to see if anyone could hear their conversation. She didn't know what pansexual was, but it seemed far more salacious than bisexual.

"Hey, Camellia, I hate to ask you this, because you have really been doing some awesome work today, but can we please cut the session short?" Lea asked from behind another forced smile.

Camellia nodded and watched as Lea made her way into the locker room to follow the passing voice. Again, she looked around to see if anyone noticed the conversation that still had her stunned. When she saw no one even cared to notice, she slid back under the bar to press out another set.

Her mind again wandered between each lift of the weighted bar. Had she forgotten to do something, and was that causing her to feel bothered? She recalled the current date—July second held no significance.

As she sat up after completing her last set, she noticed Lea standing in line at the juice bar with her arms folded, still wearing turmoil on her face. Camellia gathered her few things and headed over to her.

Lea seemed to force a smile when she saw Camellia walking toward her.

"May I ask you something?" Camellia asked quietly.

Lea nodded.

"What was it like being married to a woman?"

Lea blinked a couple times before pulling Camellia aside to a more secluded space. "Camellia, are you okay? I know we don't know much about each other, but you seem really different today. Even before you learned that I have an ex-wife."

Camellia shrugged. She didn't know if she was okay.

Lea's eyes softened as if she noticed something familiar. "I assume being married to a woman is a lot like being married to a man. There are good times and struggles as there are in any relationship. Emotions can run a little high sometimes, but it's not unbearable. Is there a reason why you asked that?"

Camellia again shrugged. "Just curious."

Lea raised her eyebrows and smirked.

"Same time next week?" Camellia asked to transition Lea away from whatever she was thinking.

Lea nodded and waved as Camellia walked away.

The orange morning sun pierced her eyes when she walked out the door. A memory of shards of sunlight streaking across a darkened, somber room through parted drapes appeared in her mind. Empress had wiped away her own flowing tears and reached up to wipe the one away from Camellia's face.

Camellia had found the source.

20.

Ruby

The pungent smell of crab wafted across the room with the aromas of fried okra and sweet, buttery yams. Empress only smelled her favorites whenever she entered the restaurant over the barrage of foods simultaneously cooking. As she surveyed the crowded room for Pops and JS, some old memories were triggered. Her sparse collection of her grandfather's image serving plates and chatting with customers surfaced. The taste of coconut-pineapple cake filled her mouth as he always slid a slice of it in front of her to initiate the few brief conversations they had. She looked over at the counter to see if there was a coconut-pineapple cake displaying as one of the desserts of the day.

"There's JS over there," Dabney said, interrupting Empress's thoughts.

Empress rolled her eyes when she noticed JS throwing his head back in abundant laughter and leaning close to the woman as they were talking.

"Excuse me," she said, as she and Dabney approached them. "JS, where's Pops?"

The woman spun around as if to size up the person attached to the voice behind her. Her brow wrinkled and her eyes narrowed as she focused on Empress's face. "I know this isn't your sister, JS."

Empress knew her immediately when the woman spun around. The pelting memories collided in her mind of others laughing around her as the woman taunted her when they were younger. She felt her jaw tightening and her fingers clenching in and out of balled fists. Her eyes darted to meet her brother's; he was silently pleading with her through his raised eyebrows. "I'm sorry, have we met?" Empress asked, pretending to not recognize the woman.

"Now, I know we haven't seen each other in quite a while, but we went to school together. I'm Gretchen Mitchell. I think we even had a couple classes together."

Empress's expression remained blank as she knew pretending not to recognize Gretchen was doing more damage to her ego than any insult would. "Nope, not ringing a bell at all."

"I used to come over to your house to study with JS," Gretchen replied and then coyly smiled at JS.

"Oh wait, did you drive a yellow car with a license plate that said Like Candy on it?" Empress intentionally mentioned something she knew would spur an unpleasant memory for Gretchen as it was another girl who drove the yellow car and came to their house to also not-study with JS.

Gretchen's light complexion gave way to the ruby color flushing her face, and her eyes narrowed. "No, that wasn't me," she answered through a strained smile.

"I'm sorry. I do remember when you won homecoming queen our senior year," Empress said, remembering the flagrant display of drama Gretchen put on, complete with tears, cuss words, and hurling the runner up bouquet when the actual winner was adorned with the crown.

Gretchen's lips tightened. "No, that was Janis Samuels."

"Oh, I'm so sorry," Empress said, trying to contain her smirk.

Gretchen's eyes shifted to Dabney. She smirked also. "You've changed so much, Empress. I hardly recognize you," she remarked, addressing Dabney over Empress's shoulder. "I guess you had to outgrow all that cystic acne and constant smell of Clearasil at some point," she said, still staring at Dabney.

"Yes, and some of us have grown a whole lot since high school." Empress straightened her posture to show how her minimal weight gain had landed in the right places unlike Gretchen's.

Gretchen's eyes shifted back to Empress.

As the two women partook in a noticeably awkward staring contest, JS interjected, "There's Pops over there."

"Why don't we meet your father at a table in the back?" Dabney added as he pulled Empress away from her stand-off. "It was very nice meeting you," he called back to Gretchen over his shoulder with Empress in tow.

As they slid into either side of the booth, Pops approached the table. He bent down to kiss Empress on her flared nostrils. She folded her arms and lowered her brow further. "Why do I have a feeling your brother has something to do with that look?" Pops shifted his attention to Dabney. "Since she was a little girl, folded arms and flared nostrils means JS did something." Pops looked around the area. "Where is he anyway? We need to get started."

"He's over there, sir, talking to an old friend," Dabney answered, nodding toward JS.

Pops seemed to also notice JS's flirty mannerisms as he rolled his eyes when he saw JS talking to the woman. He looked back at his daughter's flared nostrils and folded arms and shook his head before walking toward JS.

Pops dropped his hand heavily onto JS's shoulder, smiled as he addressed the woman, and then guided JS over to the booth by his shoulder. As they sat in the booth, Pops's face hardened and he glared at JS. "Boy, you better stop shopping for sugar when you have honey at home. And don't you ever shop for sugar again in here."

"Yes, sir," JS responded, not looking up from his phone.

As Dabney and Pops moved into talking about plans for the new restaurant location, Empress took her turn glaring at JS.

JS looked up at her and then raised his eyebrows to soften his face as if he were again pleading for forgiveness.

Empress formed a half smile to show her acceptance of his apology. When JS returned her smile, she jabbed an unsuspecting, sharp elbow into his ribs as payback for his blatant stupidity.

JS doubled over from the sudden pain of Empress's blow. As he slowly shifted himself back upright, he licked the tip of his index finger and stuck it in Empress's ear.

A loud smack caught the attention of Pops and Dabney as Empress slapped his hand away and covered her ear.

"Are you two finished now?" Pops asked his children, who were trying to contain their laughter. He shook his head and looked over at Dabney. "Maybe I should just adopt you since my children want to act like children while we adults are talking about important things."

Dabney laughed and also shook his head before continuing. "As I was saying, sir, I have a friend who is a small business expert that can lend her expertise in getting the next location up and help it to sustain continuous growth. Empress, I think it would be good if you could set up some time for JS and Nya to meet."

"What? Why?" Empress responded before realizing she, too, hadn't been listening to their conversation as she continued to wipe the wetness from her ear.

"You know some of the things that JS would like to pursue with this expansion," Dabney continued. "And I know you have shared a few ideas of your own with Nya from the financial perspective. I thought it would be good for you all to meet so that she can provide you both with some more insight."

"Oh, yes, I guess that makes sense," Empress replied, unable to think of a reason as to why she shouldn't introduce her brother to another woman she really liked.

JS looked at Empress and tilted his head before he was distracted by a wave from Gretchen as she left the restaurant. He waved back and smiled until he noticed the return of Pops's glare. "So when can we fully see the new place?" JS asked as if to show he had been listening.

"We can go right after the closing," Dabney responded. "The sellers have accepted the offer and have agreed to an expedited closing, so we should be able to do a full walkthrough soon."

"Great. I want to see what kind of storage space and prep areas we have over there, because I want to add some new items to the menu at that location that will require a bigger work area and more prep time."

Pops's eyes shifted back to JS. "Remember, we talked about keeping most everything the same at the next location until we build up a steady customer flow. Then we can talk about making a few changes."

"I really think we would be missing a great opportunity if we didn't offer some new items at the start of the new location," JS responded. "It's in a different area with a different vibe, and we should take advantage of that."

"Son, look around this room. It's packed in here because people like what we're currently doing. They're not looking for any crazy food combinations.

They know what they like, and they come here to get what they like."

JS exhaled hard through his nose. "Look at what most of them are eating: crab mac and cheese. That's not an original menu item. That was added to the menu after one of our trips to Charleston, because Mom loved it and knew it would do well here. And now it's one of our signatures."

Pops began to vigorously tap his index finger on the table.

Dabney attempted to wade through the tension. "Well, we have a lot to get through before planning the menu, so we should focus on those things first. Empress, since we will be closing in a couple weeks, you may want to contact Nya soon so the three of you can meet. Do you still have her number?"

Empress focused on her father's tapping finger and then on his face. He seemed more agitated than usual after his exchanges with JS.

"Empress," Dabney spoke again.

"What?" she answered, with the same short, annoyed tone after Dabney suggested introducing Nya and JS.

"Do you still have Nya's number?" Dabney asked again.

She nodded. "I'm sure I can find it." Her eyes shifted back to Pops's tapping finger. "Speaking of

Charleston"—she lifted her eyes to Pops's face—"how was your trip down there?"

Pops stopped his tapping finger. "It was fine," he replied. He shifted his attention back to Dabney. "So is there anything more we need to do before the closing?"

"No, sir. I think we're good. Empress has completed the needed fund transfers and signed everything. We're just waiting on the paperwork to be completed now."

"Great," Pops answered with a satisfying smile.

Still searching for something, Empress asked, "So what did you get there?"

Pops rolled his eyes back over to Empress. "I told you I had to pick up some stuff from a restaurant depot down there." He moved his hands under the table.

"What was so important that it couldn't wait?" Empress asked.

"Little girl, why are you suddenly so interested in my business trips?"

"I just found it odd that you chose to go down there this weekend of all weekends. You know Aunt Faith was here to celebrate her birthday."

Pops's eyes darted around the room. "I asked Faith if she minded, and she said she was fine."

JS looked up from his phone.

"I just hate that she spent her birthday alone," Empress continued.

"I'm sure she was fine," Pops added. "Dabney, are we finished?" he asked, again shifting his attention away from Empress's interrogation.

"Yes, sir, I think we are."

"Okay then, let me get back to running the restaurant we currently have," Pops replied before leaving the table.

As they watched Pops head to the kitchen area, Empress commented, "Well, that was weird."

"That's because he went down to Charleston to get some ass, and he doesn't want us to know that," JS said with a laugh.

"Shut up, JS," Empress replied.

"It's true. Pops suddenly had to go to Charleston to get some restaurant stuff, yet he can't tell you what he got?" JS laughed harder into his next statement. "That ass called, and it was too good to pass up."

"JS, don't make me elbow you again," Empress responded.

"Dabney, am I right?" JS asked.

Dabney laughed a little also. "It was indeed odd, and it may have been due to a woman. Men do crazy things for the right one," he added, shifting his eyes over to Empress.

"Let me go and help the old man since you got him all flustered with your cross-examination," JS said before heading toward the kitchen area also.

Dabney laughed a little again. "So did you get that thing taken care of the other night?" he asked Empress.

Empress searched her thoughts for her last lie. "Oh, yeah. It wasn't anything major, just something I needed to do."

"Do you have any plans for the Fourth? There's going to be this big festival and firework display at Romare Bearden Park, and I hear that the PopWich truck will be out there again."

"I'm sorry, but I already have plans." She read the disappointment etched onto his face. "But I'm free on the fifth," she offered. "We can get some half-priced fireworks and find that PopWich truck."

"Sounds good," Dabney replied with a nod. He paused and tilted his head. "So, who was the woman JS was speaking to earlier?"

Empress rolled her eyes and felt her nostrils flare a little. "Gretchen Mitchell. We went to school with her."

"She and JS dated in high school?"

"JS has never dated anyone." Empress rolled her eyes again. "She was just one of his many entertainments."

Dabney nodded. "She seems very ..."

"Rude, callous, asshole-ish," Empress spouted, providing him with a variety of words to complete his sentence.

Dabney nodded again. "And it seems like she was especially all those things toward you."

"That she was. She made middle school a living hell for me."

"And JS still messed around with her, knowing how awful she was to you?"

Empress nodded. "JS often lets his little head outweigh his big head."

Dabney laughed.

Pops stopped by their booth in between his rounds of checking on customers. "Hey, I thought you were going to take your aunt to the airport," he asked Empress. "She just texted me. She's been calling and texting you for the last hour."

"Oh damn, I forgot," Empress said, rummaging through her handbag for her phone. She saw the many missed texts and calls from Faith. As she scooted out of the booth, she looked over at Dabney. "See you at our July fifth celebration."

Dabney smiled. "Yes, the fifth."

She kissed Pops on his cheek, and didn't address the question on his face, before hurrying out the restaurant.

21.

Green

Faith cupped her hands around her eyes and pressed her face against the glass to get a better look into the darkened space. “It’s huge compared to the existing restaurant. I hate that I’m going to miss the opening.”

“Can you see the upstairs loft area?” Empress asked, pointing to guide Faith’s focus.

“Wow,” Faith replied after taking notice. “This is going to be an amazing adventure for you all.” She pulled her face away and adjusted the bent brim of her sun hat. “We have a few minutes before we need to head to the airport. Let’s get a cup of coffee at the place next door.”

Empress raised an eyebrow. “The last time you bought me a cup of coffee, I met my long-lost aunt. Do I need to prepare myself before going into the coffee shop next door?”

Faith threw her head back in a roaring laugh and almost lost her recently adjusted hat. “Girl, come on here,” she said, leading the way.

While Empress ordered their coffee inside the café, Faith sat at a small, round table on the sidewalk. A breeze rustled the green canopy of leaves growing from the archway of intertwined tree branches that met above the street. Her mind drifted back to the serenity of the mountain scenery at the cabin.

As Empress approached with their cups of coffee and a pastry, Faith was smiling. "For someone that hates flying, and is about to be on a plane for over three hours, you seem quite happy."

"I'm just thinking about how wonderful this visit has been with you all."

"I'm sorry you had to spend your birthday alone. I still can't believe Pops went down to Charleston this weekend to do God knows what." Empress paused to take a drink of her coffee. "JS thinks Pops hooked up with some woman this weekend."

Faith's crossed leg bounced as her dangling foot shook side to side. "Is that right?" Faith asked before taking a drink of her coffee.

"So how was it?" Empress asked.

Faith felt her skin flush at the unexpected question. "What do you mean?"

"Your birthday. How did you celebrate?"

"Oh," Faith replied with relief. Her look of elation resurfaced, spurring another wide smile. "It was wonderful." She paused to eat a forkful of the pastry and to carefully select her next words. "I was able to completely relax and just enjoy living."

"Good. I'm glad you had a nice birthday despite Pops being so selfish." Empress shook her head.

Faith again took notice of the rustling leaves and welcomed the warm breeze massaging her bare shoulders. "Don't be so hard on your father," she replied.

As Empress placed a corner of the pastry in her mouth, someone called her name. Before turning around to confirm the owner of the voice, her face scrunched.

Faith's forehead wrinkled as her brow raised due to seeing Empress's changed expression.

The sun glimmered off the woman's cheek piercings, doubling as dimples, and she wore high-top, platform sneakers that matched her lavender-colored hair. "Hey, Tandy," Empress replied through a forced smile.

"Long time no see," Tandy replied and folded her arms.

"I've been spending time with my aunt during her visit." She looked over at Faith and extended her hand in introduction. "This is my Aunt Faith. Aunt Faith, this is Tandy. She's the one I was telling you about the day you arrived." Empress raised her eyebrows and widened her eyes at her aunt.

Faith's mouth formed an O as she remembered the revealing photos.

"Nice to meet you," Tandy said, extending her hand to Faith.

"Nice to meet you also, dear. I feel like I know you on such a very personal level," Faith replied.

Empress pretended to cough to cover her laugh.

Tandy's silver dimples raised with her smile. She locked her eyes on Empress and licked her lips slightly. "Look forward to hearing from you soon," she said before continuing up the sidewalk.

Empress nodded. She waved as Tandy walked away before sitting back down.

Faith wore a coy smile as she watched Empress's performance.

"Please don't say it," Empress said, rolling her eyes to the sky.

"Say what?" Faith replied, lifting her coffee cup to her widening smile.

"You know what."

Faith shrugged her shoulders. "I don't know what you're talking about." As she casually filled her fork with more of the pastry, she whispered, "Pussy."

Empress laughed. "You just couldn't help yourself, could you?"

Faith shook her head while laughing also. "I sure as hell couldn't." She ate her forkful of pastry. "So, obviously Ms. Tandy doesn't know about Ms. Nya."

"Absolutely not," Empress responded before swallowing her last bit of coffee.

"Are you trying to keep your options open? I thought Nya was the one."

"I'm definitely not looking for any other options, and Tandy is not even on the same planet as Nya. I honestly thought Tandy would have just moved on by now so that there wouldn't be a need for an awkward conversation to end things."

"You better be careful with that one. The way she looked at you before she walked off shows that she has many more pussy pics to send you."

Empress laughed. "I should have never told you that hearing you say that bothers me."

"Nope, you shouldn't have," Faith replied before finishing her coffee. "We better get moving so I don't miss this dreadful flight."

They rode to the airport as they had when Faith's visit started with the Fania All-Stars playing a soundtrack to accompany the passing, green scenery. When Faith heard the opening piano chords accompanied by the rapid beats on conga drums, she turned up the volume. She swayed her shoulders and sung along with the lines she could remember to

Hector Lavoe's song "Que Lio." As the horns and random drumbeats closed out the song, she said, "What a mess."

"What do you mean?" Empress asked.

Faith laughed and shook her head. "That's what *que lio* means in English."

"Oh," Empress replied, nodding.

"It's about a man who wants to marry the woman he's in love with, but he finds out she is the girlfriend of his friend."

"Yep, that is definitely a mess," Empress said and released a loud exhale through her nose.

"Love usually is a mess," Faith said, looking into the distance as if she could still see the tops of the blue mountains.

"Tell me about it," she heard Empress mutter.

Faith reached over and wrapped her fingers around Empress's hand resting on the console. "It may be messy, but it's still the best thing to ever exist."

22.

Pink

The high-pitched buzzing of cicadas beckoning for mates rose as the sun sunk lower in the sky, and the sweetness of jasmine flowers was carried to her by a warm, moist wind. Empress smiled to herself as the chorus of "Summertime" played through her thoughts.

Nya patted the sweat from her brow.

Empress took notice of Nya's unconscious mannerisms, like biting her pinky nail when she came across a troubling email. They were endearing, especially because Nya didn't realize she was being watched.

As the sun disappeared behind the skyscrapers, Empress realized another day, and hence another moment, with Nya would soon be coming to an end. Empress always hated the finality of goodbye, so she stopped using that word long ago. Later, peace, or hasta pronto was all she said so that nothing ever truly concluded with her.

The warm breeze on her skin brought another unsolicited memory of Camellia. Empress again thought back to the last moment they spent together. Though she knew it was their end, she still never said goodbye in their final moment together.

Nya smiled when she caught Empress's watching eyes. "What?"

Empress smiled back. "Just enjoying the view."

"You're silly," Nya said with a playful wave of her hand.

"Sometimes."

Nya stood and walked over to Empress's side of the table. She lifted Empress's chin with her index finger. "I like sometimes silly," she said before kissing Empress. "We better get going to the party. My friend Zion can be the uptight, type-A event planner about her parties," she continued as she moved to gather her things. "She's good people, and I love her to death, but I swear you will want to throw her and her phone off of the hotel rooftop if we ever go on a vacation with her and her partner, Monnie."

Empress's heartbeat sped up and she fidgeted in her seat at the mention of meeting Nya's friends.

Nya again walked to her side of the table, lifted Empress's chin with her index finger, and met the worry in her eyes with a compassionate gaze.

"Don't worry, they will fall in love with you, too." She kissed Empress again.

The word *love* lingered in the air. Empress felt its density land on her shoulders and its lightness danced between her ears. It made her pull Nya closer and kiss her deeper, forgetting there were others around them.

"Damn, if you kiss me like that again, we will not make it to this party," Nya said, her breath heavy.

Empress leaned in to try and land another kiss.

Nya placed her index finger over Empress's puckering lips to stop her. "Nice try. We're still going to this party so you can meet my friends."

Empress turned the corners of her mouth down and pouted with her bottom lip under Nya's finger.

"Baby, I got you," Nya promised and kissed Empress's pouting lip. The long drawl of a train whistle sounded in the near distance. "Let's get the next train," she said, going back to gather her things.

As they walked from the train station through the trendy, gentrified neighborhood filled with converted, old houses that were now eclectic shops, craft breweries, and posh eateries, Empress felt that weird mix of sadness and awe. In her childhood, this area was one of the decaying, annexed neighborhoods of those people the city had chosen to forget.

They approached a renovated, Craftsman-style home that blended history with modern upgrades and was adorned with a waving rainbow flag on the front porch. “C’mon,” Nya said as she grabbed Empress’s hand and pulled her up the porch steps.

As she opened the door, Nya began singing her own words to the song that was playing to announce her arrival. “It’s some hoes in this house, it’s some hoes in this house. If you see them point them out.” She concluded with exaggerated dancing and pointing at random women standing and sitting around the living room.

“Awwwwww,” the room erupted with laughter, and hands were thrown up in welcome.

“Yo, I haven’t seen you in like a month, and the first thing you do is call me a hoe,” said a towering, slim, brown-skinned woman with wide brown eyes. Her auburn locs cascaded down the middle of her back from under her backward Charlotte Sting hat. She embraced Nya in a tight hug and kissed her on the cheek. “How you been, sis?”

“Doing very well,” Nya responded. She reached back for Empress’s hand after they finished their hug. “This is Empress.”

The woman leaned back and smiled wider. "Yo, I see you have been doing very lovely, sis. Wassup, Empress, I'm Monnie. Welcome to the Flirty Fourth."

"Nice to meet you, and thank you for having me," Empress responded, holding out her hand.

Monnie pulled Empress into a hug by her extended hand. "We all fam here, sis." She led Nya and Empress toward the kitchen, where the sounds of other guests laughing and talking flooded the air. "There's food stations here in the kitchen and in the dining room with ingredient cards in front of them in case you have any food allergies. And we have a martini barista in the far corner and a full bar serving just about anything you can think of outside by the pool," she explained, pointing out the areas. "You know how crazy and intense Zion can be about planning these things," Monnie said to Nya.

"Don't hate," they heard a woman say from behind them.

As they all turned in the direction of the voice, Monnie answered, "You know I could never hate on you, bae." She leaned over to give the woman a kiss.

"I'm loving this short cut, girl," Nya commented, running her hands over the woman's slicked down salt-and-pepper hair.

"Fifty ushers in freedoms you didn't know you needed," the woman replied. "You look gorgeous as always. I see you haven't given up on running."

Nya put her hands on her hips and struck a couple exaggerated super-model poses.

The woman's gray eyes shifted to Empress, and a broad smile exposed some of her pearl-white teeth. "You must be the reason why this pretty lady is so happy these days."

"Hi, I'm Empress," she said, extending her hand.

"Girl, please, I know who you are already, and we hug in this house," Zion said, pulling Empress into an embrace. She continued holding Empress's hand and led them farther into the kitchen. "What would y'all like to drink? Are you hungry? We have some beef and chicken patties over here that are so good I thought I was back home on the island." Zion put one hand on her stomach, the other in the air, and swayed her hips to the reggae music playing in the background.

"I'll just start with a glass of wine," Empress replied after a mild laugh.

"Red or white?" Zion asked.

"I better go with white," Empress answered and smiled at Nya, remembering her fiasco with red wine on their first date.

Zion opened the wine fridge on the counter beside them and then opened the larger kitchen refrigerator. A twinge of irritation showed on her face. "Baby, where is all the white wine? I specifically said we need to keep some bottles here in the house and not take it all out to the bar."

"Told y'all she gets berserk with the party-planning," Monnie said and kissed Zion on the forehead. "I'm on it, bae. Empress, any particular white wine you want?"

"Anything is fine, thank you."

"So, Empress, are you new to Charlotte?" Zion asked.

"No, but I feel like I am. I grew up here and then went to California for college. I just moved back a couple years ago, and everything is so different than what I remember. I can't tell you the number of times I've gotten lost trying to find my way around based on memories."

"Wow, Cali had to be nice. What brought you back here?"

"I needed to be closer to my family."

"Empress's family owns the Pops Place restaurant," Nya said.

Zion again placed her hands in a dancing position and swayed her hips to the music. "That crab mac and cheese," she said, closing her eyes and shaking her head.

Nya laughed. "That's what I said, too, girl."

"You know you can't come to another one of our parties and not bring any of that crab mac," Zion added with a smile.

"Consider it done," Empress responded. She looked over at Nya, who was struck with a sudden quiet. She watched as Nya's eyes narrowed like she was focusing on something. At the end of Nya's gaze, she saw Monnie talking to another woman about her age and with similar locs sprouting from under a backward ball cap. "You okay?" Empress asked Nya.

"Yeah, just see someone I know."

Zion turned to match Nya's gaze and then turned back to Nya with a look of concern. "Y'all come in here and check out this food. Even if you're not hungry, it's still pretty to look at," Zion said, pulling Nya by the hand.

Empress looked back out the window and then over at Nya, who was not convincing in her interest in the food on display. The patio door's high-pitched screech from being opened distracted Empress.

"I'm not much of a wine drinker, but the Mrs. seems to really like this one," Monnie said, handing Empress a glass of chilled white wine while entering the house.

"Thanks," Empress replied, still glancing at the woman sitting outside.

"So, how did you and Nya meet?"

"We literally bumped into each other on the sidewalk one evening, but we didn't officially get introduced to one another until about a week later at one of Nya's seminars by our friend Dabney."

Monnie placed the back of her hand over her mouth to hold in the sip she had just taken from her bottle. She swallowed, and through a big smile, asked, "You're the stunning one?"

Empress's eyebrow raised. "Excuse me?"

"That night Nya ran into you, she was on her way to meet us for dinner. When she got there, she kept talking about bumping into this stunning woman, who ran away like Cinderella at midnight before she could get her number." Monnie shook her head and adjusted her cap so that it rested lower on her forehead. "Damn, talk about fate. It's like y'all were destined to meet."

Empress looked in Nya's direction. She had clearly moved past her irritation and was back into her big, beautiful personality. She watched Nya's smile grow as she spoke with Zion. She saw the authenticity and genuine love in their friendship in her simple gestures, like wrapping her arms around one of Zion's as they reconnected. "Yep, fate," she said, smiling at Nya. Empress turned her attention back to Monnie. "So what about you and Zion? How did you two meet?"

Monnie's smile widened. "It was love at first sight."

"Wow," Empress responded.

"Yep." Monnie pursed her lips to one side of her mouth. "Unfortunately, though, she didn't think twice about me when we first met." She leaned back with a laugh and adjusted her cap. "But I was gone when I first saw her."

Empress grinned. "So what caused the shift?"

"Persistent chasing on my part," Monnie responded, still laughing. She reached up to touch her cap again as if to first steady herself through the story. "I was one of Nya's interns when I was getting my bachelor's degree, and Zion was one of her clients. She was opening her first store then and was using Nya's small-business platform. So when she needed help with anything on the platform, I volunteered. Even if I had no clue on how to do something, I would go over there and act like I was fixing it." She seemed to amuse herself and again had to give in to the laughter. "After about three months of me not fixing any of her issues, and asking her to go out with me at every visit, she finally agreed if I promised to stop coming out there. She needed Nya to send someone else who actually knew how to fix her issues."

Empress was now holding her hand over her mouth to hold in her wine before laughing. As she settled down and swallowed her wine, she asked, "And you two have been together ever since then?"

Monnie shook her head. "That first date was an absolute disaster. I was a broke college student at the time and very immature. Dating to me meant ordering a pizza followed by some Netflix and chill." She winked. "For her, *Netflix and chill* meant literally watching a movie."

Empress giggled.

"So after that night of eating pizza in my bedroom, because I was living in an apartment with three other roommates, and never agreeing on an actual movie to watch, she left, and we didn't go out again for about another year."

"Wow, a year?"

"Yep, and it took much more chasing to get to that point."

Empress tilted her head.

"After that first date, I went back to her shop every week and bought something just so I could see her and talk to her. Since I was broke as hell, all I could afford was these little silver key chains with different words written on them. So, after I had bought about fifty key chains, she agreed again to go out with me, but it had to be an actual date this time." Monnie turned Empress's attention to a piece of artwork on the far wall. "Earlier this year, we celebrated the tenth anniversary of that date. Zion took all of those key chains and soldered them together to make that."

Empress walked closer to the metal sculpture shaped like a curling wave hanging on the wall. Words were circling throughout it like *happiness*, *hope*, and *love*. "That is beautiful," she commented, taking in the powerful simplicity of the piece.

"See why I kept chasing her?" Monnie said and winked. "She's always been everything amazing to me."

Empress felt arms circling around her waist and a kiss being planted on her neck. The familiar warmth of Nya comforted her. "I see you're admiring 'The Chase,'" Nya said.

"Also known as 'The Crazy Chaser' before someone made me change the name," Zion added from behind them.

"Awww, you got jokes," Monnie said, kissing Zion on the cheek.

"You know you made me change the name of it. And, Empress, what kind of friend was your girlfriend to me if she kept sending a delirious person over to my place of business?"

Empress erupted in laughter before she could catch herself to contain it.

"Don't act like you didn't like my delirious ass," Monnie said, wrapping her arms around Zion's waist.

"I should have had both of you arrested."

"Arrested," Nya exclaimed, jerking her head back and batting her eyelashes. "What did I do except introduce you to the love of your life?"

"You conspired with the delirious person. You didn't know she wasn't berserk before she became the love of my life. She could have kidnapped me and used my skin as a throw rug."

Empress's laughter spread throughout the group like a contagion.

"Your skin would be a flawless throw rug, bae," Monnie said and again kissed Zion on the cheek.

"Don't get any ideas," Zion said to Monnie. She turned her attention back to their guests. "Empress, did my loving lunatic give you the rundown of the party layout?"

Empress shook her head.

"Our parties typically all gravitate to the same guest layouts." Zion raised her arm and pointed in the direction of the living room. "The living room is where to go if you feel like being informed or debating on anything from current events to the historic contributions of unsung LGBTQ heroes. We call that area the Learning Lesbians."

Empress nodded and smiled a bit at the title.

"Here in the kitchen and in the dining room are the card players. We call this area Spades All Day."

Empress again nodded and took her last sip of wine.

"And out by the pool is where you go to engage in deep philosophical conversation while getting high. We call that area the Weed Regale."

Empress's attention again went to the woman by the pool.

Nya squeezed her arms around Empress's waist. "So do you feel like being a Learning Lesbian, or would you like to join the Spades All Day gang? I'll warn you, though, the more I drink, the worse card player I am."

"Ain't that the truth," Zion added.

Marijuana had never really been her thing, and she was afraid of knowing who the woman on the other side of the window was, so Empress opted for the choice farthest away from both of those. "Learning Lesbians," she answered.

Nya looked over at Zion and Monnie and said, "Excuse us, ladies, while we go elevate our LGBTQ-plus intelligence." She led Empress by hand into the living room.

Surveying the room for an open seat, and trying not to distract anyone from the woman lecturing the group on how traditional relationship roles were inhibitors still plaguing the Black lesbian community, Empress took the only open seat at the far end of the couch. Before she could adjust her seating to ensure she wasn't crowding the woman beside her, Nya sat on her lap and folded her arms around Empress's neck. Empress felt her body stiffen at the unexpected gesture.

"You good," Nya whispered in Empress's ear.

Empress placed her hands on Nya's thighs and gave each one a gentle squeeze.

"This adversity we have to two feminine women being together or two masculine women being in a relationship with each other impedes any progress the Black lesbian community can make. It makes no sense that we subscribe to these notions that a *proper* lesbian relationship needs to have someone playing the woman role and someone playing a man's role. It's like we impose this on ourselves to be tolerated by the straight Black community since we are showing them that we subscribe to traditional gender roles. We are all women who love other women, and we don't need to adhere to only certain types of women just because we are all a certain type of woman." The woman concluded her point with a long swig from her glass of brown liquor.

"I'm sorry, but I am a true butch, and I want someone soft lying next to me in the bed," another woman responded. She laughed and slapped hands with her friend beside her.

"I'm not saying you can't like what you like," the first woman replied. "I, too, love the sexy softness of a feminine woman beside me. I am saying that we, as Black lesbians, need to recognize relationships that break from the norms of our self-imposed gender roles, which are indeed legitimate relationships. Like the two beautiful women sitting at the end of the couch." The woman raised her glass at Empress and Nya. "They don't need to have a butch woman injected into their relationship to legitimize it, just like they don't need a man to legitimize them as women. Do your thang, ladies!" The woman concluded her point with another drink from her glass. "But if you ever do feel the need to inject a butch woman into your mix, then please keep me in mind," she added before taking another drink.

The room erupted in laughter.

Nya bent down to kiss Empress in between her laughs.

"Seriously, ladies," the woman started again. "Have you all caught any hell from your Black lesbian sisters when you go out?"

"I honestly haven't," Nya responded. "And I have dated other feminine women as well as masculine women."

"What about you, pretty lady?" the woman asked, turning her attention to Empress.

Empress shifted her weight as much as she could under Nya. She was uncomfortable with the spotlight on her. "Honestly, I have dated mostly Latinas and White women, and sticking to gender roles doesn't seem to be much of an issue in those communities."

A hush draped the room, and everyone looked at the person beside them to speak their thoughts with their eyes.

"Well, damn, pretty lady, you just gave us our next subject," the woman declared. "I'm sure everyone here has dated someone of a different race at least once, but having mostly dated people of other races is interesting. Do you prefer dating others over Black women?"

Empress shifted again as she felt everyone's eyes on her. "No, it wasn't about preference at all. It was more about opportunity and proximity. Most of my friends in college, and at work, were either White or Latinx, so their friends became my friends."

"Interesting," the woman responded. "So, you didn't feel the need or urge to be around others who look like you?"

Empress did a brief mental jaunt back to her first day on the Stanford campus. As she surveyed the buildings, searching for where her first class was located, her sight caught a sign with rainbow flags in its corners taped to a tree. She walked closer to read when and where the LGBT Alliance would be holding its meetings during the semester. The same feeling of comfort she felt on that day, from finding a place of acceptance, settled into her as the eyes around the room pried at her for a response. "I felt the need to be around people who accepted me for who I was," she responded with an unwavering confidence that was rare to her.

The woman raised her glass at Empress and nodded. "I can understand that." She shook her glass to move the last bit of brown liquid around the ice cubes before taking her final drink. "And regardless of the color on the outside, they are all pink on the inside."

The room again erupted with laughter.

As folks around the room engaged in conversations with those closest to them, Nya bent down to whisper in Empress's ear. "I can't wait to get you back to my place to show you just how much I appreciate you being here with me and how happy I am."

Empress felt heat sweep between her legs, and her heart rate escalated a bit. "I'm glad you invited me," she said, smiling back at Nya.

Nya leaned in closer and kissed Empress's cheek before standing up. "Excuse me while I use the bathroom."

As she watched Nya walk through the crowd, she saw fingers wrap around Nya's wrist and pull her in their direction. At the other end of the grasp, Empress saw the woman who was sitting by the pool earlier. She felt a chill icing its way up her spine as the woman continued to pull Nya closer to her. She said something in Nya's ear.

Empress saw Nya say something back to the woman and then pull her arm away as she continued through the crowd to get to the bathroom. Empress felt the cold reach the base of her head, which caused her to shake it a couple times to remove the sudden discomfort.

"Every woman in this room owes a debt of gratitude to Barbara Jordan," Empress heard a woman in the room say as the next discussion started. She turned her body toward the speaker but kept her eyes fixed on the woman who Nya encountered. She tried to allow the many achievements of Barbara Jordan distract her thoughts.

After a few minutes of listening to the discussion transition to the next great lesbian in history, Empress spotted Nya making her way back through the crowd. She watched as Nya was blocked by the woman—this time standing directly in front of Nya. As Nya tried twice to sidestep the persistent woman, Monnie walked up and placed her arm around Nya's shoulder to guide her around her obstacle.

"I'm just trying to talk to her," the woman said loud enough to quiet some of the crowd.

"You need to chill, dude," Monnie replied, still guiding Nya across the room with an arm on her shoulder.

"Fuck that stuck up bitch," the woman responded, now loud enough to quiet the rest of the crowd.

Monnie stopped and turned to Nya. Sincerity appeared to overshadow the building fury in her eyes. "You okay, sis?" she asked.

Nya nodded and continued making her way back to where Empress was sitting.

"You gotta go now," Monnie ordered, turning her attention back to the woman. Monnie walked over to the woman and now put her arm on the woman's shoulder to guide her to the back door. "Nothing personal, dude, but I will not have anyone being disrespected like that in my house, especially her."

After Nya settled back onto Empress's lap, she again draped her arms around her, and this time rested her head against hers. Empress gave her thighs a squeeze to signal that she was once more glad for her closeness. "You okay?" she asked, not knowing what else to say.

Nya nodded but still wore sadness in her eyes.

It was the first time Empress ever saw Nya hurt. The cold of uncertainty she felt before transitioned to fire, and she blinked a few times. She had never been in a fight in her life, and she was quite sure the woman would beat the shit out of her, but she was willing to endure her own hurt and humiliation to heal Nya's.

Zion walked toward them with her own fury unmasked and well pronounced on her face. She extended her hand to Nya and said, "Please excuse us for a minute, Empress," before leading Nya up the nearby staircase.

Monnie returned from escorting the unwanted guest out. "Empress, let's get you another glass of wine," she suggested. "Who else needs a drink?" Monnie announced to the rest of the guests.

"Me," many of the guests said in unison as they trailed Monnie and Empress into the kitchen.

When Monnie finished handing out beers and topping off glasses, she handed Empress another glass of white wine and then clinked her beer bottle against it. "Cheers."

"Cheers," Empress responded, still somewhat rattled.

"I'm sorry about that, Empress," Monnie said, her voice low.

"Please," Empress responded with a wave of dismissal. "You have nothing to apologize for." She took another drink from her glass before asking the question she had been trying to avoid all night. "So that was Nya's ex?"

Monnie nodded and then rolled her eyes as she exhaled loudly through her nose. "She told me she was going to be cool." She paused to take a drink from her bottle. "If I would have even thought she was going to act like that, I wouldn't have invited her."

"So you all are friends?" Empress asked, not really wanting to know the answer.

Monnie nodded again. "We were. I met her and Nya not long after they moved here, and then when I got with Zion, the four of us were thick as thieves for a long time." She took another drink. "It all got really complicated when she and Nya broke up, especially with the way she was cheating on Nya."

They were distracted from their conversation by the sound of approaching footsteps as Zion and Nya joined them in the kitchen. Zion walked over to Monnie, folded her arms and stared at her. "I told you not to invite her."

Monnie shrugged and grabbed the brim of her cap. "She told me she was going to be cool."

Zion threw her hands up and looked upward as if to search heaven for divine restraint and wisdom. "Baby, you have got to stop being so naïve. You know her ass lies just because she can talk." She turned her attention to Empress and her expression softened. "Empress, are you okay?"

Empress nodded and then turned her attention to Nya. She saw the redness rimmed around Nya's eyes. She pulled Nya closer to her by her waist and kissed her forehead.

Nya smiled. "Let's talk." She led Empress by hand back through the living room and out the front door onto the porch.

"Nya, you don't owe me an explanation," Empress began. "I understand it can be hard to get over someone."

"It's nothing like that. I'm more than over her. It's just very hurtful to be so disrespected by someone who claimed to love you so deeply at one point." She shook her head as if she was hearing the harsh words again. "It's such a sad reminder that love can cause such a strong emotion of betrayal."

The word *betrayal* rattled Empress and caused the chill to tap on her spine again. She felt exposed by it—naked and scarred. She wondered if Nya could see her shame also. As she focused on a flickering street light across the road to distract from her self-loathing, she felt Nya's hands combing through her curls at the back of her head. She turned to face Nya and watched the flickering street light bend and blur repetitively in her brown eyes.

Nya kissed her. "Please, just promise me no betrayal."

Empress nodded.

23.

Scarlet

She twirled in a circle with the sparkler while fixating on its lingering glow like she used to do as a child. After the sparkler flickered its last glints, Empress dropped down beside Dabney on the blanket to steady herself through the remaining dizziness. "What else do you have in that bag of cut-rate fireworks?"

"I see you have jokes, as usual, Ms. Fifth of July," Dabney said, fishing through the bag. "There are some streaming fountains in here, some smoke bombs, and something called a confetti cannon."

"Well, considering I like my fingers too much to hold anything called a confetti cannon, how about one of those fountains?"

Dabney reached into the bag, pulled out one of the fountains, and extended it to Empress.

Empress raised an eyebrow and then shook her head at him. "I'm all for gender equality, and consider myself to be quite the feminist, but I'm sorry—setting up streaming fountains and lighting them is dude work."

Dabney laughed as he walked a few feet away to set up the firework.

As Empress immersed herself in devouring her PopWich bar, she paid modest attention to Dabney struggling to light the firework.

With every attempt Dabney made to light the short wick on the fountain, the wind extinguished the flame. After every failed attempt, he moved closer to light the fountain. On the last try, he succeeded.

The short wick immediately ignited the fountain, causing the air around it to be overrun with scarlet flames. As Dabney fell back and felt his face to ensure he still had eyebrows, he didn't notice the flames lapping up the linen fabric of his sleeve.

Empress looked up to enjoy the colored flames of the fountain. When she noticed Dabney's sleeve, she threw her PopWich bar and ran over to him with the blanket. Her childhood years of training to be the next *Wonder Woman* prompted her to dive on top of him and pat out the flames.

The fountain flames sputtered and died. Still lying on top of him, Empress said, "I think this concludes our fifth of July celebration."

Dabney laughed. He focused on Empress's eyes before leaning in to kiss her.

Empress figured sharing this kiss with him was the least she could do, considering he had set himself on fire trying to give her an enjoyable evening.

His face scrunched as if he still felt the flames. "As much as I want to stay here with you in this wet grass, I think I better get home to put something on this arm."

"Yes, you should," Empress replied. As they walked out of the park, Empress looked over at him and said, "You know you owe me another PopWich bar, right?"

****

JS eased the warm bread around the rim of the plate to catch some of the remaining sauce. When it was saturated to his liking, he popped the sopping piece of bread into his mouth. A satisfying smile stretched across his lips as he chewed.

EJ refilled his wine glass as JS broke off another piece of bread to continue his favorite part of the meal.

"This masala mojo sauce is absolutely amazing," JS commented, pushing the piece of bread around the other side of the plate.

EJ smiled. "Considering you have been in here almost every week since you were here with your family, I'm guessing you like it."

"Like it? I could easily drink a bucket of this stuff," JS replied. "Who crafted this recipe?"

"I guess I sort of did," EJ stated matter-of-factly. "Indian food and food made in the Caribbean islands use a lot of the same ingredients." She paused. "Maybe that's why Columbus got confused with where he was."

JS laughed.

"Anyway, I asked our chef if he would make a masala paste, but switch out the lemon juice for the sour orange juice we use in our mojo sauce. He did that, and we experimented with a few different herb combinations until we landed on this one."

"That's so cool. I wish I could experiment like that at our next location," JS replied.

"Why can't you?"

JS shook his head as he swallowed his last gulp of wine. "The old man wants to keep things as they are. He's scared we will lose business if we make any changes to the menu."

EJ nodded. "Change can be quite scary for some. But they usually get to acceptance at some point."

Disappointment tugged at the corners of JS's mouth. "My father is not as open to change like yours."

A laugh escaped EJ as she cleared his dishes. "You think my father welcomed all of this change with open arms." She laughed a little harder and shook her head. Imitating her father's thick Cuban accent, she said, "My friend, you are sadly mistaken."

JS doubled over in laughter at her Ernesto impersonation.

"I love and appreciate my father dearly, but getting him to this point took a lot of time and patience. And I can't fault him totally for that. My father grew up in a very machismo community where every decision was made by men, and the portrayal of those men was always these larger than life, gruff, masculine characters. So when his namesake revealed she was a woman, and wanted to live her true identity, it was probably like him hearing a Martian talk about the weather on Mars."

JS laughed again. "So how did you get him to this point of acceptance?"

"I had to introduce him to things slowly, like one thing at a time. Once he would get adjusted to that one thing, then I would introduce him to something else. By the time I started having my surgeries last year, he was all in because he was adjusted to seeing me as a woman."

"Wow, that's amazing," JS replied.

"Yes, it really is, because there are times when all of this still seems unreal to me."

"May I ask, why do you still go by EJ?"

"Like I said, I love and appreciate my father dearly. He has supported me so much over these last few years, and in my life overall. Before my surgeries, I had my name legally changed from Ernesto Miguel Cedro Dominguez Junior to just EJ Dominguez. And now my full name finally fits on my driver's license." EJ split the remaining wine in the bottle between their glasses. "So," she said to JS as she clinked her glass to his.

"So what?" JS asked before taking a drink from his glass.

"So, how are you going to introduce your father to change?"

"I honestly don't feel like it's worth the fight anymore," JS said, frowning again.

EJ put her hand on his and stared into his eyes. "Our parents love us, but sometimes they don't know how to love us. It's our job to show them how to love us."

"Any suggestions on how I slowly introduce change to him?"

EJ picked up her glass before saying, "Hmmm." After she swallowed her wine, she asked, "You all are having a reception at the new location the night before the official opening, right?"

"Yep," JS nodded.

"So why not introduce a few new entrees there? Your father surely won't make a scene, though I don't think it's in his nature to do so anyway. Plus, that's a way for you to try them out ahead of time. I can help you."

JS thought about her suggestion. He nodded. "I like that." A smile budded on his face as he swallowed his last bit of wine and felt the familiar rise of infatuation inside him.

"What are you smiling about?" EJ asked, removing their empty glasses.

"It's nice talking to a beautiful woman who can relate to what I'm saying."

"Thank you for the compliment, but, JS, I'm sure you talk to plenty of women all the time. Including the one you're married to," EJ replied.

He rolled his eyes at the mention of Camellia.

"Wow, is there any part of your life that isn't in turmoil?" EJ replied with surprise.

"It ain't easy being king," JS said with an empty laugh.

"Trust me, it's much harder being a queen," EJ replied.

24.

Ivory

The diamonds outlining the dangling pearls in Cammy's earrings caught a random reflection of light and broke Empress's concentration from Nya during their conversation. It was as if a beacon had been sent to signal Empress that a dangerous situation lay ahead. Her niece had inherited her mother's cascading sandy-brown hair, and it was when she used the flirty move of tucking it behind her ear that Empress noticed the earrings she had gifted Cammy last Christmas.

Empress felt her expression stiffen as she tried to place the older man her niece was having dinner with across the room.

"What's wrong?" Nya asked. She turned and looked over her shoulder to follow Empress's gaze. "You know them?"

"Excuse me," Empress responded as she stood up.

Cammy's flirty disposition shifted abruptly to shock as she noticed Empress approaching her table. "Aunt E," she stammered with wide eyes.

Her date glanced up at Empress and then looked back at a visibly frightened Cammy. "Who is this?" he asked Cammy, not bothering to acknowledge Empress.

"Right now, I'm her legal guardian. And I'm assuming you don't know how old she is, because I would certainly hope you wouldn't be stupid enough to be out in public with a seventeen-year-old girl."

"Seventeen," the man responded with alarm. "Your profile said you were twenty-two."

"Twenty-two? Seriously, Cammy?" Empress said, her face scrunched in agitation.

"Cammy," the man responded with surprise. "Your name isn't Alicia? So everything you told me this last month has been a lie?"

Empress shook her head. "Let's go, Alicia," she said sarcastically.

Empress walked back to her and Nya's table, escorting Cammy by her arm, intentionally treating her like a child. "Nya, I'm sorry, but I have to take my niece home."

"Oh ... okay," Nya responded. "Hello," she said, moving her attention to Cammy.

"Hi," Cammy responded through her gritted teeth.

"Sorry," Empress apologized. "Cammy, this is my friend Nya. Nya, this is my niece Cammy ... oh wait ... her name is Alicia tonight."

"Aunt E," Cammy whined.

Nya smiled and laughed a bit at Empress's mocking. "Hey, Empress, I'll have them pack up our orders, and you can just come by my place after you drop Cammy off at home."

"Okay, but it might be late since Ms. Cammy Alicia and I need to have a long talk about her and her new friend."

"That's fine, I'll wait up for you," Nya responded, smiling coyly. She turned her attention to Cammy. "It was nice meeting you."

"It was nice meeting you, too," Cammy replied, a small grin spreading across her face.

Empress read the calculations on Cammy's face. "C'mon, Alicia," she said, pulling her away.

The two walked in silence out the restaurant and through the parking deck. When they reached Empress's truck, she slammed the driver's side door after she got in. "What the fuck, Cammy?"

Cammy's eyes widened as they did when she first saw Empress walking toward her table. "Aunt E—"

"Have you lost your damn mind? Have you seriously been seeing that fool for a month now? And what site did you meet his pedophile ass on?"

Cammy sat quiet, still with wide eyes.

"Cammy," Empress said sternly.

"He's not that old. He's only in his forties."

As they approached a stoplight, Empress rolled her eyes over to Cammy. "Your grandfather just got out of his fifties."

Cammy shrugged and turned her attention back out the window. "He just likes for me to talk to him and to go out with him sometimes. He hasn't asked me to do anything more than that."

"Yet," Empress replied. "And I'm going to assume that ivory HERMES bag is payment for the services you have rendered so far. Or is that a down payment on future services he wants you to render?"

"Aunt E," she whined again.

"Cammy, you are not a stupid girl by any means, so I don't understand where this naïve act is coming from. Unless you think I'm the stupid one here. You know damn well no one gives a present of a thirty-five-hundred-dollar bag and expects nothing in return."

"I didn't ask for the bag or any of the other gifts. He just asks me what I like, and then he gets it for me."

Empress shook her head, "You never did say what site you met that clown on."

"It's a site called SugarForMe.com."

"Good gracious," Empress remarked and again shook her head. "A site specializing in hooking up sugar daddies with youngsters."

"And sugar mommas," Cammy added matter-of-factly.

"Yes, of course, can't leave the sugar mommas out. Where's the equality in that," Empress replied. She thought about her last statement and carefully selected her next words. "So do you only stick to the sugar daddies, or do you venture the other way as well?"

Cammy turned her attention back to Empress and replaced the grin she wore before they left the restaurant. "Are you asking if I've spent time with some sugar mommas also?" she asked.

"Yes, that's what I'm asking."

"Nope, not at all," Cammy said and turned her attention back out the window. "I only like girls my own age."

Empress's head swiveled to her niece.

"Aunt E, watch out," Cammy yelled.

The tires on the truck squealed as Empress swerved into the next lane to avoid rear-ending the car in front of her.

"Damn, Aunt E. You okay?"

"Cammy, let's just deal with one thing at a time," Empress responded, still collecting her nerves. "What possessed you to join the sugar shit site?"

Cammy shrugged. "I heard some girls at school talking about all the stuff they were getting from just going on dates with these older guys."

"And why do you need more stuff?"

Again Cammy shrugged before answering. "I get tired of hearing my mom's mouth about being more responsible and getting a job whenever I ask for stuff." She paused, and Empress saw her fidgeting with her fingers. "Just because she's unhappy doesn't mean we all have to be, too."

Camellia's face floated through Empress's mind. Empress inhaled deeply. "Cammy, there are so many things wrong with what you said. First, I don't understand where you got the notion that stuff equates to happiness."

Cammy turned toward Empress. "Aunt E, may I remind you that we're currently riding in your Mercedes AMG and that you own a banging-ass condo in the center of the city. And how much was that Movado watch you're wearing?"

"Touché," Empress replied. "Yes, I do like nice things also, but my things aren't handed to me. I have to work to maintain the lifestyle I enjoy, which is what your mother is trying to teach you."

"Well, dating sugar daddies is like work. I have to keep myself pretty for them and pretend to be interested in their boring stories."

"Honey, selling yourself comes at a much higher price than any stuff you are given."

"Aunt E, you make me sound like a hooker."

Empress looked over at Cammy again. She remembered the moment seventeen years prior when she first saw her niece's angelic sleeping face. She mentally raced through memories of hugs, laughs, and forehead kisses. She couldn't understand what had led her seemingly happy niece to her recent acts. She again shook her head in disbelief as the sleeping baby Cammy morphed into the young woman sitting next to her. "Cammy, I understand what it feels like to not know where you quite fit in your own life, despite being surrounded by people who love you and want the best for you. Is that what this is about?"

Cammy turned to meet Empress's eyes. "I'm just ready to go, Aunt E. I can't wait to leave for college next year and get away from the craziness." She paused. "I've been selling most of the stuff I've been getting from the sugar daddies so that I will have more than enough money when I go away to stay away for as long as I can. I want to do what you did, Aunt E."

Empress inhaled deeply again and let it out with a sigh, hoping that it would help her find her next words. "Cammy, I felt like I had to leave to find out who I truly was. Is that what you're feeling? And what do you mean by getting away from the craziness?"

"I feel like I need to leave for my parents to find out who they truly are, and that's the craziness I want to escape. It's no secret that Trip and I were a total accident to two people who were just hooking up and not serious about each other." She seemed to struggle with her thoughts for a second. "When they are not shouting at each other, they don't even acknowledge one another. It's like navigating a minefield when the two of them are in the house."

Empress responded the only way she could—by wrapping her hand around her niece's and giving it a gentle squeeze.

"So, Aunt E, at least I'm hooking for a purpose," Cammy said with a half smile.

Empress shook her head. "No more sugar shit, young lady. If you need something while you're away at college, then you better call me. I will not buy you thirty-five-hundred-dollar bags, but I will make sure you have everything you need. Do we have a deal?"

"Deal," Cammy agreed and squeezed Empress's hand back. "So, are you ready to move on to the second subject?"

"What second subject?" Empress asked, pretending to forget the first part of their conversation.

"The liking girls subject."

"Sure," Empress said and shifted in her seat a little.

"I like both boys and girls."

Empress nodded, not sure of how to respond to her niece's declaration.

"Aunt E, you almost ran into another car when I told you the first time that I like girls, and now you have nothing to say?"

"I guess the initial shock has worn off now. What more do you want me to say, Cammy?"

"I don't know, but I expected some kind of response."

"Sorry to disappoint you, but I really don't have anything to say about that. It seems to be pretty prevalent in your generation."

"Maybe we're just not as sexually repressed as your generation."

"Yep, that's quite obvious with all of the dick pics and sex videos being posted these days."

Cammy was silent for a couple of minutes, and Empress thought their conversation might be over. "Your friend Nya seems nice," Cammy blurted.

"Yep, she is," Empress responded.

"She's beautiful, too."

"Yep, she is," Empress repeated. "I can ask her to create a profile on the sugar shit site if you'd like to get to know her better," she added.

"Aunt E," Cammy whined. "I just thought since we're sharing so much about each other, then you would like to tell me how long you and your pretty new friend have known each other."

"We met not too long ago when Dabney introduced us."

"Oh, okay, so will Dabney be joining you all later on tonight at her place for dinner?" Cammy asked and widened her grin.

Empress scowled at Cammy's amused expression. "No, Dabney will not be joining us for dinner this evening."

"Mm-hmm," Cammy responded, still smiling. "Will her husband or boyfriend be joining you all then?"

Empress fought the urge to shift in her seat again. "No, Cammy, she does not have a husband or boyfriend."

"Mm-hmm." Cammy sounded smug. "So you two beautiful, single ladies will be having dinner alone at her place?"

"You know, you really suck at playing Twenty Questions, because you basically keep asking the same damn question."

Cammy laughed. "I just want to make sure I have a clear understanding of the fact that you, who has no husband or boyfriend, will be having dinner with Nya, who also has no husband or boyfriend, alone at her place."

"Yes, Cammy, that is correct. Two friends will be sharing a meal together."

"Mm-hmm."

The silence landed between them again as they turned the corner and approached Cammy's house.

"Go home, Alicia," Empress said with a smile after she pulled alongside the curb in front of the house.

Cammy smiled back and then looked down at her fidgeting fingers. "Aunt E, can we keep this whole evening between us?"

Empress placed her hand on Cammy's and nodded.

Cammy leaned over to kiss Empress on her cheek. "I think it's very cool that you and Nya are having dinner alone at her place. You deserve to have a friend like that, Aunt E."

25.

Peach

Nya's sounds of satisfaction as Empress explored her body with kisses, nibbles, and sucks was a welcomed ending to another shared evening. Nya's body and her moans pulled Empress's mind away from everything else .

"Baby, your …" Nya said before she trailed off into another sound of gratification. When she was again able to find her voice, she repeated, "Baby … your …" Eventually she tapped Empress on her head.

"What's wrong?" Empress whispered.

"Your phone," Nya replied, trying to catch her breath.

Empress fumbled around on the table in search of her phone. No picture displayed to identify who was calling, and the name displayed as Unknown. "I don't know who that is," Empress said and placed the phone back on the table. She turned her attention back to Nya and resumed running her lips down her abdomen.

Again Empress's phone lit up to signal someone was calling. "Your phone," Nya replied again. "It must be important."

Empress let out an exasperated huff. "Hello," she answered with clear irritation.

"Aunt E, I'm at the police station."

"Trip?" Empress asked and sat up with alarm. "What? Where?"

"I'm at the Pineville Police Department, and—"

"I'm on my way." Empress hung up the phone and then looked down at Nya. She gazed at Nya's exposed breasts down to her navel. She let out a winded sigh to show her disappointment of having to leave her favorite playground. "I have to go."

"Is everything okay?" Nya asked, sitting up and beginning to button her shirt.

Empress grabbed Nya's hands to stop her actions. "Please stay just as you are until I walk out the door. I think I might need this beautiful memory to deal with what's coming up."

Nya smiled and unbuttoned the couple of buttons she had fastened. She reached up and ran her hand through Empress's curls before pulling Empress into a kiss. "Call me if you need me."

Empress sighed again and shook her head before she walked out the door.

****

The Pineville Police Department looked more like an old high school than a place of law and order. It wasn't until Empress saw the row of marked cars with lights on top of them that she realized she was in the right place.

As she entered, she saw an elderly Black lady with her nose wrinkled up dipping a mop into a bucket before removing it to clean up a puddle of piss and vomit. The stench of the bodily fluid collided with the pungent smell of disinfectant solution and pierced Empress's nose as she walked by.

She approached the desk to talk to the officer on duty. Before she could speak, he handed her a clipboard and told her to fill out the top information. "I'm not here to file a complaint. I'm here to pick up my nephew. His name is ..."

The officer wrinkled his nose as if he got a whiff of the smell Empress passed on her way in. He flushed with irritation, and his rounded face looked like a ripened peach. "Fill out the top portion of the form," he said sternly and again thrust the clipboard at her.

Empress narrowed her eyes. She grabbed the clipboard and filled out the first few lines at the top of the form as instructed. She stopped when she got to the portion that read Reason for Complaint. She shook her head and handed the clipboard back to the officer.

"You didn't complete it," the officer said and pushed it back to her.

"I told you I'm not here to file a complaint. I'm here to pick up my nephew."

"Well, whatever he did, you need to put that here," the officer responded and forcefully tapped his finger by the Reason for Complaint section.

Empress folded her arms and refused to reach for the clipboard. "I don't know what you all are claiming he did. I just received a phone call from him saying that he is here."

The officer grew redder, and his eye twitched. "Sit down over there." He pointed to a bench.

"I'll wait here, thank you."

The officer let out a grunt as he glared at Empress. He slowly stood, sucked his teeth, and walked to the back of the room before turning to exit down a hallway.

Empress let out her own mild grunt and deepened the frown line in the center of her brow as she watched the officer walk away. She looked around the room and took notice of the people already seated on the bench. She saw a man sitting beside a woman, both wearing expressions similar to Empress's and the officer's. The woman appeared to be dabbing her eyes on occasion, probably to stop tears before they could crest, Empress thought. The man appeared to be deep in a heated conversation with himself that included many cuss words, which he emphasized with nods of his head as he muttered them under his breath.

The officer returned with another man that was dressed in plain clothes. "Her," the officer said, pointing at Empress.

The man stepped from behind the desk and extended his hand to Empress as he approached her. The badge on his waist showed that he, too, was an officer. "Mrs. Silver," he asked as he approached her.

"It's Ms.," Empress remarked, shaking his hand.

"Ms.," he said with confusion. "Are you his mother?"

"No, I'm his aunt. Is he okay? Can I see him?"

"I'm sorry. I thought his parents were coming so I could explain the situation to them."

"What situation? Is he under arrest?"

"Well, no, we are just detaining him until his parents arrive because we need to explain what happened."

The irritation that Empress felt when dealing with the earlier officer returned. "If he is not under arrest, then you can't hold him any longer. He's been in your custody at least an hour now, and twenty minutes is the reasonable amount of time for a detainee to remain in police custody if they are not being charged with anything."

"Are you a lawyer, Ms. Silver?" His face flushed and his brow lowered.

"You don't have to be a lawyer to know your rights." Empress folded her arms and planted her feet. "Now, can you please bring my nephew out so I can take him home since he is not under arrest, and his detention has exceeded the amount of reasonable time? Or do I need to contact our lawyer?"

The plainclothes officer and the one behind the desk glanced at each other. The plainclothes one let out a huff, as his colleague had done earlier before he walked back in the direction from which he came.

With her arms still folded in defiance and her jaw clenched, Empress again surveyed the room. As she looked around, she noticed the man on the bench staring at her.

His eyes bored into hers and his face flushed. When he saw something just beyond her, his nose flared and he resumed muttering under his breath.

Trip wrapped his arms around Empress and held onto her like he used to when he was a small child. "Thanks for coming, Aunt E," he whispered in her ear during their embrace.

Empress placed her hands on either side of his face to look in his eyes as she spoke to him. "Are you okay?" she asked, almost afraid of the answer.

He nodded.

"Let's go home." Empress grabbed Trip's hand.

As they walked by the angry man on the bench, he stood up and rushed over to the officers at the desk. "He needs to be arrested for what he did," the man declared loud enough for everyone to hear.

"Sir, we asked your daughter several times, and she said it was completely consensual," the plainclothes officer answered, his hands raised in a position of defense.

"I don't care what she said. I don't pay your salaries with my taxes so that some hoodlum can force himself on my daughter and brainwash her into believing it was consensual."

"Sir, based on the officer's report, and your daughter's statement, she wasn't forced into doing anything. And they are both minors who are the same age, so there isn't even a statutory issue here," the officer explained.

"I wasn't a hoodlum when I was having dinner with y'all a few hours ago," Trip remarked at the angry man.

The angry man turned and approached Trip and Empress. "Don't you talk to me like that."

Empress stepped between Trip and the approaching man as a safeguard for her nephew, though she was a few inches shorter than both of them. "You need to calm down," she warned, throwing up her arm to stop the man from getting close to Trip.

"George, let's just go," the woman on the bench said as she stood up and began to cry.

The man looked over at her and appeared to be calmed by her voice. He followed her eyes to a young lady wearing shame more natural than her long blond hair.

Empress turned to Trip and said again, "Let's go."

After they entered her truck, she ran her hands through her curls to try and shake off her agitation.

"Aunt E, I didn't force her into doing anything."

"I believe you, Trip."

"She's the one who got stuff started when we got into the car."

As they drove away from the police station, Empress contemplated if she was ready for the conversation she and her nephew were about to have. The sordid details didn't interest her, but she knew she had to listen. "Trip, what in the hell happened?"

"She invited me to her house for dinner with her parents. Her dad kept asking me about football stuff, and her mom just had questions about my family and my college plans. Everything was cool."

"Okay, so when did it get uncool?"

"When we left to go to the movies. We were about a block away from the theater, and she wanted to do … stuff."

Empress again sighed, already knowing the answer to her next question. "What stuff?"

"Aunt E, you know … stuff," he said with wide eyes and raised eyebrows.

"Okay, so I'm assuming the stuff is what led to this whole thing."

"Yep. We pulled down this dark road and started kissing, which led to other stuff. Next thing I know, a cop is shining a flashlight through the window, and sees her …" Trip motioned toward his crotch and raised his eyebrows again.

Another sigh escaped Empress before she realized it had even formed. "Okay, I think I'm caught up now."

"Aunt E, please don't tell my parents about this?"

She looked over at him and saw the same look of concern his sister gave to Empress on her late-night ride home. "Sure, Trip."

"Thanks. I just can't take hearing them argue about another thing."

"Trip, you have to promise me you're going to be smarter than this going forward. This could have really turned out bad. We have lost a lot of young men of color who didn't have the good fortune of just being detained."

"Don't worry, Aunt E. That's the last time I'm trying to see any parts of a police station. I don't even want to walk by one after this experience."

Her phone vibrated against the wood on the console between them and diverted their attention. Before Empress picked it up, Nya's picture displayed with a message, "Hope everything is ok."

"Daayyuum," Trip exclaimed. "Yo, Aunt E, who is that?"

"She's a friend," Empress replied.

"Can I meet her?" Trip laughed. "I need a new friend now."

Empress smiled and shook her head. "You don't need any new friends at all right now," she said before voicing a message to Nya about being okay and calling her later.

Trip nodded and laughed again. "So that's your *friend* sending you a text this late, Aunt E?"

"You and your sister, I swear." She ran her hand through her hair. "Yes, she is my friend."

"I'm just saying, Aunt E, it's cool to have a friend sending you a text this late." He chuckled again. "Especially a friend that looks like that."

"Oh, darn, look. We're at your house now," Empress announced.

Trip leaned over to kiss her on the cheek. "Go do some stuff, Aunt E," he teased before getting out of the truck.

"Good night, Trip," she replied, shaking her head at him.

26.

Gray

She saw Nya stand up to greet them as they approached the table. Empress scanned up Nya's sleek legs to her full lips. She licked her lips like there were still remnants of Nya there.

Nya stuck out her hand to JS. "You are definitely Empress's brother."

"Yes, and you are definitely much prettier than I was expecting," he responded, shaking her hand.

"Is that right? What were you expecting?"

"I'm not sure what I was expecting, but I'm very pleased with who I'm seeing."

"Well, thank you." Nya turned her attention to Empress. She smiled a bit as if a quiet pleasantry was just whispered to her. "Very nice to see you again, Empress."

Empress received her coy smile and returned it. "Nice to see you also."

Nya shifted her attention back to JS. "So, Empress, tells me you have some great plans for the current restaurant and the next location."

"Yes, I'm actually in the process of upgrading our current platform so that the data from all locations can be synched and accessed from a cloud environment."

"Very impressive. I see big brains run in your family," she commented, glancing over at Empress.

"Yes, brains, and other things, run big in our family," JS replied.

Nya raised an eyebrow. "So, do you have a plan for the promotional marketing of the next location?"

"I have some things I've been thinking about, but I haven't landed on anything concrete yet."

"I have some great crowdsourcing techniques to drive promotional marketing that I can share with you," Nya responded.

"Looks like you have a big brain of your own," JS said. "That's a deadly combination: beauty and brains."

"Yes, it is," Nya answered, shifting her eyes to Empress.

JS's eyes moved to Empress and then back to Nya. A grin spread across his face. "So how long have you two known each other?" he asked.

Empress read her brother's grin and narrowed her eyes at him.

"We actually met about a month ago when your sister literally bumped into me on Fifth Street. Then we officially were introduced about a week after that by Dabney." Nya's buzzing phone interrupted her, and after she read the name of the caller, she said, "I'm sorry, but I have to take this."

As Nya walked away from the table to take her call, Empress whispered, "Shut up, JS."

"Holy fucking shit," he said, shaking his head and still smiling. "I knew that bullshit Pops told us about you and Dabney dating wasn't true. So she and Dabney are friends, and he introduced the two of you? Is he in on this? I mean, does he know about you two, and he's just being your beard, or whatever lesbians call it, for Pops's sake? Or do the three of you entertain together? By the way, well done, that woman is hotter than a bowl full of jalapeños."

Empress looked across the room to ensure Nya was still on her phone. "Shut up, JS. I'll tell you everything later."

"Just tell me one thing. Does her ass look as good naked as I'm picturing it?"

Empress looked across the room again and saw Nya making her way back to the table. "Shut up, JS," Empress said through gritted teeth.

"Just say yes or no," JS replied with his smile now doubled in size.

Empress grabbed one of his fingers and began to pull it backward like she used to do when they were kids. "Shut up, JS," she uttered once again, bending the finger farther back, making him contort his body in pain.

"Okay, okay, let go with your freakishly strong man hands."

"Everything okay?" Nya asked as she sat down at the table and saw JS rubbing one of his hands.

"Yes, my sister was just showing me how much she loves me."

Nya sat back down at the table and stole another lingering glance of Empress.

Empress caught Nya's glance. "I have to go to the bathroom," she blurted.

JS tilted his head. "Thank you for the announcement."

Nya laughed. "I'll join you," she said to Empress.

As they stood up to leave, a server passed by their table. "Hey, my man," JS addressed the server. "Can you please bring me a burger and any stout beer you have on tap? I have a feeling I'm going to be waiting here for a while."

Empress followed Nya into a bathroom stall. As she fastened the door behind them, she felt Nya brush her hair to one side and kiss the back of her neck.

"I missed you last night," Nya whispered into her ear.

"I missed you, too," Empress replied, turning to face her.

Nya ran her fingers through Empress's curls before grabbing a handful and pulling her into a kiss.

Their tongues collided and their hands explored—fingertips covered with the warm wetness. Their tongues traveled—nipples between teeth led to stifled moans. Fingers prodded deeper until knuckles were soaked and sticky. Empress and Nya trembled together. A vehement, mutual climax weakened them and brought them closer to keep from collapsing.

As Empress struggled with her loss of breath and racing heart, she rested her head against Nya's.

Nya kissed Empress's forehead.

When Empress again found her voice, she whispered, "I'll go out first."

Nya nodded and kissed her again before she left the stall.

Empress continually adjusted her clothes as she walked back from the bathroom. When she sat back down at their table, she stole a fry from JS's plate.

"I hope you washed your hands after your little tryst in the bathroom," JS said.

"Nope." She licked each of her fingertips one by one as a sarcastic response.

They were laughing as Nya sat back down at the table. "Wow, that burger looks good," Nya noticed. "I am so hungry now."

JS looked over at Empress with raised eyebrows, causing them to laugh harder.

"What's so funny?" Nya asked.

"It's funny you worked up an appetite in the bathroom," JS answered.

"Your sister did most of the work," she responded and winked at Empress.

After they hailed the server and ordered additional entrees, Nya tried to resume their business conversation. "I'm sorry, JS, what were we discussing before all of these distractions?"

"Really? I'm a distraction?" Empress asked Nya with a smile.

"Damn right, you are a distraction. JS and I are supposed to be talking about business, and you walk in here with that big, beautiful curly hair, those eyes, and that body. You have been distracting me since you bumped into me that day."

"I can leave so you two can continue talking," Empress replied, feeling secure that her brother couldn't possibly steal this one away from her.

Nya reached across the table and grabbed Empress's hand. "I like being distracted by you."

"Should I leave so you two are not distracted by me," JS interjected.

"You're not a distraction; you're an annoyance," Empress replied, making Nya laugh.

"See how rude she is to me, Nya? Regardless, I love my baby sister very much. So as her much older and, much more mature, brother I have to ask what are your intentions with my little sister?"

"Six minutes doesn't make you much older, and you're for damn sure not more mature."

"Hush, little one, the adults are talking now," JS replied.

"You're an idiot," she responded.

In between her laughs, Nya started with, "Well, my main intention is to just enjoy your sister for as long as possible." She paused and looked up as if selecting her next thought. "She's special. And I would like to share more of our lives together in the future, like eventually meeting more of her other family members I hear so much about."

"If Empress brings you around the rest of the family, then you two are definitely end game. You're making history right here with me since none of us have ever met any of her harem."

"Harem? Really, JS," Empress scolded.

Nya laughed. "I knew there was no way this pretty lady had been spending many nights alone. Is her hoe-tation huge, JS?"

"I think it is, but I haven't gotten an exact number yet."

"This is the most absurd conversation I have ever heard," Empress uttered. After their server interrupted by placing their entrees on the table, Empress asked him, "Can you please bring me a bourbon and soda? I need something stronger than water to deal with these two."

"What's wrong, little sister, you don't like when the adults are talking?"

"JS, don't make me pull your finger again."

"Seriously, though, only a couple of us in the family know about Empress's harem." JS put his hand under the table so Empress couldn't grab his finger.

"Nya, please don't listen to this bull about a harem hoe-tation," Empress remarked before taking a sip from her drink. The bantering didn't bother her, only the possibility of it leading to questions of who, where, and when about her sexual exploits did. She didn't know if she'd ever been ready to lower the boom of truth, and she was certainly not prepared to do it at that moment.

"Hey, we all have a past, right," Nya responded. "I do have a question, though."

Empress shifted her legs under the table.

"What is keeping you from telling your father?"

Empress took a large gulp from her drink to stall.

"Our father is a very black-and-white man," JS explained. "He doesn't hate anyone at all, but when people fall into that gray area for him, he doesn't try to understand them. That is difficult to deal with."

"But you are his children. Aren't you all allowed to fall into the gray area sometimes and still be unconditionally loved?"

"We are loved," JS answered. "It's just tough to see the disappointment in his eyes when you live in that gray area."

Empress saw her lifelong protector drop to a place of silent sorrow. She reached for his hand under the table and cradled it in her own.

"I understand," Nya responded.

"Excuse me," JS said as he scooted his chair from the table and headed to the bathroom.

"I'm sorry." Nya looked at Empress and bit her bottom lip. "I didn't mean to upset him."

"It's fine. He just gets sensitive sometimes when he talks about his relationship with our father."

After they ate in silence for a few minutes, Empress looked toward the bathroom to see if JS was coming out. She wondered if he was more wounded than usual after talking about his relationship with their father. Her eyes darted around the bathroom area to see if she had missed him. As she surveyed, she saw a profile of his big smile talking to a woman who appeared to be on her way to the bathroom. "He's back to normal now," she informed Nya.

Nya followed Empress's eyes. "Do you know that woman?"

Empress shook her head as she chewed her food. "I'm sure she's in his hoe-tation though," she answered after she swallowed.

"I thought you said he's married."

Empress nodded.

Nya sucked her teeth then continued eating.

JS came back to the table. He picked up his glass and chugged the remainder of his beer. "I'm sorry, ladies, but something has come up that I need to attend to. Nya, it was wonderful meeting you, and we need to do this again so that we can actually talk about business." He looked over his shoulder and held up an index finger to the woman as she walked out of the restaurant.

"It was very nice meeting you, too," Nya replied as she stood up and extended her hand to him.

"Thank you," he responded, wrapping his hands around hers.

"For what?" Nya asked.

"I haven't seen her this happy in a long time," he said and looked down at Empress.

Empress and Nya watched in silence until he met up with the woman waiting on the other side of the glass door.

"So, just like that, he's going to sleep with that woman?" Nya asked, still perplexed.

"Mm-hmm," Empress responded around a mouthful of food.

"And that's okay with you?"

"It's really not my business."

"How is it not your business when over the last week you have had to rescue his children from some serious situations? Don't you think the things correlate to one another?"

Empress put her fork down and looked up at Nya. "I really feel like you are judging him too harshly, especially since you just met him." She sounded more bitter than she intended.

"Fine, I'll back off." Nya grabbed Empress's hand to defuse her.

Empress read the sincerity in Nya's eyes and dropped her guard.

They continued with their meals, and Nya asked, "How are your niece and nephew doing, by the way?"

"They're good. Both are ready to get through their senior year and move on to college."

"Yes, that is quite an exciting time in life. I couldn't wait to get to college, just so that I could be more so me."

"I know what you mean," Empress said, a feeling of nostalgia rising in her chest.

"So, will I see you tonight?"

"Yes, but it will be sort of late. We have a meeting this evening to talk through the closing in a few days. And I have to leave early in the morning, because Pops and I have to meet up with the contractors to see how soon after the closing they can start."

"I just want to spend some time alone with you to show you how much I really missed you after you left last night. That time in the bathroom was nice, but it just made me want more of you."

Empress felt a warm throb between her legs. She smiled at the feeling Nya stoked in her. "You will definitely see me tonight."

27.

Indigo

The past month was a beautiful blur in her mind, like looking at lights through a window covered in cascading rain. Empress sat up in bed and waited for the sun to break through the surrounding buildings as she often did in the mornings from Nya's bed. Daylight slowly lightened the room, and Empress blinked as her eyes adjusted. In the far corner of the room, she noticed her most recent gift to Nya—a dozen indigo calla lilies in a white vase sat on a small pedestal table. A laugh escaped her as she looked closer; each one looked like a little vagina. *How fitting,* she thought and wondered if that was the real reason they were Nya's favorite flower and not the reason she gave of them symbolizing regal beauty.

Nya stirred as the sunlight streaked the room.

Empress laughed again as Nya pulled the covers over her head. Within seconds she heard the deep breaths and felt the settling stillness of Nya lulling back to sleep—a sensation she had grown a longing affinity for.

Peering back at the rising sun, she thought about the word happiness. The day Camellia stormed out of their makeshift relationship a year ago, when Empress told her she could do no more, she looked up the definition for happiness. Good fortune, pleasure, contentment, and joy were the words used to describe it. Empress now realized she had stumbled onto happiness again when she assumed her only chance at it left a year ago.

As the beams of sunlight now stretched to the calla lilies, the flowers caught her attention, and again she quietly chuckled. Nya's body stirred beside her as she pulled the covers from over her head before fluttering her eyes open.

"What's so funny?" Nya asked as she yawned and stretched.

"I was just admiring your bouquet of vaginas."

Nya scrunched her face.

Empress bent down to kiss her puckered lips. "I have to leave now to get ready for our meeting with the contractors."

Nya sighed and pouted.

Empress bent down to kiss her before getting out of bed.

As Empress walked around the room naked to retrieve her clothing, Nya said, "Mmmm. I hate to see you go, but I love to watch you leave."

****

The mixed smell of maple syrup, coffee, bacon, and pastries wafted from the restaurant next to Nya's building and pulled Empress's attention. She stopped and considered going in to get something to eat on her way home.

Through the sounds of silverware clinking on plates and the restaurant patrons' muddled conversations, Empress thought she heard her name. She looked around and heard the rich baritone of his distinct voice getting closer. Her body tingled with panic.

"Well, this is a pleasant surprise," Dabney said as he approached her.

Damn my weakness for breakfast foods, she thought as she greeted him with their customary hug. "What are you doing over this way?" she asked, trying to mask her panic. "And how is your arm?"

"The burn wasn't serious, so my arm is good. And I'm meeting Nya for a run. What brings you over this way early in the morning?"

"There was this thing, and I ... had ... to ... go to the thing," Empress stuttered, knowing what she said made no sense and wasn't convincing at all.

As Dabney's eyes squinted, Nya exited her building wearing capris and a razorback sports bra. Though she had seen her naked quite a few times already, Empress stared and her panic briefly subsided.

Nya looked surprised to see Empress standing there. "Empress, I thought you—"

"Hi, Nya, it's nice to see you again. Do you live here? I was just telling Dabney I had to attend a thing over here, and now that it's over, I'm going home. You two enjoy your run," Empress said and turned to walk away.

"Empress, wait," Nya called and walked after her. "It's okay," she assured Empress and grabbed her hand.

They walked back to Dabney hand in hand. He stood with confusion etched into his face, and his mouth gaped open.

"Dabney, the thing Empress had to do was me," Nya said, then paused. "That sounded a lot better in my head than when I said it out loud. What I meant was Empress was with me this morning and last night."

"I don't understand," Dabney responded. "I mean, I understand for the most part, but, Empress, I thought—"

"Empress isn't completely out to her family," Nya said.

"So you were just using me?" Dabney asked as his expression hardened.

"No, she didn't use you exactly," Nya answered. "She—"

"Nya, please," Empress pleaded. "Dabney, I'm sorry I didn't tell you sooner."

Dabney shook his head and held up his hand. "This is really fucked up, Empress," he said before turning to walk away.

Empress sat down on the steps outside Nya's building. She ran her fingers through her thick curly hair a couple times. The sounds of silverware clinking on plates and the patrons' muddled conversations in the restaurant next door made her cringe. *Why didn't I just keep walking,* she thought.

Nya sat down beside her and rubbed her back. "It's going to be okay," she assured her.

"Nya, I'm not you," Empress snapped. "I almost lost my father once, and I can't even fathom possibly losing him again."

"Empress, your being gay is not going to kill him. He may be disappointed for a little while, but he loves you, and that will be more important than anything else he feels."

"I don't want to lose him on any level or for any period of time." Empress stood. "I have to go," she said and walked away.

The distracting aromas of breakfast food didn't pull her attention this time as she walked by the restaurant. This time, she smelled nothing, heard nothing, and saw nothing as her mind ran through the what-if questions and their possible answers. Every result she came up with ended in permanent rifts in the relationships with people she loved.

She sat silently in her truck. Her thoughts went to the first time she inadvertently came out. It was the first time JS came to visit her at Stanford. His unexpected knock on her dorm room at six in the morning was a startling interruption to her activities with a lady she met the day before at the library. To her surprise, JS showed little surprise. He assured her then that Pops could keep holding on to his hallowed hope of her finding a nice guy to settle down with one day as he would tell their father nothing different. She wondered now if that promise would hold up against her truth.

28.

Graphite

They all had become a collage of body parts to him—tight asses, round hips, long legs, and supple breasts. With the only purpose of fulfilling his many missed opportunities by marrying at a young age, faceless infidelities had become an intricate part of his life. The current opportunity was no different to him.

"How long before I see you again?" she asked as JS gathered his clothes from the floor.

As it always did, his interest left with his orgasm. "I don't know," he replied, still getting dressed.

The woman threw the bedding off her naked body, and the sheets snapped in rebellion. She crawled across the bed and began to unzip the pants he had just put on.

JS placed his hands on hers and said, "I'll call you," before walking out the room.

He started his rendezvous ritual of rolling the windows down after lighting a cigarette on his ride home. The argument with his wife about smelling like smoke was a better one to bear than the actual truth.

There were five inhales and exhales in each cigarette; with each one, he took in a distant memory of his early adulthood years and then expelled the possible outcomes that never occurred. Since he was faced with manhood long before he was ready to grow up, he was forever clinging to the moments before Camellia told him she was pregnant. He gripped the couple years of freedom he experienced in college with such tightness that they would crumble to dust if they were tangible.

Camellia was nothing more than a pastime to him then, and now he saw her as nothing much more than a responsibility. He had grown to love her over the years, he guessed, but never grew enough to fall in love with her. "We wear the mask that grins and lies," he recited from his favorite Paul Laurence Dunbar poem.

His mind wandered to when he first heard that poem. He remembered the booming sound of each word as they dropped from his father's voice. The words pounced into his ears and echoed between them like the bass root of a jazz song. He didn't understand what he was hearing at the age of five, but he never grew tired of hearing the words of Maya Angelou, or Langston Hughes, or any of his father's other favorites.

His mind took a turn down a desolate path where graphite rubbles of his aspirations were the pavement. "Hold fast to dreams," he recited from another favorite in a voice that mocked the baritone of his father. He tried to count the infinite times his father spoke and wrote those words to him. They accompanied every accolade his father bestowed on him. They were written in every celebratory card he received from him; they hung in every hug and prideful gesture given to him. As the second exhale of smoke clouded in front of him, he realized those words could only be found in his distant memories.

He found it ironic that the man who told him to dream was also the man who told him to stop dreaming. His thoughts went to the day when his life forever changed. The only day he could remember seeing beads of sweat running through the crevices in his palms under the unsettling gaze of his father.

After he delivered the news to his father of Camellia's pregnancy, his father placed one of his large hands over his eyes and shook his head. JS felt the disappointment draping him from his father's eyes, though they were no longer fixated on him. The distinct baritone that had soothed him through childhood rolled with weight over a long sigh that seemed to elevate from his father's soul. When he was able to find his voice again, the only thing his father said was, "Man-sized choices come with man-sized responsibilities."

"Bullshit," he yelled after the fourth exhale of smoke from his cigarette. It was bullshit how his father's disappointment deepened as JS went on to tell him about his plans of continuing to play football at UNC and then entering the NFL draft before his senior year. It was bullshit how his father slammed his hand on the table to disrupt JS from talking about following his dreams. It was bullshit that his father told him he needed to get a job and think about Camellia and their child first and everything else was a long, distant second. It was bullshit that he made JS come back home and work with him in the restaurant to ensure he was working to support his child. It was bullshit that his father went from being his ally to his adversary at that pivotal moment.

At the bottom of his final exhale, he paused his breathing and waited before taking his next inhale. He felt his chest tighten. *This is what my responsible life feels like,* he thought to himself before giving in to his body's pleas to resume breathing.

As he turned onto the street where they lived, he pulled his car alongside the curb. He looked down at his house and saw only the kitchen lights on through the front window. A small smile broke on his face at the thought that possibly no one was home.

When he pulled his car into the driveway and pushed the button to open the garage door, the tightness returned to his chest. Camellia's truck was in its designated spot on the left side.

"Fuck," he yelled. His mind swiped through the excuses he had used over the years to lie about his whereabouts and lateness. Late customers at the restaurant, traffic accident, a game at a sports bar, hurricane, inept employees, explosion, Internet outage, flooding, power outage, or any other outlandish mishap.

He sat in his car after parking it in the garage. He took three deep inhales between long, emptying exhales to try and remove the tightness from his chest. "We wear the mask," he said again. It was time for his next performance as responsible husband and father.

29.

Hazel

It was not the fact that tonight was yet another night he would traipse in smelling like smoke, hoping it covered the smell of his latest fling. It was not the fact that their years together seemed like a sentencing of consequences instead of building a life together based on love. It was not even the fact that she barely remembered the last civilized conversation between them. It was the simple, honest fact that she was now done.

She did not feel the normal tension aching through her shoulders and up her neck when the front door opened and closed to signal JS had arrived home. Camellia remained still on the edge of their bed as he entered the room and began his spiel about traffic being bad while removing his clothes to go straight into the shower. "Shut the fuck up, JS," she said in a monotone voice.

"Huh?" He paused with his shirt halfway off.

"JS, I'm tired, and I'm done with this, so save your bullshit for someone who gives a damn about it."

Her calmness seemed to paralyze him. Her words were not new, but they were often shouted or said through tight lips and gritted teeth.

Camellia placed her head in her hands as if to hold it up from the strain of her weighted mind. She spoke aloud to herself. "I knew who I was years ago, but I could not accept myself on those terms. I was loved by someone that I truly loved, and I couldn't accept them either."

JS stood in silence.

She lifted her head and looked around as if she saw everything for the first and last time. She nodded as she confirmed to herself that she was good with her decision. "I'll come back later for my things," she said before standing and leaving their eighteen years of life together.

****

JS placed his head in his hands just as he had watched his wife do when her mind became too heavy. He tried to make sense of her words and how his life had leaped to this point. He often thought about the relief he would feel if he wasn't shouldered with his forced responsibilities. In the face of this freedom now, he was simply baffled.

From behind his closed eyes, he saw the furrowed brow on his father's face when JS would hand him yet another disappointment. The loss of his wife paled in comparison to the further loss of his father's approval.

He thought about Camellia's final words to him. She couldn't accept herself or the person she loved. He always felt both he and Camellia belonged to other people. His others were one-night stands and short-lived girlfriends on the side, but he had never considered she loved someone else. He actually wanted to apologize to her for derailing her life with a falsehood of love.

The memory of when they first spoke of love to each other flooded his already drowning mind. After a few months of them secretly meeting, when he would come home during his school breaks and exchange orgasms with her, his unintended words led to unintended consequences. As it often was, his judgment and words were clouded from physical pleasure. At the height of his climax, as the euphoria washed over his mind and body, he released the words, "Shit, I love you."

As the tremors settled out of him, and the room filled again with light and silence, he heard Camellia ask, "You love me?"

JS saw the sadness rimming her eyes as she waited for his response. He noticed the gray-and-green flecks weaving through the brown to give her eyes their hazel color. He ran his hand over her sandy-brown hair. For the first time, he saw how beautiful she was. He kissed her and began to feel his desire rise again. "Yeah," he said before kissing her again to move on to their next orgasmic exchange.

He looked around their bedroom as Camellia did before she announced she was leaving their marriage. He saw her in the long mirror across the room, modeling her new suit in preparation for her first management position. JS saw her sleek, naked body through the glass in the bathroom shower. He saw her brushing back her thick hair as she put on his mother's earrings before they attended the gala in his family's honor. He saw her tempting him, lying across the bed in lingerie during those moments when they both tried to love each other as husbands and wives should.

He knew now that he didn't lie in that initial declaration of love. He just didn't understand what it meant to love her until now when she was no longer there for him to try and love.

He reached over to pick up his phone and sent a text. "Meet me for a drink."

****

Something was wrong. Though they were going through their usual motions of ogling at passing women between drinks and clinking their glasses when they agreed on the aesthetics of one, Empress still felt a disconnection.

"Time travel, baby sis," JS murmured with a slight slur in his words brought on by his sixth beer. "The year is 1975; Pam Grier or Lonnette McKee?"

"Damn that's a hard one," Empress replied, tilting her head in thought. "Can I opt for a me sandwich on that one?" She asked with a smile.

JS laughed as if it was the medicine he had been needing. "You're crazy, but I think I'd exercise that option on my side as well."

They clinked their glasses together.

Silence fell as it had been doing throughout the evening. Empress saw beyond the mask her brother had been wearing all night. She could see how he tried to distract himself by systematically peeling the label from his beer bottle to keep it intact. She placed her hand on his to distract him from his distraction.

"Camellia is gone," he said.

A chill inched over Empress's body as she tried to make sense of his words. "What do you mean, gone?"

"She left." He took a long sip from his bottle as if he needed its contents for his next sentence. "She told me she couldn't do this anymore and said something about loving someone else."

Empress pulled her trembling hand away from him and rubbed it with her other one under the table. She looked away from JS and took her own long sip from her glass. Thousands of questions hit her at once, and their possible answers frightened her.

"Shit," JS muttered.

His statement brought some focus to her current blurred reality. Empress looked up at him and saw the truth he was wearing behind the mask. "I'm sorry, JS," she said.

"You," he declared, and again drank from his bottle.

"JS ... I ..." Empress stammered.

"You were the only one," he said, nodding as if agreeing to something unspoken.

Empress lowered her head in shame. She started to sweat and her head began to throb.

"It was you I should have listened to," he continued. "You were the one who told me not to marry Camellia."

She lifted her head to read her brother's eyes and was relieved when she saw no malice or scorn. She took a deep breath. "Time travel, JS," Empress said. "Eighteen years ago; Camellia or you?"

"I love my children, and I appreciate my wife, but ... me," he admitted, dropping his head. "When I told Pops Camellia was pregnant, all he said was,

'Man-sized choices come with man-sized responsibilities.' I knew in his mind, that meant I needed to marry her and be a father." He paused to drink the last swallow from his bottle. "We're alike in so many ways, E, because I also can't bear to see the disappointment in his eyes."

She placed her now steadied hand back on his and cradled her fingers around it.

"I've lived this moment in my mind for years. I thought it would be such a relief when one of us finally said they wanted out. Right now, though, I don't know what to think. I know neither of us has been happy in a long time, if ever, but I hate the thought that I've failed at yet another thing."

"JS, you've raised two beautiful children, you're a successful entrepreneur, and you have a good heart."

He looked down at the bottle in his hand and continued peeling its label. "I have cheated on my wife for most of our marriage, I didn't finish college, and I've been vaguely present in my kids' lives." Tension lines etched deeper into his face as if his truthful words were carving them.

"Have you talked to Camellia since she left?" Empress asked.

"Nope, she hasn't returned any of my calls or texts," he replied, still focusing on removing the label. "And why should she," he added.

They finished their drinks and settled the bill in silence.

"I have to get home, JS. I'll drop you off, because you're in no condition to drive," Empress said as she stood.

JS staggered behind her out of the bar. As the stench from a nearby trash can—rimmed with rotten food and stale beer bottles—hitched a ride on a swirling breeze, he bent over to throw up. After spitting the last remnants of his dinner onto the pavement, he slumped down into Empress's front passenger seat and whispered, "Sorry."

Empress heard his soft snores soon after they left the parking lot and used that as her queue to search for her phone in her handbag. "Where r u," she typed after she found it.

The bright city lights passed in blurred streaks as if she were pushing the boundaries of this reality and being forced into a new dimension. A dimension, it seemed, where everything she had been holding together with plastered patches of lies would soon be the decayed ruins of her relationships. She felt the familiar blanket woven of anxiety and panic weighing on her limbs and chest.

JS let out a loud snort as he shifted in his seat.

When she turned onto his street, she narrowed her eyes to search for any signs of Camellia in the house. There were no lights on in their bedroom or her office. Empress felt her heartbeat in her throat.

As she parked in their driveway, she nudged JS awake. “Hey, JS, wake up.”

JS let out another snort, and he blinked several times. He fumbled out of the car and stumbled to his front door.

Empress walked behind him and watched as he fidgeted his key around the keyhole. She felt nauseous.

The darkness in the house greeted them. Empress watched as JS dropped his head in defeat. She pulled him into a hug and, as her tears fell on his shoulder, she said, “I’m so sorry.”

“Thanks, baby sis.” He wiped away one of her tears. “Don’t worry, I’ll be okay.”

Her phone was buzzing when she got back into her truck. “I’m at our spot. Room 1020,” the text read.

Since her unexpected visit at her place, Empress hadn’t seen Camellia, which was before Nya came into her life. She wondered if Camellia would be able to see Nya in her.

30.

Yellow

She had always loved so much without ever knowing it. She loved unpredictable seventy-degree days in a Carolina December. She loved the slow, reluctant way the leaves fell during the transition from autumn into that first month of what southerners know as winter. She loved the mixing aroma of books and coffee on those Saturday mornings when she disappeared to a hidden corner of the bookstore to enjoy anything that was an escape from her reality. She loved the actual onset of spring where occasional warm winds accompanied brisk April mornings to signal the approaching scorch of summer. She loved the lingering aftertaste of honey when she dribbled strings of it onto her tongue.

It was not until the sweet acidity of her rum and Coke washed over her taste buds and eased the ailing of her thoughts that Camellia remembered all she had loved over time. She circled her index finger around the edge of the glass and allowed her finger to dip into her drink. She watched the reacting liquid disturb the ice cubes and, for some reason, smiled at that. She scanned the room as she sucked the sweet acidity from her finger.

She knew why her aimless driving landed her here. It was here that was more home to her than the house she lived in with her family. Compacted into a few hours at a time, here was where she experienced seventy-degree December days, the aroma of escape, warming spring winds, and the lingering taste of honey.

They met here often after JS paid Empress an unexpected visit and almost found Camellia in Empress's bed. He had come over that evening hoping to clean himself up to ward off the smell of his latest fling before going home to his wife. When Empress told him he could not shower away the stench because she had company, he started his ritual of smoking a cigarette on his way home.

After paying for her third drink, she made her way to her hotel room. She flung her body across the bed and allowed her shoes to dangle on her feet until they gave way to gravity. The noise they made when they hit the floor was the only signal that someone was there.

For the first time in her life, she was truly alone, and it scared her. There had been so many plans laid for her life before she was even blessed to live it. Since her inception, she was always expected to be a spitting image of her parents. She had been predestined to live her life with the strict moral standards that came with being the child of a third-generation minister. She would always be a top student breezing through higher education, a young lady in waiting with her virtue intact for only the most worthy suitor, a wife and mother whose life rivaled that of Mary in the Bible.

But long ago, she met the fortunate misfortune of falling in love beside a lake. Since that day, she knew she would always fall short of her destined expectations and plans no matter how hard she tried. As she listened to the silence bounce off the surrounding walls, she wondered if there was a single word that described her feeling of simultaneous love and hate. At that moment, while the rum seeped into the uncharted memories she kept under lock and key, she blamed Empress for making her broken. It wasn't her that wanted to fall in love with Empress; it was Empress that grabbed her heart with both hands and refused to let go. Even during those times when either of them walked away, Empress still held her heart hostage.

She played her own mental game of what-ifs and explored the possible outcomes of different decisions she had made. She painted a picture of Stanford in the spring, where she and Empress sat on a lawn, studying each other more than their assigned work. Again, as she often asked herself over this last year, what if she would have just said yes to what scared her most?

Her phone buzzed. She lifted her head to read the message. "Where r u."

****

Empress knocked on the door to Camellia's room for a couple minutes before she finally answered. Her stumbling back to the bed let Empress know she was in the same condition as her husband.

After Camellia flopped across the bed, she asked, "Are you only here because he sent you?"

"No," Empress replied. "He doesn't know I'm here."

"Then why are you here?" Camellia replied with her mouth half muffled in a pillow.

"I wanted to make sure that you were okay."

"Bullshit, Empress!"

Camellia's voice had a sudden clarity that jarred Empress. "Camellia, what's going on?" Empress asked, her voice calm.

"I'm fucking done with this shit. I'm tired of his shit. I'm tired of my shit. I'm tired of all this stupid shit that's been going on for years."

Empress sat on the bed beside Camellia.

Camellia turned her head to look at Empress's face. She gazed into Empress's eyes. With abruptness, she sat up and leaned in to kiss Empress.

Empress backed away as Camellia leaned in to kiss her. "Camellia, you don't want to do that. You're just angry right now."

Camellia reached up and touched the side of Empress's face. "I love you."

Empress stood in an attempt to escape the complicated, confusing space before her. "Camellia—"

"I know why you couldn't keep going with what we were doing, but things are different now. We can be together. I can be yours now, just like you wanted in the beginning."

Empress briefly indulged her dreams from yesteryears, when she had crafted her utopia. It wasn't until the current moment that she realized she hadn't thought about anyone else beyond herself back then. As much as Empress always wanted Camellia, that reality carried the weight and power of a wrecking ball if it were ever to come to fruition. "Camellia, we can't," was the only way she could respond.

"I know you still love me, don't you? Don't you want to be with me now just as you always did?" Camellia grabbed Empress's hands and circled them around her waist. She pulled herself into Empress's forced embrace, and this time landed a kiss.

Empress felt herself succumb to the possibilities she had weighed over the years. She felt the summer sun at Lake Wylie on her skin again and the scent of vanilla hitting her nose. Nostalgia pulled her deeper into the kiss and all that Camellia was offering.

"I want you so bad right now," Camellia whispered into her ear before kissing Empress's neck.

Empress's buzzing phone brought her back from the yellow glow of her utopia's dawn. She broke away from Camellia to read her latest text. "Camellia still isn't home," was sent from JS. She turned her attention back to Camellia, who now wore tears in her eyes.

"Is that from your new girlfriend?" Camellia asked with a tone of contempt that cut the air between them.

Empress's eyes narrowed.

"Pops told us you were spending a lot of time with Dabney. Fortunately for you, he doesn't know you as well as I do."

"It's from your husband," Empress snapped back, holding the phone up for Camellia to read. "Fortunately for you, he doesn't know you as well as I do."

The thought of Nya forced Empress back to reality. The summer sun at Lake Wylie was replaced by the heat Nya stoked inside her. Empress looked into the red-rimmed hazel eyes that initiated her quest for the impossibility of eternal love and said, "I have to go."

She felt as if she were walking in slow motion toward the door as each step was weighed down with uncertainty. The cold steel of the doorknob felt as if it were burning her hand when she turned it. As she walked down the hall away from her figment of utopia, she felt her phone vibrate.

"Been thinking about you. Are you ok?" Nya had texted.

Again Empress saw bright streaks of light surrounding her as she passed through the boundaries of this reality and into the next dimension. "I'm ok. Will be at your place soon," she replied.

31.

Ebony

Empress leaned away from Nya's hands as she reached to play in Empress's curls after opening the door.

"You okay?" Nya asked as she stepped aside and closed the door.

"Yeah," Empress replied, making her way to the couch.

Nya took a seat beside Empress, folded her arms, and gazed at Empress's stoic face.

Empress combed through her curls with her fingers as if she were trying to shake her mind loose from something. She looked up at Nya. "What?"

"I'm just waiting you out," Nya responded.

"Waiting me out?"

"Yes, waiting you out," Nya reiterated. "Obviously, there's something wrong, so I'm just going to wait you out until you feel like clueing me in on what it is exactly."

Empress weighed distractions against the truth. Choosing a distraction, she moved closer to Nya on the couch and leaned in to kiss her.

"No," Nya said and leaned away.

"Fine," Empress replied before standing up and walking toward the door.

As she passed Nya's end of the couch, Nya grabbed her hand to stop her. "Empress, talk to me," she said, a plea in her eyes.

Again, Empress sat at the other end of the couch and combed her fingers through her curls. She sighed and blurted out her first point of the truth. "There's someone else in my family who knows I'm gay."

"Okay," Nya responded. "So how is your father handling it?"

"It's not my father," Empress answered.

"Okay," Nya said, the word drawn out.

To break the uncomfortable rise of silence between them, Empress blurted out the second point of truth. "My brother's wife also knows."

"Okay." Nya narrowed her eyes. "Why is that a problem, Empress?"

Empress's curls received another vigorous finger combing. She took in a deep breath to steady herself. "She knows because we were together."

"You were together before her and your brother?"

“Yes and no.” Empress turned to read the inevitable question on Nya’s face. “We started as friends in high school, and that grew into much more before we graduated. Then when I left for college, she and JS started hooking up, and then they got married when she got pregnant.”

Nya motioned with her hand for Empress to keep speaking. “I know there’s more because something that happened that long ago is not why you are so restless this evening.”

Another deep breath flowed in and out of Empress. “Not long after I moved back here, we started seeing each other again.”

“For how long?”

“About a year until I broke it off last year.”

Nya looked away from Empress’s pleading eyes and shook her head. “Why do I feel like there’s more you’re not telling me?”

Empress’s curls suffered through another raking as she searched for her next words. “Tonight she left JS, and he was worried, so I went to check on her and ...” Empress carefully chose her next words. “I got really confused.”

Nya nodded before raising her eyes to Empress’s. “Define confused, Empress,” she said, her words direct.

“She kissed me and wanted us to be together now, and I started thinking about that. And—”

"Do you still love her?"

Empress swallowed hard as if she were choking back the words. "I want to say no."

"But you can't say no."

Empress looked away from Nya's gaze.

"Okay," Nya said. She walked over to the door and opened it. "You need to leave."

"Nya, I—" Empress started as she approached the door.

Nya held her hand up to halt Empress's words. "Empress, I asked you for one thing, and that was no betrayal. Plus, I can't compete with someone that you refuse to let go." She reached to feel Empress's long, ebony curls again, slowly running her fingertips to the end of each curl she connected with. "Take care, Empress," she said as she closed the door.

An unseasonably cool wind met Empress when she exited Nya's building. As others on the sidewalk huddled together to ward off the sudden chill, she welcomed the crisp air onto her hot skin. With another breeze, her falling tears gave the appearance she wasn't crying at all.

Her buzzing phone sent hope throughout her body as she walked to her truck. She hoped Nya had a change of heart.

The text was from JS. "Camellia said she's fine." She stared at the phone for a few seconds, expecting more to follow. When she received nothing more, she considered responding with how she already knew Camellia was fine.

32.

Pewter

The night air was thick with moisture and carried a bewildering chill. The quiet disturbed him. Pops missed Empress's many words swirling through the night air and making his walk home not only tolerable but enjoyable.

He reread their last text exchange and looked for anything hidden in her responses. The few words offered no more insight than they had when he reread them a few minutes ago.

He approached the streetlight and thought about when Empress talked about what-ifs. He wondered if her many what-ifs were the motives spurring the distance between them. Or maybe it was merely the entrance of Dabney into her life.

Fighting his urge to call her, because he was sure he would be disturbing whatever had taken her attention, he opted to talk to his own current what-if.

"Hey, Sterlin."

He heard her smile through the phone and hoped she was receiving his also. "I miss you," he admitted to Faith.

"Awww, I miss you, too. It seems like it's been much longer than a week since I was there."

"Yeah, it does." He paused.

"What's wrong? You seem troubled."

"I don't know. Just thinking about Empress. I haven't heard from her much in these last few weeks. I'm sure she's just enjoying her time with Dabney, but I'm worried about her." He waited for Faith to inject some assurance to appease him. When he heard nothing on the other end, he asked, "Are you still there?"

"Yep, I'm still here."

"You don't have any of Faith's famous wisdom for me?"

Faith let out a tense sigh. "I do, but I don't think it's what you want to hear."

"Well, now I'm curious, so please go ahead."

"Sterlin, your children aren't children anymore."

"I know that," he replied defensively.

"Let me finish," Faith responded. "You are a wonderful and devoted father, but you have to start respecting your children for the adults they are."

"I do treat them like adults," he stated.

"Sterlin, you asked to hear what I had to say. Are you going to listen?"

Pops let out his own dense sigh. "Yes."

"I love Empress like she were my own daughter, and I understand why you worry about her, but, Sterlin, she's much stronger than the little girl in that hospital bed who didn't know how to cope with the loss of her mother. She's the beautiful, intelligent woman you raised her to be."

"I know she is."

"Well, if you see that then you also have to see how easily she reverts back to that fragile little girl whenever she feels like she's disappointing you."

"I've never been disappointed in her."

"Then maybe you should ask her if she really is enjoying her time with Dabney, or is she spending time with him because she knows that makes you happy."

He was disarmed. "I just want what's best for Empress," he admitted.

"Then trust her, and respect her for the woman she is." Faith paused. "Now," she continued, "let's move on to JS."

"Good Lord, woman. I didn't prepare for a lecture this evening."

"You asked for Faith's famous wisdom, so I'm giving it to you straight with no chaser."

He laughed a little. "Fair enough."

"I know JS walks a different path, but did you ever think that maybe he behaves the way he does because of the way you treat him?"

"I have nothing to do with JS cheating on his wife. I showed him how to be a husband and father."

"I'm not saying you have anything to do with that. But Sterlin, didn't you insist on him getting married when he told you Camellia was pregnant?"

"Actually, what I told him was man-sized choices come with man-sized responsibilities and that I wasn't paying for another one of his man-sized mistakes. Camellia was the third girl he had gotten pregnant while he was in college."

"Okay. I'm not going to make any excuses for his bad behavior. But, I will say if you treat someone like you only expect them to mess up, then all they will ever do is live up to your expectation."

He sighed again. "I'm afraid to ask, but do you have any other observations you would like to enlighten me with?"

"Just one," Faith replied.

"Dammit. Why did I ask?"

Faith laughed. "We only see each other when I come there."

"Yes, but I thought you liked coming here?"

"I do, but if you want us to move forward as you said, then you need to show me. The cabin was wonderful, and I appreciate you sharing it with me, but it was still on your terms and your turf."

"I understand, but I can't promise anything until the next location is up and stable."

Faith exhaled loudly. "Sterlin, I love you. I've given you many years to get to this point. Just know that I'm not going to give you many more."

"Is that an ultimatum?"

"Nope, it's just one of Faith's famous pearls of wisdom that also happens to be the truth."

The pewter-colored clouds in the night sky had reached their swelling point and he smelled the falling rain. He stood under the awning of his building, consuming her last piece of truth. "I love you, too. I can't promise you when, but I promise I will show you."

33.

Ashen

Daylight peeked through the slivers of the heavy drapes that were failing at their duty of barricading out all light. The sweet smell of coconut evoked the memory of Nya lying beside her. She felt her face harden and frown at the unwanted intrusions of dawn and adoration.

Empress's last couple of days had been full of memories and emotions flashing through an ashen fog. Tears could not find their rightful place as the many moments of bliss with Nya and Camellia meshed with the last night she saw them both.

Empress picked up her phone and found hope in the number ten, displayed on top of her messages app. Her hope was immediately doused when she only saw unread messages from Pops, JS, and Tandy.

It was easy to respond to Tandy first as she no longer cared about hurting Tandy's feelings. She scrolled to the bottom of Tandy's revealing selfies to type her reply. "I started seeing someone." She figured there was no need to detail where things stood now, especially since she was still optimistic about hearing from Nya.

"Really," Tandy replied. "Is it serious?"

"Yes," Empress responded. The dull ache of loss was a painful feeling for her right now. And the realization that happiness may again be only a memory was even more serious.

When she saw no flashing dots indicating a return message from Tandy, she moved on to JS. "Told the kids that Camellia is taking some space right now. They weren't surprised. Haven't heard from Camellia since the other night when she said she was fine." His messages resumed a few hours later. "Dabney called, they moved the closing to 2:00 tomorrow. Pops asked about you. He seems worried if you're ok. R u?"

She had forgotten about the closing and dreaded the thought of seeing any of them, including her father. Empress didn't know how much he knew already. "I'm ok. Just not feeling well," she replied to JS. "Think I have a stomach flu. I can't come to the closing tomorrow." She saw the flashing dots as he typed a response.

"Damn. Stomach flu. Yuck. Do you need anything?"

"No. Don't come over. You might catch it, too."

"Ok."

The tears welled in her eyes as she thought about the significant part she had played in contributing to her brother's transition into single-parenthood. Yet, her looming fear of when her secrets would come to light still didn't goad her into wanting to tell the truth. She chose the option she always gravitated to: self-preservation.

JS answered before she heard the first ring. "Hey, sis. You okay?"

"Yeah. I just need to rest for a few days, so you will need to handle everything. I'll let the contractor know to meet you at the restaurant after the closing, and I'll get the deliveries moved up. He said the work will only take a couple weeks. So, I'll send the invitations out for the reception."

"Cool. No problem." He paused. "Are you sure you don't need anything? You sound like you have something much worse than a stomach flu."

"Yeah, I'm good. Just tired." Empress said, trying to muster a cheerful tone.

"Okay." JS responded, but still didn't sound convinced. "I'll holler at you later." She scrolled to Pops's text and felt fear pulsing through her before tapping on his name. "Are you ok, baby girl? Haven't heard much from you lately. Have to walk home by myself now." He followed his last statement with a sad-face emoji.

Her welling tears broke and streamed her face. All she wanted at that moment was to see her father dancing to "Feeling Good" for her amusement until she felt obligated to join him. "Hey, Pops. I'm ok. Just not feeling well. Think I have a stomach flu. I can't come to the closing tomorrow." The ease of lying concerned her. She wondered if it was now a trait woven into the strands of her DNA.

Instead of seeing the flashing dots, her phone rang. "You're sick, baby girl?"

She cleared the remorse and regrets from her throat before speaking. "Yes, I think it's just a stomach flu though."

"Peanut butter, banana toast, and lots of water."

"Excuse me," she replied.

"You need to eat some toast with peanut butter and bananas on it. Just a little peanut butter so that the bananas will stick to the bread. Or if you feel daring, you can eat some banana-rice. We used to feed you all that when you were babies and had upset stomachs."

Empress felt a tear race down her face. She cleared her throat before speaking. "I don't think I'm banana-rice daring anymore," she replied.

Pops laughed. "Do you need me to bring you anything? Do you have any bananas?"

"I'm good, Pops. I think I have a couple bananas. I'm going to lie back down to get some rest."

"Okay, baby girl. I'll call you later to check on you. I love you."

"I love you too, Pops," she responded around the lump in her throat.

Empress sighed and got out of bed. Her bedroom looked dissimilar to the space it was before Nya made her entrance. Nya's positive energy lingered in the air and shot needles into her heart.

Her sneakers beckoned from the corner, still showing signs of their newness. *Time to trade some pain*, she thought in reflection of her aunt's words.

****

As always, during these periods of pain trading, she wanted to quit after the first half-mile. Just as on the first day when Empress started this ritual with her aunt, her heart pounded in her ears, her breath was lost between her lungs and mouth, and her legs ached. She even heard herself say, "I can't."

Empress thought back to her aunt telling her that the physical pain goes away sooner than the emotional pain. So, she welcomed the focus on her irregular breathing until the rhythm of her breath smoothed into a tolerable cadence. She was pleased with hearing the gravel crunch under her steps. She felt refreshed by her cascading sweat. All those things culminated in her not thinking about Nya or Camellia.

She slowed her pace as she neared the end of the trail, which totaled to her three miles. As her breathing and her pace slowed, her thoughts returned to Nya and Camellia. All the pain had not been traded.

She walked back to her place and noticed something else that might distract her. She wasn't in the mood for banana pancakes, but she also hadn't been in the mood to run.

The diner was modestly crowded, so she couldn't sit at her favorite booth. In her previous reality, that would have bothered her. In this new dimension, where she awaited the demolishment of all she held dear, a little impediment like that didn't resonate.

She shook her head as the server extended a menu to her. "Just banana pancakes and milk, please."

As she fiddled with the wrapped silverware on her table, she felt a comforting hand on her back. "Tell me something good," she heard the familiar voice say.

Empress pushed a deep breath through her nose before admitting a truth she had been trying to avoid. "I'm in love with two women."

“Oh,” Ms. Evelyn said and raised her eyebrows. She sat down at the table. “Well, honey, if that’s a good thing, you certainly didn’t make it sound that way.”

She took further comfort in the mixture of kindness and concern on Ms. Evelyn’s face. “It’s definitely not a good thing, but it feels good to finally say it out loud.”

“Well, I can’t say I fully understand about being in love with a woman, let alone two of them, but I do understand how freeing it is to talk and be heard.”

The server returned to the table with her banana pancakes and milk. Empress stared at the plate of nostalgia.

“You better dig in, honey, before they get cold,” Ms. Evelyn urged.

Empress carved a triangle from one of the pancakes, topped the fork with a banana, and dipped it into the whipped cream. As always, that initial forkful sent her back to Saturday morning cartoons with her mother.

Ms. Evelyn returned the smile budding on Empress’s face and patted her hand before leaving the table.

Two women. A fact she knew before the night when she last saw them, but didn’t want to lend it any space. She assumed that fact would eventually transform into loving only one of them. At least, she hoped so.

34.

Black

The walls were black and mottled with red, gold, and orange flecks to depict the rising embers from a simmering fire. *She is here*, he thought. Pops looked through the many attendees to the far wall to see the words *Hope Hearth* written with the same style of rising embers. A perfect imagery of the lasting, comforting warmth his late wife bestowed on all she encountered.

Life echoed throughout the new restaurant with the sounds of laughter and other exchanges. Though he was surrounded, Pops felt alone without Faith by his side to share this moment. Hope had been just as much to Faith as she had been to him.

"Aaayeee," a man bellowed a few feet away from Pops. "My friend," Ernesto said. He pulled Pops into a hug and gave him a vigorous pat on the back. "Congratulations."

"Thanks, Ernesto," Pops replied, hugging him back.

"This place is incredible, man. So upscale yet inviting."

"Thanks, man." Pop's canvassed the room again and smiled. "This was all due to my children, though. They made this happen."

"It's amazing what they can do when we get the hell out of their way, isn't it, my friend?"

Pops nodded. "It sure is."

"And oh, man, the new food is great. Those picadillo rolls with the black bean sauce are so good. I have never had anything like that in my life."

Pops nodded and smiled his way through Ernesto's last statement to cover his lack of understanding. "Hey, Ernesto, can you please excuse me?"

"No problem, my friend."

Pops tried to greet his way through the crowd to get to the kitchen, but he stopped when he happened upon Dabney.

"Hello, sir," Dabney said and greeted him with a hug.

"Dabney," Pops responded, prolonging his hug as he whispered in his ear. "Thank you so much for all of your excellent work."

"I'm just glad you are pleased, sir."

Pops noticed the woman standing beside Dabney after their embrace. "Hello," he acknowledged, extending his hand to her.

"I'm sorry. This is Alexis," Dabney stated.

"Very nice to meet you," Pops replied with a slight nod to her. "Will you both please excuse me. I have to tend to something in the kitchen."

"I hope you're going to have more of those seafood scampi meatballs brought out. I didn't think anything could top the crab mac and cheese until I had those," Alexis commented.

Pops nodded and again tried to cover his confusion with a smile.

As he scouted a clear path to the kitchen, he noticed a modified version of his daughter. Sadness was rimming her eyes, and she was fidgeting with her earring. He wanted to rescue her from whatever was weighing on her but remembered Faith's wisdom of allowing his children to be adults. He forced himself to turn away and continued scouting out the new food everyone was raving over.

****

As Empress greeted guests and tried to keep up her façade of happiness, Cammy approached. "Hey, Aunt E," she said and greeted Empress with a hug.

"Hey, my beautiful niece," Empress responded. "Are you staying out of trouble and off the sugar shit site?"

"Aunt E," Cammy whined.

Empress took notice of the young lady beside Cammy and redirected her attention. "Welcome to our little event."

"Thank you," the young lady answered.

A familiar light was in Cammy's eyes as she grabbed the girl's hand. "Aunt E, this is my girlfriend, Lila." Her smile widened.

Empress's smile became genuine. "It's wonderful to meet you, Lila."

"Nice to meet you, too," Lila said, her cheeks flushing.

Cammy embraced Empress again. "Thank you for not being weird about this, Aunt E, like my parents were. I thought my mom's head was going to explode a few minutes ago when I introduced her to Lila."

Empress's happiness faded at the mention of Camellia. She tried to hold on to her smile. "A few minutes ago? Your mother is here?"

"Yep." Cammy turned to point in the direction where she last saw Camellia. "She was right over there."

Empress felt her heartbeat speed up as she scoured the area for Camellia.

"She must have moved to somewhere else," Cammy said. "Aunt E, we're going to see if we can find some more of those meatballs. Daddy really did his thing tonight."

Empress nodded as they walked away. When they were no longer in sight, Empress pushed her way through the crowd to find JS.

"Wassup, Aunt E," Trip shouted, wrapping Empress in a tight hug when they happened upon each other in the crowd.

"Hey, Trip," Empress returned, hugging him back.

He smiled. "I found a new friend." He put his arm around the waist of the young lady beside him. "This is Gabrielle."

"Very nice to meet you, Gabrielle," Empress said with a quick handshake. She turned back to Trip. "I'm sorry, but I need to find your dad for something."

"He's right over there." Trip pointed behind him.

"Thank you," Empress replied before continuing through the crowd.

She spotted JS on the outskirts of the crowd talking to EJ. She wasn't sure what she would say to him, but she figured it would be best to tell him before Camellia did.

"Hey, momma," EJ said when she saw Empress approaching. "You are rocking that dress, girl. And I'm loving the updo."

"Why thank you," Empress replied. "You look amazing as well."

JS bent over to give Empress a side hug. “Baby sis, isn’t this amazing? And people are really digging the new food,” he expressed with excitement.

“Yes, big brother, you really did your thing.” She pursed her lips. “Hey, JS, can I talk to you for a minute?”

“Yeah, sure.” He tilted his head. “Are you okay?”

Empress nodded.

As JS searched the room for somewhere quieter where they could talk, he squinted. “Is that Nya?”

“What?” Empress answered, looking in the same direction.

“I’m surprised you brought her,” he replied, smiling. “Are you using this as your defining moment also?” he asked with a slight laugh.

“She didn’t come here with me,” Empress said, frowning.

“Did y’all break up?”

“Something like that.” Empress dropped her shoulders. “Let’s just talk later.” She walked off before he could stop her.

Empress strode toward the kitchen. She figured she could slip out the rear entrance without encountering anyone else. As she rounded a corner, she was met with her first what-if. She took a step back. “I didn’t expect to see you tonight.”

"I didn't expect to be here," Camellia responded. "The kids are never home these days, and JS has been so busy preparing for tonight. This was the only place I knew I could see all of you at once."

Empress's panic morphed into confusion. "All of us?"

"I just came to say goodbye," Camellia answered.

"Goodbye?"

Camellia nodded. "I was accepted into a global journalism internship, and it starts in a few days. I'm leaving for South Africa tomorrow."

Empress felt her breath quicken. "You're really going to leave just like that?"

Camellia nodded and looked at the floor. "I have to start living my own life now."

Empress felt a lump pulsating in her throat. "I have to go," she muttered.

As Empress turned another corner and passed the entryway to the restrooms, she was met with her last what-if. "Nya."

"Empress."

They gazed at one another through an awkward silence.

"You look beautiful," Empress said, blurting out her first thought.

"Thank you. So do you," Nya responded with a curt tone.

"I didn't expect to see you here."

"The Charlotte Regional Business Alliance asked me to attend as their representative. I originally confirmed with them weeks ago that I would attend this reception, but of course, I asked them to find someone else after everything that happened between us. Another member was supposed to be here, but they had a last-minute emergency. So, they asked could I still attend since they wouldn't be able to find anyone else on short notice."

Empress reached up to rifle through her curls, but quickly remembered they were tucked away on top of her head. Her hand moved to her earring. "Nya, I'm so sorry."

Nya shook her head. "I don't think it's me you need to be apologizing to."

Empress bit the corner of her bottom lip.

"Empress, you act like you're the victim who has to live this secretive life due to the fragility and judgments of others," Nya continued in a sharper tone. "The truth is you're the main one hurting all these people you say you love."

Empress opened her mouth to reply, but no words came out.

"Do you understand how fucked up it is to silently encourage your brother's sleeping around, because it was helping you to sleep with his wife? And what's even more so fucked up is I bet you felt justified in what you were doing."

Empress felt Nya's words swimming in her stomach. The nausea made her feel light-headed. She lowered her head, hoping to not hear the words so loudly.

"Empress, you think you know how to love, but that's just another lie you tell yourself."

Empress looked away from Nya and saw JS walking toward them. Her hand dropped from her earring as her limbs became heavy.

JS turned his attention to Nya. "You are missing out on an amazing, beautiful woman that you would be lucky to have."

"I know." Nya gazed at Empress. "She is amazing and beautiful, and I would love to have her in my life, but she doesn't have room for me in hers right now."

As Nya walked away, JS turned to Empress. His mouth fell open. "You broke up with her! And what does she mean by you don't have room for her? Do you really have a harem stashed somewhere?"

"JS, I have to tell you something."

****

The darkness in the office made light seeping from under the door look like a warning flare. He heard the murmur of conversations and laughter outside the door, but none of those noises echoed as loudly as his last words to his sister. "Get the fuck away from me."

Tonight was not supposed to be that.

He heard the squeak of the door inching open and squinted at the light it ushered into the room. "Son," he heard his father call through the darkness.

"Yeah, Pops," JS answered, sniffing back his tears.

Pops entered the office. "You okay?"

"Yeah," JS responded, quickly wiping his eyes.

"Great turnout tonight," Pops said.

"Yeah."

"I saw the new food."

"Uh-huh," JS answered, awaiting his lecture.

"Son, you've done something unimaginable tonight."

JS tried to find his father's face through the darkness to understand what he was saying.

"You proved me completely wrong tonight, JS." Pops walked closer to him, details of his face appearing in the dim light. "I'm so proud of you."

JS's anguish subsided momentarily when he heard his father's words. "You're proud?"

Pops nodded. "Very much so, son."

JS stood up to hug his father. The embrace took him back to the feeling of them as allies. He buried his head into his father's shoulder and expelled the tears he had been trying to hide.

Pops kissed him. "You held fast to your dreams, just as I knew you always would."

After they parted, JS again wiped his eyes and sniffed back his remaining emotions.

Pops wiped his face with his handkerchief and then shoved his hands in his pockets. "Have you seen your sister? I have something I need to tell you both."

JS clenched his jaw at the mention of Empress. "I think she left," he said flatly.

Pops's head jerked. "She left?"

"Yep."

Pops looked at the floor. His hand moved around in his pocket. "I'm going to call and check on her." He motioned his head at the door. "Get out there and enjoy the moment you earned, son."

****

He watched his son walk out of the darkness. The click of the closing door bounced through the shadows and affirmed his solitude.

The broken expression Empress wore when he last saw her weighed on him and pushed his shoulders down. He rubbed his eyes.

Pops picked up his phone and scrolled to find his favorite picture. Empress wore her mother's smile as they huddled together under a streetlight to pose for a selfie during one of their many walks home. The picture pulled a smile from him as it always did.

Empress didn't answer the first time he called, so worry and fear made him immediately redial. When she answered the second call, he heard the same weight in her voice that he wore on his shoulders. Even if he had been able to do so, he knew playing "Feeling Good" for her at that moment would not mend her wound. "What's wrong, baby girl?"

He heard her pain deepen in the long breath she exhaled. "I had to leave, Pops."

"Yes, JS told me." Again, he heard a long breath at the mention of JS. He rubbed his eyes. "Did something happen with JS and that lady I saw you talking to earlier near the bathrooms?"

"Her name is Nya."

"Okay," Pops replied. "Did something happen between JS and Nya?" He heard no long breath this time. "You still there, baby girl?"

"Yes, I'm still here." She sighed. "Nya and I have been seeing each other over the last couple months."

Pops expelled a long breath of his own. "I don't understand."

"Pops, Nya was my girlfriend until a couple weeks ago."

"Girlfriend?" Pops questioned as he again rubbed his eyes. "But I thought you and Dabney—"

"I was only going out with Dabney because I didn't want you to know the truth."

Now he was quite sure that "Feeling Good" would do nothing for this open wound. A dusting of anger covered him as he pondered his failure. He never considered that while he was trying to protect Empress from the world's cruelty, she was defending herself from him. "So ..." he started with caution as he attempted to wade through this unknown territory. "... did JS have something to do with things not working out between you and Nya?"

Her long breath returned. "No, this was totally my fault."

He allowed the silence to sit between them this time.

"I have been in love with Camellia since the first moment I met her," Empress confessed.

His hand rested over his eyes, and it took him a moment to absorb what Empress said. "I'm sorry, baby girl, but I'm really not understanding any of this."

"Camellia and I were girlfriends in high school, and we planned to go to Stanford together. When her parents wouldn't let her go, she became resentful about me moving on without her. Then she got pregnant by JS, and so they got married."

"I still don't understand what this has to do with you and Nya."

"Camellia and I started seeing each other again shortly after I moved back here until I broke it off about a year ago." She paused. "The night she left JS a couple weeks ago, I went to check on her. She kissed me and implied we could be together now." He heard her swallow. "And for a few minutes, I seriously contemplated that because it's what I always wanted."

He heard the hurt in her words. His sense of failure deepened. "So, Nya found out about that night?"

"I couldn't hide it from her, just as I could no longer hide the truth from JS."

Silence. Words were lost as they both retreated into their own thoughts.

The picture he looked at before calling her was sketched behind his eyes. He focused on the smile passed on to her. The smile Hope and Faith shared. Faith replaced the picture in his thoughts. He chose words stemmed from Faith's wisdom. "Baby girl, it doesn't matter who you love. It only matters that you love."

Empress sobbed. "I never meant to hurt anyone."

Pops felt helpless like when he had to carry her limp body into the hospital all those years ago. Since he wasn't with her this time, he resorted to the only Band-Aid he could apply at that moment. He recited the words to "Feeling Good."

35.

Golden

A cold wind pushed against her and carried the smell of approaching rain. The sudden downpour made the existing puddles around her dance and sent everyone scrambling into buildings and under awnings for cover. As she hurried to the nearest covering while wrestling with an unruly umbrella, she collided with someone also seeking shelter. "I'm sorry," she uttered, still fixated on her umbrella.

"Empress?"

The familiarity of the voice jolted her. A vanilla scent clung to the moistened air and ignited areas in her that had dulled. Empress raised her head hesitantly and was greeted with the hazel eyes she saw on her way to her Linear Algebra class all those years ago. "I thought you were gone," she responded.

"I was," Camellia replied. "I loved Johannesburg, but I came back immediately after the internship was over. I missed the kids. I've been back for a couple months now. JS didn't tell you?"

Empress pursed her lips at the mention of her brother. Her truth had resulted in so many emotional casualties over these last few months, and he was her most significant loss. Though the animosity he emitted toward her when they were forced to be in each other's presence was still prevalent, she remained optimistic about Saturday mornings when his Count Chocula box would again sit next to her Franken Berry one. "We don't talk much anymore," she said simply.

"Oh." Camellia nodded.

"So do you live here in uptown now?" Empress asked.

Camellia smiled and shook her head. "I wish. I can't afford anywhere up here on my modest salary. I work here at the Observer as a regional travel writer." She pointed to the building they were huddled beside.

"Wow, so you're really doing the journalism thing now?"

"Yes." Camellia emitted a glow Empress hadn't seen since they were teenagers. "It's only a step above entry-level, but I love it."

"That's awesome, Camellia. I'm so happy for you." Empress stared at the flecks of brown and green in her eyes. She still saw the golden Lake Wylie sun reflected in them. When she realized the uncomfortable silence she had ushered into their conversation, she said, "I better get over to the restaurant."

Camellia nodded. "It's good that you're still walking home with Pops."

Empress shook her head. "Pops is still in California with Aunt Faith." She paused; their relationship was still difficult for her to understand and digest. "That's another long story. Apparently, our family is a bunch of master secret keepers." She shook her head again to loosen the thought from her mind. "We're doing some upgrades to Pops Place, and my team is running the project," Empress continued.

"Your team?"

"Yes, I started the construction management company. I have a small team, and we are getting started with a few quick projects."

"I knew you would make it happen," Camellia replied with a budding smile.

After another awkward pause, Camellia said, "Well, don't let me hold you up."

Empress smiled and nodded. She took a couple steps into the slowing rain before feeling the weight of the looming what-if that had been in her life since the day she left for Stanford. "Camellia, maybe we can catch up over lunch or dinner sometime."

Camellia widened her smile and nodded. “Sure.”

Acknowledgments

My daily acknowledgment, "Thank you, Creator, for my life."

This story was inspired by the Toni Morrison quote, "If there is a book that you want to read, but it hasn't been written yet, you must be the one to write it." My hope is this is a contribution in elevating stories about queer people of color so that we can finally overcome under representation in media.

Thank you to my mother Annie Knight for giving me unconditional love and support, especially as I build my life outside the traditional structures of society.

Thank you to my sisters-in-life Kay and Lisa who constantly remind me that we are the embodiment of bosses. Our annual affirmations in the form of girls' trips allows me to take self-inventory and fills me with the needed encouragement to grow into my next level.

A special thank you to the beautiful women who helped to raise me and showed me how strength and perseverance lives daily. Aunt Ora, Aunt Maxine, Aunt Staree, Aunt Rean, Aunt Dorothy,

Aunt Shirley, Aunt Dorothy-Jean, Aunt Pearl, Aunt Nell.

To my many extended family members, thank you for always making me feel included and loved. The Osborne-Haynes family, the Harper-Ivy family, the Summers family (love you Ms. Sherry and Jermaine), the Knight-Weathers family, the Humphrey family, the Williams family. Special shout to my brother Tracey and my many many cousins: Keisha, Roz, Regina, Shaunita, Kendra, Alyssa, Cynthia, Valerie, Qunita, JJ, Benny, Kenny, Terry.

For my many wonderful friends who have been a constant cheering section since I started this project and who have been readers throughout it. Candace, Otelia, Tara, Rita, Vanessa, Kiki, Nicole, Steve, Boyd, Kim, Cola, Shamiya, Sara, Elisa, Shonda, Demetria, Erik, Aaron, Will.

A special salute to the beautiful Black women I served with who showed me the impossible is always accomplishable. Sharon, Laveda, Yolanda, Sharon, Pam, Tanya.

Thank you for the much needed reprieve from the workday the Potty Crew provides me. Felicia, Nadia, Princilla, Katie, Kelli, Uchenna.

Thank you in advance to the next generation who will lead us beyond the troubles of now.

Keyante, Kayla, Jayla, Kimmy, Karen, Sheena, Destiny, Jada.

A very special acknowledgment to two men who indirectly made this writing journey possible. Thank you Michael Crab for recognizing my craft in your 7th grade class and for encouraging me to continue writing. Thank you to Onyeka Nchege who re-ignited the spark with my first love.

For my community of queer peers here in the Charlotte area thank you for living your truths unapologetically and for providing good times in safe spaces. Big shout out to the White Party board members, the Charlotte Pride board, the Charlotte Black Pride board, the LGBTQ Mecklenburg Democrats, Time Out Youth, Transcend, RAIN.

For the women who built this story into a book. My publisher Debra Funderburk (Burkewood Media). The editing services of Monique Mensah (Make Your Mark Publishing Solutions).

A depth of gratitude to some of my favorite LGBTQ writers who paved the way for this story. James Baldwin, Octavia Butler, Audre Lorde, E. Lynn Harris, Lorraine Hansberry, Jewelle Gomez, Alice Walker, Cheryl Clarke, Bruce Nugent, Nikki Giovanni.

About The Author

Retha Knight is a long time resident of Charlotte, NC where she lives with her partner and daughter.

Most of her work is contemporary fiction with references to, and attributes of, historical places and context. Through writing, her goal is to bring light to stories that are overshadowed by everyday living, and, hence, often go untold.

There are many people who are celebrated everyday for doing extraordinary things, and there are many extraordinary people who live their everyday lives uncelebrated.